THE
MAÑANA KID

Center Point
Large Print

Also by Francis W. Hilton and available from Center Point Large Print:

Grey Sage
Skyline Riders

This Large Print Book carries the Seal of Approval of N.A.V.H.

THE
MAÑANA KID

FRANCIS W. HILTON

CENTER POINT LARGE PRINT
THORNDIKE, MAINE

CHAPTER ONE

LIMESTONE walls suddenly blocked his advance along the trail that had grown dimmer, more matted with yucca and mesquite with each succeeding hour—sheer-rising walls, purple in shadows that lay long on the dun-colored earth of the canyon.

The rider drew rein, turned in his saddle—a quick movement for all the weary sag of shoulders, the grim set of thin lips. Nothing stirred behind save dust scuffed up by his own horse—far-flung dust drifting along the canyon's rim. Up on the gyp-rock crown any movement would have been a flash against the skyline.

The rider eased booted feet from sweaty stirrups, stretched legs long cramped to saddle-leather. But his eyes never left the back trail; sharp, black eyes brittle in their hardness, eyes that veiled more or revealed more in a single glance than any word that ever passed his thin, close lips.

His garb might have set the fashion wherever vaqueros rode. It was silver-mounted, bangled-studded. From the crown of his hat—telescoped after the manner of riders of the far west—to the rowels on his heels he flashed with silver. His shirt was of silk; his black chaparejos stamped, rosetted, tied with white whang. The tooled-leather holster, strapped low on his lean thigh, was notched away from the trigger guard of a pearl-handled forty-five.

From cantleboard to tapaderos, silver inlay gleamed through a film of dust. Silver studded was the bridle, martingale and breast-band of his palomino which, for all the weary miles it had pushed behind, still strained at a frothy silver bit.

The rider slapped the dust from his shirt, settled the ornate cartridge-belt at his slim waist. Then he fell to stroking the palomino. Under his caress the brute arched its neck, pawed the ground with impatience to be on, even though its golden coat was streaked with sweat and lather that fringed the saddle-skirts. But the rider paid no heed. Never did his eyes leave the back trail. For once, however, there was no one there. Again, apparently the palomino had outrun his past.

Miles back a man lay dead. Through no fault of his to be sure. Yet . . .

He shrugged. By no means was it the first time he had felt wind sting his cheeks, had heard lead whistle past his head as he laid along the palomino's neck and raced into the sheltering darkness of night. But now, at least, there was not the soul-sickening sense that comes of spilling human blood.

Death had struck with the suddenness of lightning back there in Guadalupe. Now that he could somewhat relax his vigil, the events stalked before him with amazing clarity. He had sauntered into Cantina El Paseo after nightfall, the danglers on his inlaid spurs barely tinkling so easy was the movement of his lithe body. He had bucked a chair against the side wall, to sit half facing an open door through which strayed a breeze—hot as a flame yet sweet in the odor of stale beer, sweaty leather and cheap perfume. For a time he had surveyed the reward notices that littered the wall. One in particular. Even now thought of the thing brought a smile. For that notice pictured a lean-faced youth with the barest trace of a mustache on his thin lip—a youth, handsome in a dark, wind-whipped way, with black hair, black eyes that reflected the recklessness of the border.

$1,000 REWARD
THE MAÑANA KID

Wanted on a fugitive warrant
Suspected of bank robbery
Officers take no chances
Julio Montagues, Sheriff,
San Ysabel, California

At the memory, the rider threw back his head and laughed. Startled, the palomino lunged away to stop short and nose a tapadero as though in apology for its raw nerves.

Now the man could laugh. But back there in Cantina El Paseo it had been no laughing matter. A hard lot had been the motley mob that filled the border dive: gunmen who played tag with the law across the line from Tijuana to Mexicala, shifty, suspicious eyes on every newcomer; swarthy-faced breeds in gaudy scrapes who padded about mooching drinks and lights for foul-smelling *pitillos* that clung to flaccid lower lips as they talked; sailors in "civvies," who still had the roll of the sea in their walk; vaqueros fresh from the mesquite, reeking of sweaty leather and garlic.

Dance-hall girls had moved in and out of the mob. Some with young-old faces that still were pretty in a hopeless way, some with faces brittle and seamed in the bluish-white glare of gasoline lamps, all preening wantonly for the greedy gazes of boisterous men.

He had taken no part in the revelry, had no eyes for the girls who regarded him admiringly and found occasion to brush against him as they passed on the arm of a vaquero. Time and again he had refused to drink, chuckling at the snarls of men that met his refusal, smiling at the pouting plea or smothered curse of some girl who edged close to lift her glass to his lips only to be shoved aside.

As the sultry night wore on, to push into the cantina breathless heat from desert wastes, one of the group had caught his gaze—a slim young fellow in gaudy chaparejos and flashy shirt. He was spending recklessly for the benefit of the tallow-kneed group at the bar, and hoarse-voiced women who swarmed about him. Yet the liquor he drank stimulated within him no hilarity, only deepened the chalky hue of his boyish features, set him to twitching.

It was obvious that he was trying to avoid a girl in red velvet; a shapely girl as slight of build and age as himself; a girl whose big black eyes were sincere and soft and pleading. Her features were delicately molded, bore no stamp of riotous living that marked the faces of the other creatures in the resort.

He had wondered about that girl from the moment he laid eyes upon her. She had seemed so out of place among the others. Somehow she had reminded him of a rare bloom struggling for existence in the blistered chaparral of the desert. Her movements had been graceful, with the grace of innocence. Her eyes, when occasionally they met his, were frank and sincere. Yet in their depths had lurked a gleam of fright—almost terror. Plainly she was fearful of something. He had determined to find out, but . . .

Her sole interest had been in the flashily-garbed youth, who made no move that escaped her. Time and again she crossed over to the bar and led him onto the dance floor. Always he seemed to find an excuse to break away. Not so the others, many of whom had singled her out. For vaqueros constantly harassed the pair as they danced, attempted to cut in when the pianist paused for a drink or the wilting woman sought a moment's respite from the heat.

Came a time, as the youth and the girl in red danced, when a drunken vaquero did tear her from his arms. As though by signal the dancers halted.

The pianist crashed out a discordant chord, ducked from sight. Glasses clinked onto the bar. One shattered with a resounding crash. Rowels raked gratingly as men spun about. Then silence; silence that cloyed men's throats and sent women edging away, stifling shrieks, rouged lips suddenly grown pallid and drawn.

A shot blasted the stillness, roared down on taut nerves. The youth beside the girl in red, his gun halfway from its holster, threw up his arms, pitched headlong to the floor. No need to ask if he were dead. The stain that popped out between his eyes as he went down, the one convulsive shudder that racked him was enough. Yet the gun of the drunken vaquero who faced him, one arm still around the cowering girl, had not cleared its holster.

• • •

The rider slackened rein, gave the pawing palomino its head. It fell to snipping at the parched grass in the canyon. He tossed a leg carelessly over the saddlehorn, twisted and lighted a cigarette, which he held upright in the first two fingers of his left hand—the studied move of a gunman who, even when smoking, had clear vision and a free right hand.

Seated as he had been there in Cantina El Paseo, he had glimpsed something that had escaped the others—a smoking revolver jerked back from the open rear door. He had bolted to his feet, forty-five in hand, bounded toward that door to stop directly beneath the reward notice for the Mañana Kid. The killer had vanished. But he caught a clatter of hoof-beats out of the dark. . . . Two running horses, his quick ears told him, horses running in opposite directions.

As he edged away from the lighted frame of the doorway, he made mental note of another thing. The knuckles of the hand that had fired the shot had been toward him as he sat on the right side of the door. The first hoof-beats had sounded from the right. The killer had been outside and on the opposite side. For only one reason would he have risked detection to cross the path of light in the alleyway. Because he had shot with his left hand. An unusual thing, a thing to remember.

Then pandemonium broke the awful silence

11

that comes of violent death. Women began screaming, talking wildly. Men lunged about, shouting. The vaquero who had dared precipitate the play that ended fatally for the flashily garbed youth slunk back. But even the drunken crowd was quick to observe that his gun never had left its holster. Bloodshot eyes swept the cantina, finally to focus on the stranger as he stood just beside the door, forty-five in hand.

There had been another momentary silence. Then a surly growl had gone up, to rise to a threatening roar.

Again the rider laughed. But now the hard, dry sound went unheeded by the grazing palomino. . . .

"Hang him!" had come a thunderous shout. "*Sangre de Cristo*. He's the one. He has his gun in his hand. Bring a reata. He's the . . ." This time the rider's laugh sent the palomino lunging away. For that reward notice and picture had been on the wall just above him—the reward notice for the Mañana Kid.

"He's . . . he's . . . Down him!" The shout had ended in an awesome whisper, the insucking of breath as the vaquero who had cried out dodged to cover behind a dance-hall girl.

"Mañana!" Even now he recalled the word he had hurled at them—a purr on his lips as he stood, lithe body suggesting a puma in its supple grace. He looked around for the girl in red. She had disappeared. Hers was not among the chalk-white faces that flashed under his darting glance. Her face—the eyes in which terror had lurked—alone was missing. But there had been no time to ponder it. He had reached out quickly, ripped the reward notice for the Mañana Kid from the wall, sent it sailing into the crowd.

"You have him now, señors, as you will never have him again—under your very feet. As for me . . . *adios*, *amigos*. We'll meet . . ." His gun had spat. The great pendant light over the bar had crashed to the floor, plunging the dive into darkness. Fingers of flame licked up from trickling oil. ". . . *mañana*." The last he had sent tauntingly from the alleyway.

Not until he had flattened himself against the 'dobe wall of the cantina did a hail of lead riddle the door frame. Again pandemonium—curses, shouts, bellows of rage, terror.

He had dodged between two buildings, leaped out in front to the deserted street, a sepulchre in its darkened silence—silence broken only by the drum of running hoofs out of the far dark to the right . . . and to the left.

"One will be the vaquero who shoots with his left hand," he had chuckled softly as he now chuckled at the recollection. "A left-handed gun-man—a real curiosity and a señor with whom I have much business. But which one?"

Inside, angry feet had pounded toward the front of the cantina. Leaping to the tie-rack, he had jerked loose the reins of his palomino, vaulted into the saddle. Pulling the nervous brute about, he had given it rein, touched it with the spurs. It was gone, a golden meteor into the night, its sleek coat bright as the gleaming silver of saddle-rig. He wondered about the youth who had been killed, his name, where he was from, if he would have a decent burial. More he wondered about the pretty girl in red. Who was she? Where had she disappeared? But these thoughts were only flashes in his brain. Bullets whining after him in the dark were more important at the moment.

"Buenos noches, Guadalupe amigos." He still recalled the taunting laugh he had sent drifting back to the cursing crowd. "You may meet me . . . the Mañana Kid . . . *mañana."*

Dawn had found him still riding, the speed of his big palomino reduced to a mechanical, stiff-legged lope, which it seemed capable of maintaining endlessly. Occasionally, during the hours of darkness, he had caught the hoof-beats of a horse ahead. But he had lost them in broken country when, long since the Guadalupe posse had been outdistanced by the lather-smeared palomino.

A June sun had come swimming up in a sea of fire-yellow to turn the wild and desolate

14

Cuyamas into a bake-oven which radiated heat like a griddle. Dust rose chokingly from the trail to parch his throat, powder him with a thin gray film and glisten on his lean face. Utter weariness took toll of his endurance.

Once during the day he had found water. He had slaked his own thirst and that of his tired mount. Then he had gone on, toward evening to reach the end of the trail where limestone walls of a box-canyon blocked his advance.

CHAPTER
TWO

T HERE at the head of the box-canyon the Mañana Kid swung down from the saddle to stretch stiffened legs. Bridle reins free, the palomino eased its arched neck, shook itself and went back to grazing. For all his weariness, the Kid with easy, confident stride moved off, his gaze whipping the rimrock as he sought a way up the side walls of the canyon. A short distance below he found a cow trail. Again he took careful stock of his surroundings before he started up.

A hard climb in the loose, sliding dirt. Then he raised his head over the rim. But apparently caution was needless for he went unchallenged. Straightening up, he made his way along the dusty trail that meandered through a gap in the rimrock. Half crouched, one thumb hooked in his cartridge belt, he moved out onto a mesa.

A vast brush-clotted tableland stretched off into the face of the setting sun. Here and there great manzanita and chaparral reared up thirstily from jagged ravines as though to escape the merciless aridity of the sun-cracked beds sapping the life from their twisted forms. Ugly, weirdly shaped

17

buttes stepped away to the red-glowing horizon, finally to become but dim and hazy etchings in the lengthening purple shadows. A mile or so below spread out a boulder field which finally broke off in a wild and rugged area of arroyos and barrancas.

A sound alien in the whirring of hoppers, the shrill song of the cicada, the lazy buzz of flies, brought him whirling about, hand on the butt of his holstered gun. A short distance to the right, beneath a cut bank, he could hear the lapping of sluggish water. On the very edge of the mesa, where it pitched down into the barranca, a great white stallion, whose short arched neck was proof of Arabian strain, startled by his sudden appearance, had gotten to its feet to let forth a whistling snort and stand eying him belligerently. For a moment he sized up the huge, hostile brute which fell to slapping the ground savagely as though warning him to stay his distance.

Suddenly aware of a burning thirst at sound of the water, the man started forward. The white stallion snorted again, reared on its hind legs to meet him.

Still the Kid advanced. The horse came down shaking its head, started to back away. The cut bank on which it stood gave way with a boom. The Brute somersaulted backwards from sight.

The Kid stopped. But the horse did not reappear. And he could hear it threshing about in water.

Suddenly he realized the brute's predicament. It was bogging down in one of the quicksand bars jutting up in the stream.

Leaping to the head of the trail the Kid whistled softly. The palomino below threw up its head, located him, left off its grazing and came on a trot, head cocked sidewise to keep clear the trailing reins. A few vaulting lunges and it crawled through the gap of the rimrock to stand with nose outstretched for the caress such obedience commanded.

"Always are you at hand, Rey del Rey, *amigo*," the Kid chuckled, stroking the brute's neck, crusted with dust. "And again we have work together!"

Swinging into the saddle, he took down his reata, slid out a noose with the effortless ease of a practiced vaquero. He rode as near as he dared to the caving bank. Sucked to its stifle joints in the treacherous quicksand of the stream, which at that point widened out into a small pond, the white was managing to keep its threshing forehoofs free of the ooze. But its struggles were growing weaker. Inch by inch its flanks were settling. Wild-eyed, nostrils flaring, body streaked with mud, it was waging a desperate but losing battle.

Tossing the rope over the brute's neck, the Mañana Kid took a dally around his saddle-horn, laid the rowels against his palomino's side.

Rey del Rey lunged ahead. The choking reata set the white to fighting its head and bucking. The palomino laid low to the ground, clawing for a hoof hold, the muscles of its shoulders standing out in knots.

Plunging, pitching, snorting, the white stallion kicked itself loose from the quicksand, struggled up the bank to stand, head down, dripping, trembling.

"A fine-looking caballo are you to keep a thirsty man from drinking," the Kid taunted the quivering animal. "The fight is gone out of you— *si, amigo?*"

Flipping loose the reata, he crowded the palomino closer. Dog-tired though it was, trembling violently from its struggles, the white stallion suddenly came to life, reared to strike.

"Careful, *amigo*," the Kid cautioned, setting spurs to the palomino and jerking up the slack in the rope with a suddenness that whirled the brute end for end. "I choose to look you over."

The white planted its mud-smeared front legs, laid back on the rope. The palomino straightened about to face its quarry, then sat back almost on its haunches. Slowly the white stallion went down, breath rasping croupily, sides heaving. The reata grew tighter as it sank.

"Hold him, Rey del Rey," the Kid commanded as he dismounted. "We shall look him over for marks. And you, *señor bianco caballo*, have been on the business end of a reata before, yes?" He worked his way to the side of the brute, which began to lunge wildly, only to be choked down. He walked about the animal, examining it for marks. It was unbranded. But worn places on its withers indicated that at some time or other it had been under a saddle.

Cautiously the Kid stroked the horse's nose, scratched its forelock. It curled its lip, attempted to rise. But the rope held taut by the palomino kept it powerless.

"*Sangre de Cristo*, but someone has treated you badly," the Kid observed grimly. "And you have taken it into your head to repay everybody for it." The brute groaned, squealed, tried to strike lying on its side. The Kid dodged the threshing hoofs, continued to rub its forelock, run his fingers through its muddy, burr-matted mane. Under the patting and crooning voice, which inspired confidence instead of antagonizing it as others apparently had done, the white stallion began to quiet down, submit sullenly to the caresses. Having satisfied himself that the animal was unbranded, yet puzzled over the saddle marks, the Kid went back to his palomino, slackened the rope.

The stallion struggled to its feet, trembled a moment and charged. With a word to Rey del Rey, the Kid stepped aside. His quirt sliced the striking hoofs. The palomino made two or three quick lunges. The rope sang with tautness. Saddle leather creaked. The white stallion crashed to the ground.

"Lesson number one," the Kid said soberly. "We're not trying to hurt you, *amigo*. But you are much too old and savage to be running around the range thinking you are the *primero*—or even the *segundo*. I am fearful that you will kill someone. Therefore I take the time and the trouble to teach you, you are not the boss of this range— or any other. Now we had better let him up again, Rey." The palomino promptly slackened the rope.

Again and again the white stallion got to its feet to charge only to go down as Rey del Rey turned it end-over-end with the singing reata. Time and again the Kid's quirt wrapped around its flailing forehoofs, opening the flesh and nipping tufts of hair from its sides. Sweat trickled across its heaving sides. Its eyes, rolled back to the whites, grew glassy with weariness. Its efforts to trample the persistent, quiet-voiced man, who dodged it with careless ease and who seemed utterly oblivious to fear, were becoming more and more feeble.

When the brute had reached a point where it was almost ready to topple with fatigue, the Kid advanced, hand outstretched. It snapped at him savagely, then reared back on the rope to stand eying the quirt, front legs spraddled wide like those of a locoed colt's. Dumfounded at the temerity of this man, it waited, muscles bundled to strike him down. Still he came on, straight for its head. Once, twice, three times the white stallion slapped the ground to warn him to keep his distance. But he paid no heed. And his pleasantly crooning voice made the brute prick up one of the ears plastered tight against its shapely head. When he was within reach it struck. The stinging quirt sliced the blood from its fetlocks before they hit the ground. Still the man came on.

Fear clutched at the heart of the outlaw stallion. Never before had a human dared meet it face to face. All the others had taken to their heels when it bared its flashing teeth. It began to understand that the merciless quirt at the man's wrist did not bite nor did the rope cut off its wind and send it somersaulting when it was docile.

Then before it realized what had happened the fingers were scratching its forelock again. Violent trembling seized it. The tables had been turned. For the first time in its life the white stallion was pitted against a human it could not frighten; a human who terrified it, yet . . .

There was something reassuring about the soothing voice. From enduring the caresses the brute began to like them. It stood stock still, fearful to move and experience the lacing pain of that quirt.

Then the man did a thing that made the white stallion quiver with rage. He slipped an arm about its mud-streaked neck, whispered in its ear, tickled its nose. Blind anger gripped it. It snorted, reared to strike. The quirt sliced the blood from its fetlocks. It came down with a thud, beaten, completely at the mercy of this fearless man. After all, the petting was not nearly so painful as the stinging lash. And the fingers on its nose were cool and gentle.

Hatred gave way to submission which quickly grew into a confidence that this stranger, unlike all the rest, meant it no harm. It craned its neck to look after him, nickered softly.

"Well, it took you quite a while, *amigo*," the Kid said. "Now that it is over and we understand each other. I'm going to try and buy you—if I can find your owner. You have had a good lesson on how to treat friends. I'll be back again before long and we'll play some more, yes? Meanwhile, don't forget that I only laugh at your bluffs as I laugh at the bluffs of men of your type." Reaching up, he took the rope from the white stallion's neck, coiled it leisurely while the animal looked on, then walked back to Rey del Rey. Once the outlaw started to charge. The Kid whirled. The brute stopped dead in its tracks.

"*Adios*," the Kid said. "We are *amigos*, remember. If it were not for the gathering darkness I would take you with me until we found a rancho, and ask about you. But we shall meet again." He swung into his saddle to stand in his stirrups and sweep the country. Then he reined out onto the boulder field, shadowed now in the lowering light.

Of a sudden, off to the right, his eye caught the twinkle of a light—now gleaming sharply, now completely obscured in the shimmering heat waves of falling night.

Grimly determined to have rest, not so much for himself as for the leaden-legged Rey del Rey, he struck out for the light that blinked like a will-o'-the-wisp ahead. His quick ear ever tuned for the sound of hoof-beats that would signal the approach of the posse from Guadalupe, he rode on through the thickening night.

After a considerable time he pulled up before a cabana, the 'dobe walls of which stood out dimly in the darkness. From a single sack-covered window filtered a soft light.

"Hallo, *amigo*," the Kid shouted. "What chance for rest and food—for my horse and myself?"

A moment of silence. Then the covering that was the door moved. An old man stood silhouetted against a light. "You are welcome, señor," he said. "Alight. Such as I have is yours."

The Kid got down warily, the butt of his forty-five tightly clenched in white knuckled hands. But apparently he was safe. For the old fellow had stepped back to light a lantern, with which he came forth presently and led the way to a barn under an overhanging cliff.

Rey del Rey unsaddled and munching on grain, the Kid followed the old man to the 'dobe cabana.

CHAPTER THREE

THROUGH the June dawn the Mañana Kid and his grizzled host of the cabana rode back over the mesa the Kid had found the night before. Little conversation had passed between them since the Kid had ridden into the retreat of the old fellow, who for all his taciturnity made no attempt to conceal his joy at human companionship.

The Kid had found rest for himself and Rey del Rey, who now stepped along with a vigor he had lost in the weary miles which lay between them and Guadalupe.

Ever quiet, the Kid—a sharp eye in every direction—was sunk in his own thoughts. What had become of the left-handed killer of the youth at Guadalupe? What had become of the posse that had started out from the desert town sending lead after him? And what had become of the girl in red who had disappeared so mysteriously from Cantina El Paseo after the shooting?

He made no attempt to answer the questions flashing in his brain as he rode through the dawn beside his new-found companion. But his mind was in a turmoil. Not so much for the slain youth, not so much for the posse—but for the girl in red velvet. Two horses had pounded away from Cantina El Paseo. One had been the killer, the other the girl. It was the girl he wanted to find— not the killer. Had he followed the wrong trail?

"Down yonder a good many miles is Rancho Diablo, my friend," the voice of his companion cut in upon his thoughts. "But if I were you and didn't have any good reason for going in there I'd just ride along this mesa and pass it up."

"Why?" There was careless indifference in the voice of the Kid who had spoken scarcely a dozen words since he had ridden into the cabana of old Jim Brown the night before. Yet for all his silence it was evident the Kid had missed nothing of what the old man had said. But if the warning now interested him he gave no sign. For suddenly he had caught sight of the white stallion he had encountered the evening before.

The brute had popped into the skyline, nagging a bunch of mares to water at the stream from which he had dragged it. Proudly defiant, he had taken up a position commanding a view of the mesa while his herd drank.

Old Jim shifted sidewise in his saddle. "For a right smart of reasons," he observed, cryptically. "That might be one of them."

The Kid took his gaze from the white stallion long enough to glance in the direction the old man indicated. Nailed to a tree ahead was a weather-blasted placard.

$2,000 REWARD

will be paid for "Blackie" Ware, alias Hank Cranston, alias Tony Rodriguez *DEAD OR ALIVE*. Wanted for murder and horse stealing. Take no chances. This man is a killer. Six feet tall, dark complexioned. Likely to be found around a ranch, employed as a bronc-rider. Communicate immediately with

Julio Montagues, Sheriff,
San Ysabel, California

When the Kid had finished reading he shrugged, shot an inscrutable look at his companion, and turned back to watch the stallion which had spied another bunch of grazing horses, splashed through the stream and come up on the near bank, prancing and squealing a challenge at a black stallion leading the herd.

"I ain't saying Blackie Ware's down yonder at Rancho Diablo," old Jim remarked, "because we fellows who live neighbors to that outfit don't do any more talking than we have to." He found a foul-smelling pipe, crammed it full of cheap tobacco he took from a sweaty pouch in his hip pocket, and lighted it. "Some folks call the Rancho Diablo spread 'Break-Neck' Rancho."

"Why?" The abrupt query was the only evidence the Kid was listening.

Old Jim sucked until the pipe was sending up a cloud of smoke. "It's the out-neck-breakin'est place in southern California, that's why."

If his words were calculated to claim the interest of the Kid they failed completely. For the Kid's black eyes were riveted on the white stallion which was bouncing around like a ball, striking savagely at the leader of the second herd.

Having surveyed the scene of combat casually, and apparently found it to his liking, the black snorted a challenge, advanced on hind legs. The white stallion circled it warily a couple of times, then launched into battle with grunts, bawls and squeals.

"Pedro Rodriguez used to own Rancho Diablo. He broke his neck," volunteered Jim. He was nettled by the unconcern of the Kid who sat his mount far straighter than the young eucalyptus about them, the thumb of his right hand hooked in his cartridge belt. Old Jim had wondered about that hand. The arm did not appear to be crippled, yet he noticed his companion seldom changed its position—probably a habit, he concluded.

"Pedro had a foreman, an American named Johnnie Bender. Johnnie got his neck busted too, just like a sheriff and a deputy and a pile of horse-buyers that have gone in yonder. But those goin's on aren't any of my affair. What I'm getting at is this: You look a heap like Johnnie Bender. You don't happen to be kin of his, do you? It wouldn't be healthy for any kin of Johnnie's down yonder."

The Kid dragged his eyes away from the struggle in the valley to meet the old man's inquisitive gaze. "I'm called the Kid," he said shortly. "I don't remember any of my folks. Down on the Pecos where I grew up, the fellows said my father was killed by an outlaw. But I never heard the particulars. For which I am sorry, on your account, *amigo*." He turned back to watch the horses which were fighting grimly inside a circle formed by the mares comprising the two herds. "How far would one guess this Rancho Diablo lies?"

"Forty miles down the Santa Ynez valley, there where you see that dust," replied Jim. "But it's a hard bunch. Young men like you are—are—well, those hombres are looking for young men like you—some young men, understand."

"*Gracias, señor.*" The Kid's voice was not insolent, yet it carried a cold, disinterested note; the tone of a man who had seen the rawest of frontier life and had learned to rely upon himself in every emergency.

"Yeah," snorted Jim. "Pedro Rodriguez had a kid. Cutest little shaver ever you run across. Was only two when his pop got busted, some ten years ago. He hasn't been seen since. Some say Pedro sent Brownie—that was his name. Brownie

Rodriguez—east for kinfolks to raise. Me, I'm not saying. And then there was a girl. . . . And her older brother—a nephew and a niece of Pedros'. Nobody knows what's going on down there. But if Brownie Rodriguez was alive he would own Rancho Diablo, wouldn't he? I'm warning you again, Kid, that unless you got pressing business down yonder you'd better steer clear of Break-Neck Ranch."

The Kid gathered up his reins. "*Gracias, señor, y adios*," he said. "I'll be riding back this way some day. If I do, and you don't mind, I would like to put up with you again."

"You're sure welcome, Kid," exclaimed the old man, extending his hand, and dragging his pony about on the back trail.

After he had disappeared, the Kid rode out onto the mesa and drew rein to sit sidewise in his saddle, twist a cigarette and stare out over the brush-clotted tableland that ended in a jumble of barrancas to the south.

His idle gaze wandered back to the fighting horses. Snapping like a wolf, its teeth bared and dripping with bloody foam, its body splattered with lather and streaked with sweat, the white stallion was slowly conquering the black which was bleeding from several gashes in its glistening hide.

Urging Rey del Rey along the trail that wandered toward Rancho Diablo, the Kid rode as close as possible to the circle of mares and pulled up to watch the deadly contest. A vicious sweep of the black's hoofs left a crimson streak across the white stallion's withers. Squealing with rage and pain it whirled. Its hind hoofs beat a tattoo on the black's ribs.

A pause. The brutes stood nose to nose, lips curled, forefeet planted, ears plastered against their heads. Somewhere a mare whinnied her approval. The black closed in, striving to set its teeth in the neck cord behind the white stallion's ears.

The white met the onslaught. Up on their hind legs they reared, balanced. Then their fore-hoofs became deadly, crushing flails of bone and muscle.

Shaking its head fiercely, the black attempted to retreat. The white straddled its rump, tearing away tufts of hair with its teeth, ever straining nearer to a neck cord, a grip which would down the other in a paralytic heap. The black fell. The white bounced around on legs stiff as stove bolts, its dancing hoofs peppering the mares with chunks of earth.

"Give him hell, *bianco diablo*," cheered the Kid under his breath. "I hate a horse of your type. But I'd like to own you. I'll wager I'd take more of the fight out of you." Completely absorbed in the contest, he tossed a leg over the saddlehorn and rolled another cigarette. The black struggled desperately to rise. The white stallion stood above, slapping its bleeding head back to the ground with terrific force each time it came up.

The black groaned and stretched out. Satisfied with its victory, the white threw up its head and tail, trotted around the circle of mares. The black struggled to its feet. The cordon broke. Unprepared for a renewal of hostilities the white backed off.

The black charged, teeth grinding under the pressure of viselike jaws, forehoofs hammering the ground. Waiting until it was within reach, the white stallion reared. His hoofs came down across the black's head. His teeth sank into its neck cord. The black went down to jerk spasmodically, then straightened out to lie still.

"Lesson number two," the Kid said under his breath. "But a lesson in killing I shall have to correct. I go now, you white devil, but I shall return—to claim you."

He loped away, the black stretched prone on the ground, the mares circling the white stallion, nickering their praise.

Through the day the Kid rode. But never did Rancho Diablo come in sight. The way was weary—an endless stretch of boulders, mesquite and chaparral. The hot wind whining across the mesa sapped the life from him. But the palomino struggled on gamely, pushing the weary miles behind with monotonous ease.

Then toward dusk, as he dropped down off the mesa toward a labyrinth of barrancas he became aware of some incomprehensible thing that tightened his nerves. Pulling rein, he glanced about. Save for the grasses swaying among the boulders nothing moved. Prey to a disquieting sensation of being watched by unseen eyes, he roweled forward. But as he advanced the ominous quiet seemed to increase.

CHAPTER
FOUR

"THROW down your gun!" came a command from beside a boulder flanking the trail. "I've got a bead on you—and I'll shoot." A figure moved in the shadows ahead.

The Mañana Kid swore softly. One of the posse, was the thought that flashed to his mind. He jerked straight in the saddle. But he did not throw down his gun. Instead, his Colt spat from its holster. Rey del Rey sun-fished away to land, snorting. The Kid's challenger reeled out from the shadows of a boulder. His weapon fell to the ground. He clutched at a bleeding hand.

"I am sorry, *amigo mio*," the Kid apologized in a soft tone that still rasped with hardness. "But the señor should ever guard against leaping into range of a riding gun. Now that we have met, so unfortunately, I ask who you are, why you challenge me?" He lifted in his stirrups. The figure ahead had crumpled to the ground. And was crying!

For a moment the Kid sat motionless, one hand on the nervous palomino's neck. Then he got down. Careful against trickery he moved forward only to stop. At his feet stretched a slightly built, freckle-faced boy decked out in the gaudiest of range clothes—a bolero, conchas, rosettes of every description.

"I'm dying," the youngster sobbed. "What did you want to shoot me for? I didn't have no gun?"

The Kid flushed guiltily. The object he had mistaken for a blue-barreled Colt in the dim light, was a straight-stemmed briar pipe.

"I'm sorry, *chamaco*." There was real concern in the Kid's voice. He stooped to examine the boy's bleeding hand.

"No, you don't!" the lad snarled, springing to his feet and backing off. "You can't double-cross me. Juan never lets a hombre get the edge, you bet. I'm on to your game."

A smile of pity tugged at the corners of the Kid's mouth. "Your name, *chamaco*? And where did you come from?" he asked. "I have hurt you . . . I am sorry. My only excuse is I am weary and thus easily excited. I need rest, as does my horse."

"They call me Toughy," sobbed the boy, eying the Colt that never had come away from its holster. "I'm from Rancho Diablo."

"Toughy who?"

"Just Toughy," sullenly. "Don't know any other name."

"In that respect we are much alike, Toughy," the Kid observed soberly. "What were you thinking to do when you leaped into the trail and ordered me to throw down my gun? Rob me?"

"No," reluctantly, through teeth chattering with pain and fear. "I'm no hold-up. But I figured— Juan was telling me about how they used to stick 'em up down on the Pecos. And . . . and you scared me, mister. You see, I was . . ." He caught himself quickly. His childish air of bravado returned. "If I'd of been Juan though, you can bet your life you wouldn't of shot me."

"Who's this Juan?" the Kid asked. Not that he cared, but this boy puzzled him. It was obvious the youngster was holding back something. And he wanted to help him.

"Don't you know Juan Lopez?" Toughy stared in astonishment. "He's the best hombre you ever met up with in all the Santa Ynez . . . and the toughest. Why, he can shoot the ace of spades out of a playing card from his hip without half trying. And ride! Say, he's the out-ridin'est hombre that ever came into these parts or any other. When I grow up I'm going to be just like Juan. But then, that's none of your business. What are you nosing around here for, anyway?"

"I said I was in need of rest. But your hand, *chamaco*?" the Kid said softly. "It is bleeding. Please, to let me bandage it, yes?"

"Yeah, and you'll probably shoot me again." Toughy backed farther away to eye him with the mistrust of a young animal.

39

Determined to have a look at the wounded hand, the Kid reached out suddenly. For all the boy's kicking and fighting he drew him close and held him between his legs while he examined the wound. Satisfied that his bullet had no more than sliced the flesh, he bandaged the bleeding hand with his kerchief. Once having felt the strength of the Kid's iron muscles, Toughy offered no resistance.

"Now get your pipe," the Kid ordered curtly, releasing him. "I'm sorry we had this little—misunderstanding. But it might teach you a lesson, *chamaco*—a lesson in not going around trying to halt strange travelers."

"Don't call me *chamaco*," Toughy snarled. "I ain't no little fellow. I'm growing up fast—and getting hard enough to take care of myself—and others."

The Kid wondered at that, but said nothing. He wanted the boy to talk. But apparently the youngster had no such intention.

"What's your name?" the boy demanded presently.

"They call me the Kid. And right now I'm tired to death. So is my horse. We must find rest and water. I have but a small canteen, which will keep us going but a short time longer."

"You're just four doors from the desert here, hombre. And Juan says the desert has taken care of a lot of snoopers. But—is the Kid your real moniker or just a phoney? Juan says all bad hombres have a lot of names they use in a pinch."

"They call me the Kid—everywhere," softly.

The boy shrank from the black eyes into which suddenly had flared a cold, hard gleam. He looked about, his own gaze presently to fall on Rey del Rey who stood, ears cocked forward as though he, too, were listening in on the conversation.

"That's a beaut of a palomino you're forking, hombre. And that saddle . . . say, you must be somebody. I never saw a saddle-rig nor a horse like that—and look at that silver martingale and bridle. Can I look at 'em close, *amigo*?" The Kid was quick to note the *amigo*, the change in the tone of the youngster, who was striving so valiantly to maintain a hard front. But Rey del Rey, his golden coat dulled with dust, was quickly forgotten. It was the silver rig that had won him.

"You can ride the horse and the silver rig, too, if you'll take me to shelter . . . where we can have rest, *chamaco*," the Kid said. "But not now. Please. . . ."

With the inquisitiveness of youth Toughy rushed on. "Say, mister Kid, how did you shoot without drawing your gun? I never saw Juan do that. Not even when he . . ." Again he caught himself.

The Kid pinned down his roving gaze. "When he what?" he asked.

"Nothing," Toughy hedged. "I'm the biggest

41

liar in these parts or any other. But how did you do that shooting—huh?"

In his abstraction of pondering his own predicament the Kid scarcely heard the boy.

"How did you do that shooting, mister?" Toughy was not to be denied.

"It's an old trick." The Kid dropped down cross-legged on the ground to pluck a stalk of bunchgrass. After all, there was no hurrying this youngster, much as both he and the horse needed water. And he was hungry—and dog-tired. But the bags slung behind the silver saddle always carried enough to stave off starvation. And ever since he could remember the vast open spaces had been his home. His saddle blanket, a plot of earth—and he could sleep. But water . . . "A Mexican gunman taught it to me down on the border," he found himself saying. "I shoot from my holster to save the time of drawing. Where is your horse?"

"Over yonder." The boy jerked a thumb toward a boulder.

"Get him and ride on to your rancho with me."

Toughy held back. "They'd kick hell out of me for not coming in and telling them you were heading that way. Are you a horse buyer?"

"No. Why?"

"If you was, I could go in with you. They don't object to horse buyers—or even cattle

42

buyers, if they know who you are. Because they always . . ." Again he stopped.

"Always what?" the Kid encouraged.

"I was just lying some more. Juan's warned me about that, too. But it just seems like I can't help it. Gosh, this here's a foxy handkerchief you tied around my hand. Could I have it, mister? I'm saving up to get some duds out of the catalogue. But the loboes don't pay me only a dollar a week. And they won't trust me with a gun. That's how come I used this pipe. It's better than nothing if a hombre gets his bluff in first. Juan says always to get your bluff in first. But if I was you and wasn't a horse buyer I'd turn back. The foreman, Mert Bradley, and Juan won't be none too tickled to see you. And your fancy shooting won't be worth a damn if Juan gets sore at some little thing and cracks down on you. Juan's funny that way. And he's fast—he'll tell you so."

"One should never boast of their shooting, *chamaco*," the Kid said. "It only leads to trouble. For always among men there is jealousy. And jealousy leads to needless gunplay. You are certain you dare not go into the ranch with me?"

"Gosh, no," the boy said in alarm. "Why if old man Pearson and those others thought I'd seen you and hadn't dropped rock on you— hadn't come and told them, they'd beat hell out of me. You won't tell on me, will you, mister— Kid?"

43

"I'll keep your secret if you will keep mine."

"What's yours?" demanded Toughy.

"I'm none too proud of this shooting, *chamaco*," the Kid confessed.

"Why do you keep calling me *chamaco*?" angrily.

"Because it means little fellow and you aren't very big." The smile the Kid essayed froze on his sun-parched lips. "But in this case we'll say it means friend, partner and little fellow too. And if anyone asks you concerning that bandaged hand tell them you fell down—or something, yes?"

"You're danged right I will," the boy agreed warmly. "And I'm much obliged to you for not plugging me when you had a chance. If it had of been Juan he'd of . . ." The youngster broke off shuddering. "If you're bound to go into the ranch you'd better travel. But you're cooking your own goose, as the fellow says. And don't ever say I didn't tell you. I'll come in after a spell and eat in the cook shanty. The cook'll feed me—sometimes. Then I'll skin off to bed. I'll come by a different trail so they won't get wise we've met up before."

The Kid got up, walked over to secure the trailing reins of the grazing Rey del Rey. "Here's my hand, Toughy," he said, coming back, leading the horse, to gaze down into the wide blue eyes of the forlorn boy. "You and I shall be *amigos*, while I'm in these parts—forever, perhaps, yes?"

The lad swallowed hard. Tears came into his eyes.

"Do you really mean it, hombre?" he whimpered. "I never had any vaquero do that before. Juan is always kicking hell out of me. And Mert—the rest of 'em treat me like a dog. Of course, old man Pearson ain't there so much— and—well, he'd be all right if the others would let him alone. That's why I want to be like Juan—so when a hombre busts me I can beat him to the draw and shoot hell out of him. Sure, Kid, here's my hand. I'm much obliged to you for not killing me. And I'm right proud to call a hombre as handles a gun like you, *amigo*."

The Kid clasped the dirty hand warmly. "I don't know this Juan you speak of," he said. "But if he dresses like you are attempting to, and goes for his gun at every excuse, I would suggest you give up trying to follow his example."

The boy's eyes flashed.

"Don't you dare say a word against Juan," he flared, backing off. "I'll—I'll . . ."

The Kid smiled.

"No need that we should resort to anger now, *chamaco*. Who am I to try to belittle your friend, Juan? All three of us someday may be *compañeros*. Who knows?"

Toughy shook his head.

45

"You don't know Juan. There aren't many hombres besides me he'll team up with. And even then he kicks the devil out of me."

"Well, *adios*, Toughy," the Kid said. "This Rancho Diablo interests me—so much so I'll just ride in and look it over. Rancho Diablo! A strange name. Why Rancho Diablo?"

"I never could figure out," the boy said seriously. "Of course, there's strange things . . ." he stopped shortly. "We brand a pitchfork."

"Perhaps that is the reason—who knows, *chamaco*?" The Kid smiled. "After all, pitchforks have been mentioned in connection with devils. But me—I believe, perhaps, there may be other reasons. *Adios* for now. I'll ride straight in. You can come by some other trail. And remember—we have secrets, yes?"

"You're danged right we have," the boy returned importantly. "And Toughy will keep yours as long as you keep his. If we meet again—you never saw me before, you know."

"If we meet again?" the Kid repeated softly. "Sure, we will. Compañeros stick together—always. For there is no telling when compañeros may need one another. Your horse?"

"I said he was over yonder aways. You just be riding along first. I'll take care of myself."

Wondering, the Kid put Rey del Rey down the trail. A short distance and he looked back. The boy stood watching him, a pitiful figure in his homemade, gaily decorated chaps and bedraggled bolero.

"Poor little *chamaco*," the Kid told the palomino, which cocked back one ear as though to catch his words. "Never had a chance. He thinks raising the devil is all there is in life. Nicknamed Toughy and spends his time trying to live up to the name. And this Juan—I presume he is the one responsible for that."

He rode on, again to look back. Toughy had disappeared. The Kid pulled rein to watch until he had located the boy riding through the boulders above where he had left him. But, in the opposite direction to which he had said lay the ranch! The Kid shrugged and went on.

"A strange country," he told Rey del Rey after the manner of men of the silent trails who talk to their mounts as they would a human. "Already we have met the old man of the cabana who warned us of Rancho Diablo. Already we have encountered a white stallion and a *chamaco*, both aching for a kind word. Perhaps we shall make friends here. They seem hungry for friendship. But again, we may . . ."

CHAPTER FIVE

H ALT!"

Again the startling command came from behind a boulder flanking the trail to check the Kid's words to Rey del Rey.

Now an oath ripped out from the Kid's dry lips. He came up taut in his saddle to peer through the waning light. Positive that Toughy had not cut in ahead of him to repeat the command as a prank, yet unwilling to shoot for fear it might, indeed, be the youngster, in a single leap he was off the palomino, which at a word whirled and raced back up the trail. In a half-dozen bounds the Kid went sprawling to cover behind a great rock. Picking himself up, he crouched motionless as the stone that concealed him.

He pondered that voice. It had not been Toughy's. Neither had it carried much authority. Yet . . . again thought of the posse flashed to his mind. For all his caution on the trail it was possible that some lone posseman had tracked him. And always he had to be on his guard against the killer who had pounded out of Guadalupe.

He waited tense, motionless. The command

was not repeated. No sound broke the gripping stillness. Inching a dried stalk of mesquite toward him with his foot, he hung his hat on it, stuck it from the side of the boulder. The crack of a small caliber revolver broke the almost throbbing stillness. His hat went spinning.

The Kid jerked to closer cover.

"The enemy shoots well," he observed laconically to himself, recovering his hat. "But does he shoot wisely?" For by that shot he definitely had located his challenger—behind a big boulder directly across the trail. He took a quick survey in the gathering gloom about him. He was on slightly lower ground than his challenger. Boulders were all about, great hulking forms that offered a natural breastwork in every direction. And the swiftly failing light made any target uncertain. He could wait until pitch dark or unless his adversary was as well versed in trickery as himself, he could worm his way around behind the boulder which sheltered him.

On his hands and knees he moved cautiously backwards, careful always to keep the barricade of his foe from sight behind his own protection. Presently, without drawing the fire of the mystery gun, he succeeded in gaining another boulder. By a series of catlike movements he wormed his way around again to the trail where, from behind another boulder, he could make out the figure of his challenger in the dim light.

Skylined in the gloom it offered a perfect target. The Kid watched for a few moments, chuckling to himself. Then:

"Come out, *amigo*! I do not want to kill you. It would not be sportsmanlike. For too good a target you offer. But as you come out do not forget I will shoot if you force me." The command was soft. Yet it carried with a singular crash in the stillness of the dusk, echoed hollowly among the boulders.

From his vantage point the Kid saw the form stiffen, saw it come up, whirl to look in all directions.

"One false move and I will shoot, señor, much as I would dislike it," the Kid crooned. "Please to step out—there in the trail. And drop the gun as you come. After all, to shoot you from here would be—almost murder."

He had the satisfaction of seeing the figure jerk straight. Then it was moving cautiously out into the trail. A sound and a puff of dust told him the gun was down. When presently, the stranger stood silhouetted in the wan light, he stepped from his place of concealment, gun in hand. The figure recoiled.

"And now, señor," the Kid asked softly, "what was it you wanted when you challenged my advance? Was it that . . ."

He peered through the dim light. This figure too, suddenly had wilted to the ground. Wary

51

against a ruse, he moved forward. Then he stood directly above, waiting for some sound, some word. But no word came. He holstered his gun, leaned over the inert form only to straighten up quickly. It was the figure of a girl!

The Kid whistled sharply for Rey del Rey. Twice, thrice, before he heard the hoofs of the palomino crunching on the trail. As the brute neared the prone form, the Kid went forward to halt it.

His mount within easy reach again he stooped over the prostrate figure. Sure now that the fall was not intentional, that no trickery awaited him, he placed his arms gently about the girl, lifted her from the ground. She lay limp and lifeless against him. She was light in his arms—a wisp of a figure, her face dead white. Her features were pale, beautiful, the Kid thought. He wondered who she was. Surely not one of the posse. That was too wildly improbable. She must belong somewhere close by. But why had she challenged him?

No answer was forthcoming. The girl apparently had fainted. There was nothing he could do. He didn't even know where she belonged. And how to find out . . .

Much as he hated to, he took to slapping her wrists. They were soft, slender, finely delicate. He worked her arms, which were limp in his grasp. He laid her out flat, tried to restore her to consciousness. Still she made no move.

"We must have water, *amigo*," he told Rey del Rey who stood at his elbow, watching curiously. "But even now I hesitate to share our meager store that may mean life or death to us. But—we must, *caballo mio*. Even though we suffer more than we already have."

By now it was quite dark, so dark the Kid could scarcely see what he was about. But securing his precious canteen from the saddle, he unknotted the silken neckerchief from his throat, dampened it, dropped to his knees beside her to bathe her forehead. And somehow he found a secret sense of satisfaction in bathing that forehead. It was high and dead white save for one black curl that persisted in getting in the way and which he found himself touching gingerly as he laid it back among the others on her shapely head. Her face was oval, her features fine, smooth as agate—now that he had time to study it—a small aquiline nose, a well-shaped mouth, tiny ears that were revealed as he brushed back her hair, long black lashes that framed her closed eyes. He observed her appraisingly as she stretched limp and motionless; a trim little thing he had handled her as though she were weightless.

Then of a sudden he recognized her. She was the girl in the red velvet who had ridden away from Cantina El Paseo in such haste after the murder. But now she was garbed in a corduroy divided skirt and shirt which, open at the neck, revealed a white and shapely throat. Her broad sombrero had fallen askew on a mass of black ringlets. He wondered how she had gotten here, who she was, from whence she had appeared, how she had changed—a thousand things. But she was not reacting to his awkward ministrations. He was positive she had only fainted. Yet for all he had done she still stretched prone on the ground with no sign of returning life.

He took her wrists again, cuddled a slim small hand in his own. It felt warm. He leaned over to place an ear to her mouth. She seemed to be breathing naturally from between lips the color of which shone even in the dull light. He laid his ear against her breast. Her heart was pounding.

A grim smile moved the Kid's lips. He straightened up, got to his feet.

"Come, Rey del Rey," he said. "*Chamaquita* who sham thus with one who tries to help them should be left alone, to find their way home as best they can. The señorita tried to shoot me. Who am I to give her help—or pity? I shall bind her here, and here I shall leave her. Perhaps after a night of terror she will learn something of the courtesy the Cuyamas of old held for the traveler." He strode over to the palomino.

The figure on the ground bolted upright.

"Please don't," the girl begged in a tiny, frightened voice. "It's my ankle. I wrenched it just before you came along. It will not bear my weight. I have tried to stand on it. While you were with—while you were dodging around those rocks I thought I couldn't stand the pain. And when you ordered me out—I was so terrified I forgot the pain for a moment. But I can't stand on it. Please . . . Don't . . ." Her voice trailed off.

CHAPTER SIX

THE MAÑANA KID lifted his bullet-punctured hat to bow politely in the darkness.

"A thousand and one pardons, señorita," he apologized. "Had I for an instant realized . . . but one knows only what one is told. Or can see. The way we met I had so little time for inquiries concerning your personal well-being. There is something I can do, yes?"

For all the mockery in his tone his shuttling thoughts were deadly sober. Who was this girl, whom he last had seen the night of the murder in Cantina El Paseo at Guadalupe, and whose unexpected appearance had upset him strangely. He entertained little doubt that she had been an accomplice of the mystery killer; had never doubted that it was she who had ridden into the night from the cantina. Yet, as he recalled, the riders who had left Guadalupe so precipitously, had gone in different directions. Still, that could have been a blind to throw off a posse in case they were followed.

"There is something you can do," her petulant voice broke in on his thoughts. "I tell you, it's . . ." She pulled her corduroy riding skirt to the top of a fancy-stitched boot. ". . . it's this ankle." She extended her right foot. "I can't get the boot off. I've been trying ever so hard. And it hurts so badly. Then—then you came along. I was frightened, fearful that you . . . Perhaps if you—if you'll pull—"

Came to him to ask her of what she was afraid. For he had seen the light of terror in her eyes even before the killing at the cantina. But that, too, was obvious. As an accomplice of the slayer she had decoyed the flashily garbed youth to the dance floor where he had afforded a better target. And now, as a fugitive, she was fearful that a posse, or perhaps, he himself, had trailed her. After all, she was only a dance-hall girl, else why had she been at Cantina El Paseo? Yet, her fresh young face, the sincerity in her eyes had struck him at sight of her. Her accomplice! He jerked straight to whip the darkness, his ears straining for any sound. He saw nothing, heard nothing save the thin, still sounds of the deepening night.

"The señorita should have said she would accept my help before, without shamming," he chided, trying for the moment to dismiss from his mind the conjectures that only whirled in a bewildering circle. He would find out who she was, where she lived—which must be nearby as evidenced by the changed clothing—and then. . . . But there would be time enough later to ferret out her connection with the Guadalupe killing, and uncover the left-handed gunman. His chief concern now must be to avoid stepping into a net spread by trickery.

He dropped to his knees to take her tiny foot in his hand. With all the care he could exercise he attempted to draw off the boot. She tried to stifle a cry, sank back onto the ground.

"My ankle is swollen so," she panted.

"But the boot must come off, señorita. . . ." He hesitated on that señorita, hoping she would tell him her name. But apparently she did not notice for she said nothing. And after all, she would be foolish to divulge it, he reasoned. Surely she had recognized him, remembered seeing him in the cantina, knew that he knew of the killing. "I dislike hurting you. I dislike hurting any lady—especially one who is so kind and gentle as to shoot at travelers from under cover of a boulder, yes?"

"Please," she begged. "I didn't . . ."

"I know," he said. For all of him a contrite note slipped into his tone. "And I was only making fun. After all, it is not every day that a vaquero has the adventure of a pretty woman challenging him along the trail and shooting the hat from his head. Forgive me," as he felt her tremble. "Forever I say the wrong thing at the wrong time—especially when pretty ladies are within hearing to muddle my thoughts and tongue."

His bantering tone changed to one of sternness. "The boot, señorita. It must come off. It will hurt terribly. But once it is off we can bathe the ankle and bandage it tightly. And so—I shall play the bootjack, yes?"

Still holding her foot he turned his back to her, suddenly thankful for the gloom that hid the flush darkening his face. He cursed himself for his sudden embarrassment. He, the Mañana Kid, whose face was on reward posters from San Diego to Mexicali; the Mañana Kid, who had scorned women in the border dives as he scorned rattlers on the blistered desert. And here was a dance-hall girl, touch of whose tiny foot had set him trembling. Yet of all the women he had encountered along the border there had been none such as she. The others had not so much as caught his fancy. But here, at last, was a girl—a different sort of girl. She had reminded him of a desert flower among rank weeds there at Cantina El Paseo, he recalled. Yet it was this girl—the girl in red—who had ridden away into the night after the murder in the resort.

"Play the bootjack?" she was demanding in a voice that quivered with terror or pain, he couldn't decide.

"But, yes, señorita. I hold your injured ankle between my legs, thus." He backed up to her, his hands on her foot held tightly between his knees. "Let us call it a game—a game we two shall play

60

here in the dark of the night. The game is for you to put your other foot . . ." He stopped, suddenly embarrassed. ". . . put your other foot—against me—and push as you want to, and feel able. If it gets too painful, you can ease the pressure yourself. See, is it not a game, señorita?"

In silence she did as he instructed.

"Is the señorita ready, yes?"

"All ready."

He felt the pressure of her other foot against him. He pulled gently.

"It has to come off," he heard her sobbing. "Please, take it off—even though it hurts terribly. I can stand it. Pull!"

Putting real strength on the boot he gave it a quick jerk that brought a cry of pain from the girl. But the boot slid off. He held a silken clad foot in his hands, fingered the swollen ankle gently.

"I'll light a fire," he said, for the moment forgetful of the risk he ran in his eagerness to help this girl. "It is too dark to examine it otherwise."

"Oh, no. Please don't." There was new terror in her voice.

"Why not, señorita?"

"They will see it?"

"They?" The posse was the thought that flashed to his mind. The posse or her accomplice. "But, señorita, why should you be afraid if I am not."

"Please don't light a fire, that's all. Just help

me bandage it as best you can—so I can make it to—to the ranch."

Then she did live nearby? That accounted for the change of clothing. He would find that ranch even at the risk of his own freedom. He would, but she was not as easy to talk to now as she might have been back there in Guadalupe. Somehow he had liked her best in the red velvet dress there in El Paseo. It had been daring. But it had brought out every line of her fine young figure. And the high-spiked heels, and the silken hose had increased her natural charm.

"Not only shall I bathe and bandage your ankle, señorita, but also shall I take you to your rancho." With misgivings he thought of the precious little store of water in the canteen slung on his saddle.

"You wouldn't dare—take me there." Her dark eyes gleamed at him through the gloom. "Sometime, I may explain. But right now, you've just got to trust me and help me ease the pain in my ankle."

The increasing fear she could not conceal aroused a pity within him. What if she was a dance-hall girl—the accomplice of a killer? She was unusually pretty. He had noticed that at Cantina El Paseo. She was possessed of an appeal that had kept the vaqueros swarming about her. He himself had been conscious of it, had determined to find out about her even before the fatal shot was fired. A dance-hall girl who, here in the still Cuyama night, perhaps miles from human habitation, was pleading with him to trust her—trust her, the accomplice of a killer. The whole thing was without sense or reason. Still, here they were, two alone in the darkness, the girl he perhaps had followed through the night from Guadalupe, instead of the left-handed killer. And she was appealing to him. And strangely, the thing was so real, so sincere, he found his doubts dissolving even while new questions piled into his mind.

"It is best the señorita slip off her stocking," he suggested timidly.

She raised up. And presently the stocking rolled down. But she was unable to get it over the swollen ankle. Taking her bare leg in his hands— which felt terribly awkward and rough against her velvet smooth skin—he worked the stocking off over her foot.

"I shall hurt you only if I cannot help it, señorita," he assured her. "But I cannot bandage it unless—unless I feel—unless I find exactly where it is wrenched."

"Go ahead," she said. "Don't mind me. I'll just lie back. I feel kind of—faint."

With gentle fingers he felt of the swollen ankle. Then taking the dampened scarf with which he had bathed her face, and wetting it again from the precious water in the canteen, he bandaged it tightly. He felt her wincing under his awkward touch. But he went ahead, silently, all too conscious of her nearness, wondering who she was, fearful that she would not tell him.

When he had braced the ankle as best he could he laid it down gently and raised up.

"Perhaps now it feels easier, señorita, yes?"

"Enough so I can get to the ranch. I've been a bother to you, I know. Now I wonder if you'll be good enough to get my horse."

He glanced about in the darkness. He had seen no horse, had heard no sound. Her words again had put him on his guard. Strange that his ear had not caught the movement of a horse nearby. Unless in his preoccupation, his anxiety to help this girl, who stirred him so strangely, he had, for the first time in his life, forgotten caution.

"But was not the señorita thrown?" he asked. "Your horse would not have remained."

"I wrenched my ankle walking through the rocks in my high-heeled boots. I left my horse here in the boulders. If you'll just help me—I'll show you."

He lifted her to her feet. In spite of his protests she insisted on hobbling along. With an arm that tingled about her he moved along slowly.

"And now your horse, señorita?" He smiled into the darkness. "Where would it be?"

"Over there." She pointed off into the gloom. "He's picketed. You should have no trouble finding him."

"And you, *chamaquita* . . . you will be all right?" solicitously. "I could spare you so much pain if you would but let me take you to your rancho."

"No, thank you. You've already done enough. If you'll just get my horse."

He set off in the darkness, reluctant to leave her, determined upon his return to demand her name, find out something of the mystery concerning this rancho where she belonged.

On and on he walked. But he came upon no horse. When he had completed a great circle he came back to where he had left her. She was nowhere in sight.

"Señorita," he called softly, thinking perhaps she had laid down to rest her ankle. "*Chamaquita.*"

No answer. He came near shouting, but thought better of it. After all, he knew nothing of her. Even now she might be working with the posse that had raced after him from Guadalupe! He had every reason to doubt her, none to believe her.

He called again. Still no answer. Against his better judgment he cupped lighted matches in his hands, made a thorough search of the ground about the boulder. Then presently he discovered fresh horse tracks. Not one set, but two.

He straightened up. The girl had tricked him, had sent him in the wrong direction after her horse, then had secured her mount and ridden away. Her accomplice probably had had him covered every minute.

The Mañana Kid sat flat down and cursed—cursed himself for a fool. Probably under the menace of a mystery gun he had helped her because she was pretty; because he had pitied her from the moment he had seen that light of fear in her eyes in Guadalupe. She deserved no pity now. She had tricked him. He would show her up for what she was—a dancehall girl and the accomplice of a murderer. But why had she done this? And who was the rider who had come up in the short time he had been away?

Presently he succeeded in shrugging the thing off. The Kid had not lived his life on the border for nothing. Women were all the same whether he met them in a dance-hall or, like this, far from nowhere in the night-shrouded Cuyamas. There were more important things at the moment. Eating right now was vastly more important. And drinking. But he had used all but a few drops from his canteen to bathe the girl's ankle. And Rey del Rey needed water. Not that he cared for himself. He could get by for a time . . . but his faithful palomino . . .

He whistled shrilly for Rey del Rey. What mattered it if anyone heard—the posse, or anyone else. His nerves were raw, his mood ugly. He welcomed action—any kind of action, even though it now was so dark he could scarcely see a foot ahead of him. Rey del Rey came up, snorting. The Kid swung into the saddle, to sit staring into the gloom. Once he thought he caught the sound of hoof-beats throbbing on the air. But he could not be sure for the sound was that of a horse moving slowly through the wild arroyos and barrancas about him.

"That'll be her, and her companion who, no doubt, had me covered at every move," he said grimly. "*Sangre de Cristo*, Kid, what an ass you are to let down your guard thus because of a pretty face. But I shall find out who she is and of what she is afraid—as well as the identity of this mystery vaquero who comes so conveniently to her aid. However, we shall eat first, *compañero* . . . and choke the food down without water, thanks to the señorita."

Giving Rey del Rey rein, he headed into the night in the direction of the occasional distant hoof throbs.

CHAPTER SEVEN

T OO LONG had the Mañana Kid been on the trail to be caught hungry without food. He pulled up presently to swing down and undo one of his saddlebags. From within he pulled a carefully wrapped tortilla, found himself some jerky and stretched out on the ground. To follow the girl in the darkness was impossible. The hoof-beats of her horse traveling slowly in broken country offered no lead. Even the direction in which the old man of the cabana had said lay Rancho Diablo was lost to him in the darkness. Possessed however of an uncanny sense of direction, he refused to give up. Those hoof-beats had come from below—down there somewhere in the breaks he had sighted during the day.

The meager snack finished, while Rey del Rey nibbled at the sparse grass beside him, the Kid caught up the palomino and again climbed into the saddle.

By now stygian darkness had settled down—darkness more intense because of the stars that seemed to hang almost within reach in the black void that was the sky. The sound of hoof-beats long since had been lost on the night air.

He rode on. But once his quick ear had lost even the throb of those dull hoof-beats, he determined not to get too far from the place where he had encountered the girl. He pulled rein again, and finding a sheltered spot behind a boulder, dismounted, unrigged Rey del Rey, made the palomino secure with a pair of rawhide hobbles and stretched out on the sweat-damp saddle blanket.

Once free of the saddle, the palomino shook itself thankfully and got down to roll. Always amused—as is any vaquero by the rolling of his horse—the Kid cheered softly the brute's attempts to go completely over. But the weary Rey del Rey was satisfied to dust his golden coat, then lurch up to shake again, blow his nose and fall to seeking out the stray bunches of cured grass with the optimism of a desert horse.

The Kid twisted a cigarette and touched a match to it in the darkness, careful to shield the flare of light with cupped hands. His *pitillo* glowing, he stretched out again and fell to mulling over the events of the day. But the strange things he had encountered from the time of his arrival in Guadalupe defied solution. The more he tried to make sense to them the drowsier he became. Finally utter fatigue claimed him. He fell asleep, to dream of a girl laying prone on a prairie while he attempted to ease a sprained ankle. A pretty girl, a girl he would see again, he hoped. But a girl who apparently had no intention of seeing him if she could avoid it. For after his kindness she had left him without so much as a thanks. And she had tricked him to do it.

The Mañana Kid awoke in pre-dawn darkness to whistle for Rey del Rey. The palomino nickered softly. Locating the brute presently in the gloom, he stripped off the hobbles and led it back. Shaking out the blanket on which he had slept, and rubbing Rey del Rey's back to be careful against any piece of dirt that would start a sore, he resaddled and swung up.

Early as it was he was tormented by thirst—horrible, haunting thirst that drove all else from his mind. There were a few drops in the canteen slung behind the saddle—a few precious drops he had saved after he had wet the kerchief—the kerchief that bound the ankle of the girl who had tricked him.

Getting down after a time, he secured the canteen, shook it. Less than a third full. Rey del Rey nickered piteously. Carefully he poured a few drops into his hand, held it before the horse. It lapped eagerly at his moist fingers. Time and again while his own parched throat cried for water, he let Rey del Rey lick the moisture from his hand. And then, finally when only enough water remained in the canteen to make a sound, he wiped his hand dry on the pleading animal's nose, slung the canteen behind the cantleboard and mounted.

Dawn found him well on his way, plunging deeper and deeper into the badlands which reared up about him. No hoof-beats ahead now. They had been lost forever—the hoof-beats of the killer of Guadalupe or of the girl who had tricked him and her companion. No hoof-beats behind that would signal the approach of the posse, long since outdistanced by Rey del Rey, who for all his thirst was jerking and sawing on the bit.

The sun came swimming up in a sea of metal to turn the Cuyamas into an inferno. Ugly mesquite-covered buttes stepped away finally to become but dim etchings in the smoke-blue air. Here and there gnarled oaks gave promise of water—a promise that was not fulfilled by the sun-cracked beds of writhing barrancas. Occasionally an oasis rose ahead—a verdant, oak-spangled patch that defied the ravages of the scourging sun. Time and again he dismounted to stretch out in the cooling shade and gaze up at the barren, ugly Cuyamas that towered above him. But never did he find water. He only stopped that Rey del Rey might pick at the scrub oak and the grass that grew rank in the shade, perhaps gather a little moisture from their leaves. Then again he would mount and rowel ahead.

Dust rose chokingly from the trail to parch

his throat, powder him with a thin gray film and glisten on his lean face. Thirst put a sag in his shoulders. But the trace of a smile still hovered on his lips.

CHAPTER EIGHT

W ITH daybreak, prowling cattle had taken to following him. First a lone critter that drifted out from a barranca to amble along in the dust scuffed up by the hoofs of the weary Rey del Rey. Others came singly and in small bunches until a considerable herd was strung out behind him. Twice during the morning the sniffing brutes circled him. He attempted to rout them. They only backed away to paw dirt and shake their spike horns savagely. Then when he moved on, like a pack of wolves they resumed dogging his tracks. There was something sinister in their actions, something terrifying in their utter fearlessness.

Ever keeping a sharp eye on the brutes the Kid rode along. Wild cattle, no doubt. Yet far too many for safety. Frantic, hostile cattle that sight of a human seemed to goad to a frenzy. Yet the brutes were no wilder than the region through which he was passing—a region devoid of beauty where even the mesquite about him was shriveled with the blistering sun, the earth baked hard as flint.

Still no sight of Rancho Diablo, which the old man of the cabana had told him lay below. But he was positive of his direction even though darkness had intervened. Reared as he had been in the outlying wastes of deep California, the Kid's direction had developed into a sense as acute as that of his nostrils which now burned and smarted with the stench of a parboiled land; a sense as keen as that of his eyes, shot with blood and film by the sultry wind constantly whining across the region—eyes whipping the wild country for a glimpse of some habitation, straining to keep in sight every head of the cattle that milled about threateningly.

As day advanced his thirst became almost unbearable. And Rey del Rey had taken to coughing violently; spasmodic convulsions that stopped him in the trail until they had passed to end in a hollow groan and pitiful nicker. But the few precious drops in the canteen must be saved until the last. Even then they would be of no avail to aid the palomino who struggled on so gamely beneath him.

The Kid fell to cursing. Again he had allowed his chivalry to get the better of him. Had he ignored the youngster, Toughy, and the girl and ridden on he might have made Rancho Diablo. Had he not given her the most of his precious water it might have seen him through. She deserved no help. She had proved that by the way she had tricked him.

A grim smile braced his sun-cracked lips at thought of her. She had won the first round by speed. Probably the second by trickery. She could have helped him by directing him to a rancho. What of it now? A pretty face had gotten him into a predicament that at the moment seemed hopeless. It was not the first time. Nor the last. In this case there would be another time. He would meet her again. And then . . .

Where the dusty trail pitched up over the base of a butte the Kid pulled rein to stand in his stirrups and let Rey del Rey blow. But he heard nothing that would account for the sudden tightening of his nerves, saw nothing save the hounding range cattle and other small bunches scattered about a great basin into which he had ridden.

Still, warned to caution by some innate sense, he dismounted. Himself thankful for the respite from the sticky saddle—as was Rey del Rey, who shook himself with relief as the load was lifted from his back—he moved up the trail. With every step his nerves grew tighter. Shifting his bridle reins to his left hand, his right fell to the butt of his forty-five. Slower now he moved. For over that rise lay danger. Perhaps the posse. Perhaps the girl and her companion who had sent the youth to his death in Cantina El Paseo at Guadalupe. But whatever it was, he was going ahead. His one hope lay in reaching water. The thirst that left his throat dry and aching, now kept him licking cracked lips with a feverish tongue, made him desperate.

A few more steps. He stopped short. Directly ahead a great white-faced bull with a gigantic sweep of horns appeared to let forth a grumbling challenge. The Kid whirled to mount. The move frightened Rey del Rey. The palomino shied violently. The reins burned through the Kid's fingers. His forty-five swung up, fell. Now that no human faced him there was no need to shoot. Fugitive that he was a shot might betray his whereabouts.

He chuckled aloud at that. What difference did it make who found him. He would welcome any posse if they had water, then risk shooting it out later.

A cracked bellow from the bull. The pawing brute downed its head and charged. The Kid leaped aside. The animal thundered past. Almost before the Kid could recover from his amazement at the unprovoked attack by the brute on the open range, the bull slid to a halt, lurched about and came back. Running blindly as it was, eluding it was an easy matter. Again the Kid bounded aside—this time to the side of Rey del Rey who, once ground-picketed by the dragging reins, had stopped. Securing the reins, the Kid vaulted into the saddle. Mounted he felt more secure. He had heard of wild cattle who would attack a man on foot. Never had he heard of range stock that would molest a horseman.

By now the scattered herds he had sighted in the basin were closing in on a lumbering run to join the brutes that had dogged him through the day. They came bawling and pawing dirt. And the bull had stopped a short way above to watch him from white-rimmed eyes almost concealed by the horns that lashed the trail.

Thoroughly aroused to his danger, the Kid roweled forward. The brute held its ground. Then, to his amazement, it let forth a bellow of rage and charged again. Too late the Kid attempted to rein about. One of the sweeping horns gouged the palomino's shoulder. Rey del Rey lurched back under the impact.

For all its film of dust the Kid's face went white. Snatching his forty-five he fired. But the terrified Rey del Rey lunged away. The bullet went wild. The bull whirled and disappeared over the pitch.

Consumed now by a cold fury, the Kid set to routing the collecting cattle, his cracking revolver sending screaming lead over their backs. Even that lead failed to stampede the brutes, which only backed off a short distance to throw dirt and shake their heads savagely. Presently a steer broke. Turning, they all lumbered away.

When the last animal had taken refuge in the

barrancas—from the rims of which they eyed him belligerently—the Kid got down again. This time to examine Rey del Rey's shoulder, the wound in which was pulsing blood.

"*Sangre de Cristo*," he cried, holding fast the terrified horse and dashing dirt into the wound to stem the flow of blood. "This would happen to you when you are so thirsty—and when you have been so brave. What wouldn't we give for water now, *caballo mio*? But we have no water. And you are hurt. . . ." He buried his face against Rey del Rey's wet neck. "And to think, I missed. Me—the Mañana Kid—and I missed." He fell to stroking the nose of the nervous brute that nuzzled him pleadingly.

Not until now did the Kid realize to what extent thirst had reduced him. He was trembling violently. His legs could scarcely support his weight. His tongue felt swollen. He could hardly bring it back into his mouth when he licked his hot lips.

With an effort he jerked himself together, collected his almost incoherent thoughts. Ahead, somewhere over the mesquite cacti-clotted land lay a rancho. For once his sense of direction seemed to have deserted him. He was not so sure. And there might be a posse—warned by his shots—lying in ambush for him. To seek aid at any rancho—if indeed there be one close at hand—was to risk capture. Yet ahead somewhere might be the girl, and her accomplice killer. Of that left-handed gunman he had no fear. The girl . . . he had a score to settle with her.

Perhaps Rey del Rey could not go on. The wound in his shoulder looked ugly, although the blood flow had stopped. But even if Rey del Rey could not proceed he had to have water. That meant abandon the faithful palomino. Abandon the horse that had carried him across endless miles of blistering trails! Better that they stay together even though it meant death. Besides, the wounded animal would only betray him to the possemen if, indeed, they still were on his trail. He glanced around glassily. The cattle were bunching again, starting to circle him. They would make short work of him now that he was afoot.

For all of his predicament, the Mañana Kid smiled, a grim tightening of lips across braced teeth. Together they would go down, if they must. Mounting, he urged Rey del Rey up over the pitch. The palomino went gamely. A short distance and it fell to limping. Completely fagged, it stopped in its tracks. The Kid's rowels bit deep. For the cattle were milling about again on a lumbering trot, bawling as they came. Sharp rowels goaded Rey del Rey on. The brute, too, seemed to sense the seriousness of the thing. For straining muscles told the Kid of the effort it was making. Not until the cattle had wearied of the pursuit and left off to graze did he dismount to lead the limping palomino and seek cover from the scourging sun under the cut banks of the arroyos. Gone now was his puma-like grace. He moved heavily, tormented by thirst and aching weariness.

The sun crawled through the coppery sky, started its downward course. Panting, sweating, choking, the Kid trudged on, only numbly alert now to signs of danger.

Late in the afternoon he dropped rein and crawled to the rim of a barranca to sweep the region with bloodshot eyes. Far below in the deceptive distance was a large ranch. Hope flared within him. Yet . . . suppose the posse already had reached that rancho? The real killer? But he, too, probably would try to avoid all habitation. Besides, what did it matter now? Unless he found water quickly no posse would take—him—alive.

CHAPTER NINE

On and on the Mañana Kid stumbled, hoping, praying fervently that the rancho he had sighted had not been a mirage—the image of a distorted brain that he had known before. Those other times, when like this, he had lurched along on the desert the mirage had been only of water—cool, inviting pools that had increased the torment of his thirst. Thirst!

He seized the canteen. With trembling fingers he finally succeeded in undoing the saddle straps that held it. Rey del Rey nickered pleadingly, turned his head to watch.

Once the canteen was free the Kid shook it. Less than a quarter full. Yet even that little might mean life for him. But the palomino?

Careful lest he spill a single drop, the Kid filled a cupped hand. But instead of carrying it to his own lips that burned for a taste of it, he carried it to the lips of the nickering horse.

"I drank last, *caballo mio*," he choked out. "Or did I? What matters it? What I have is yours—*compañero* of countless trails."

Rey del Rey lapped the water eagerly. Then

like a dog he licked along the Kid's arm. When he had finished the Kid drew back his hand to suck the still moist fingers. Time and again he repeated the process, doling the precious water with miserly care, while his own throat ached at the sound as it gurgled from the canteen. The last drop he gave to the nickering palomino, then rubbed his damp hand over its nose and up under the sweaty bridle.

The Kid tied the empty canteen onto the saddle.

"That is all, *caballo mio*," he said, stroking the brute's arched neck. "You needed it more than I, yes? Now we go on. Surely . . . as the horse held back on the tightened reins, ". . . surely you too, are game. Never have I known you to fail me. We have been thus before, *compañero*. You have yet the first time to see me lie down and curse circumstances. Nor will you now, although that small drink would have given me new life. Come *caballo mio*—a song. What would one sing, dying of thirst. Why not . . . I have it—the trail song of Los Rancheros. Why not, *caballo mio*? Too bad you cannot sing. For that matter neither can I. But I sing anyway. Always have we done this when the breaks are against us. Listen—

"Oh, we'll drink, drink, drink to Los
    Rancheros
To Rancheros who have gone . . ."

A sharp whinny from the palomino stopped him. They had come up to the rim of an arroyo. Directly ahead in a wide canyon, its floor studded with bunchgrass, its steep walls capped with colored gyp rock lay a rancho. Cattle were grazing about. But unlike those in the basin they only stared at him inquisitively.

"A rancho, Rey del Rey," the Kid muttered thickly. "Never do I get to sing my songs to the end. And me such a nightingale, yes?" He threw back his head and laughed. A chortle that presently swelled loudly in his thirst-closed throat. "Never do I attempt to sing, *compañero*, only when we have tossed in the last chip. And always something happens. Like this. It means water for you, *caballo mio*. It means water— water—and life even if we must claim it with bullets."

He lurched on toward the rancho that suddenly took to swaying before his glassy eyes. But this was no mirage. A short distance ahead was, indeed, a rancho. His thirst-distorted mind might conjure up an image of fancy. But Rey del Rey knew, for he was nickering constantly now.

As for the Kid, he still wasn't sure. Through glazed eyes that seemed blistered in his head, he could see it. But as he blinked swollen lids over those eyes to open them and peer unseeing until the haze had cleared, there was nothing, only swaying buttes and barrancas from which heat poured up in shimmering waves. He wanted to sing again, as he had before when he and the palomino had all but given up on some waterless waste.

The song formed on his lips. He tried to voice the words. They stuck in his parched throat; refused to roll across his tongue that was terribly thick, too large for his aching mouth.

Finally he got them out, scarcely audible to himself, yet strangely loud and metallic in his ears.

"Oh, we'll drink, drink, drink to Los
    Rancheros—"

He broke off again. This was no mirage ahead. It really was a rancho . . . a place of many well-kept buildings nestled on the gyp-crowned canyon. And Rey del Rey still was nickering with every step—a continual, pitiful pleading.

The Kid stopped to rub his aching eyes that suddenly seemed incapable of focus. The palomino went on to tug at the reins. Directly ahead loomed a rambling adobe ranchhouse, its walls somehow reminding him of a row of white tombstones.

Still not daring to trust his sight—too many times the Kid had stumbled over hopeless miles toward mirages—he reached out. There was no doubt now. For the side wall of that 'dobe ranchhouse before him was rough and real.

He clapped a hand over the nickering Rey del Rey's nose. Even though there was water here, there also might be trouble. Now that help was close at hand he waited until he could pull himself together, get some control of his singing nerves. When presently the blood had stopped drumming in his ears, and the scant moisture of his licking tongue had given some relief to his swollen lips, he listened. But the rancho might have been a place of the dead for all the sound he heard at the moment. Hugging the side wall, he edged around toward the front of the building. The shadows of evening now lay long in the canyon. But still he could see through eyes that burned and tortured him. At the corner he dared a glance. A girl in a crisp, white house-dress stood on the front porch; above a man sprawled on the steps. Her back was toward him.

He heard the girl speak. Angrily, he thought. But the blood pounding again in his ears might have tricked him. He cared not for their conversation. What mattered it to him? He wanted water. Not so much for himself, although he could not force his swollen tongue back between his sand-dry teeth. Water! Water!

He was barely conscious of Rey del Rey's piercing whinny. He saw the man leap to his feet. The girl whirled. He pitched forward on his face, his knees suddenly turned to tallow.

Summoning his last strength the Kid got shakily to his feet. A hand fled to his throat to claw open his shirt.

"My horse, señorita," he heard himself croaking in a strange unnatural voice. "Rey del Rey, the finest caballo, the truest amigo in all California, is dying of thirst. And he is hurt. Please, señorita. Not for myself—I ask nothing for myself. But have someone see to him. *Gracias* señorita . . . *La chamiquita* cannot refuse."

"*La chamaquita!*" She swung around on the porch. "Juan," she cried, "attend to him. See—he needs water . . . and his horse shall have the best. Look to his horse. Quickly!"

He saw her then through eyes filmed with haze. It was the girl from Cantina El Paseo at Guadalupe—the girl with the injured ankle with whom he had shared the precious water that had brought him to this state—the girl he had determined to find after she had tricked him.

Everything was growing black. He backed over against Rey del Rey. She was the accomplice of a killer. Even now that killer might be . . . he reached for his forty-five. A numb right hand could not find it. And the girl—the girl who had tricked him, was coming down off the porch. She was beside him. He tried to turn on her, to tell her what he thought of her for leaving him out there without water. But the words choked in his throat. Try as he would he could not get them past his swollen tongue.

Now her hand was on his arm, cool and fresh and reassuring. He tried to jerk away. She was just a dance-hall girl, the confederate of a killer. She had tricked him out there in the darkness, left him without sufficient water.

The Kid reared back on his heels. But he couldn't seem to stop there. Again he reached for his gun. But his hand only slapped empty air. The girl was trying to support him. She was talking to him—had her arm around his shoulders, was trying to lead him somewhere.

"*Gracias, chamaquita,*" he found himself muttering thickly. "All I ask is water . . . for my horse. Afterward, or not as you care, I would drink. Surely, *chamaquita*, you cannot refuse water to my horse. For he has been hurt—gored by a bull . . . water for him . . . water . . ."

A suffocating wave of blackness engulfed him. He strove desperately to stay on his feet. For all he could do he pitched forward, half conscious that it was the girl who was supporting him in her arms.

CHAPTER TEN

THE MAÑANA KID'S first conscious thought was of heat—blistering, paralyzing heat that wilted his brain, seemed to sear his soul, left him fearful to rouse himself from this stupor that, at least, obscured the sight of desert wastes his eyes no longer could withstand.

For his eyes ached violently. He seemed incapable of opening them. Heat welded the lids. His cracked lips and tongue were swollen. His head sputtered and popped. The infernal din of hot blood throbbing against his ear-drums deafened him. He tried not to move lest pains shooting through him again send the dark mantle of insensibility down upon him.

His body was bathed in perspiration. His silver-mounted rig weighted him down. The fancy-stitched boots were shackles on his feet.

Dreading to shake out of the lethargy that possessed him, yet fearful the torture would only increase if he gave way further, he managed to open his eyes. Instead of the glaring wastes he expected, he was in semi-darkness—hot darkness that seemed to stifle him.

He attempted to sit up. The effort brought forth a whistling sigh. He dropped back, fighting for breath, clawing at his throat. Realizing he was only wasting what strength he possessed, he quieted down, presently to raise himself slowly to a sitting position. When his eyes had accustomed themselves to the gloom he looked around.

Apparently he was on the floor of a little used storeroom. Beside him he could make out a heap of old saddle-rigs, pieces of harness and a pile of sacks. The room had the fetid smell of unused places. With no ventilation the heat was terrific.

The Kid wondered how he had come there. Then, as things drifted back to him, he fell to blaming the girl. He recalled now that he had lurched into the rancho half dead for water, had appealed to her and then collapsed. But he had been given no water. His parched throat and swollen lips were proof of that. Instead he had been bundled off into this airless storeroom—his return for sharing his last precious water with her.

The grim smile the border knew and feared refused to form on the lips of the Mañana Kid. He had put his faith in a woman—one of the few times—and lost again. There at Guadalupe she had seemed so sincere. Even back there on the mesa, when he was bandaging her injured ankle, she had seemed like a frightened girl. But, he had appealed to her, asking only for water for . . .

Rey del Rey!

Clenching his teeth on the pain, the Kid braced himself against the wall to outwit his spinning brain, and lurched to his feet. She might treat him thus if she chose. After all, she was only a dance-hall girl, the accomplice of a murderer, of whom one should expect little. But Rey del Rey had been wounded by the sweeping horns of the bull they had encountered back there in the glaring wastes. If they had him cast into this breathless storeroom without drink, then Rey del Rey, too, might have been denied attention and water. For himself he did not care—but for Rey del Rey . . .

"*Sangre de Cristo*," he hissed through lips swollen until they beat back the whistling breath into his aching lungs. "Shall she pay for this if *caballo mio* has not been given proper care. Rancho Diablo, truly it is. It could be no other place. There is no mistaking it." The words of the old man of the cabana began ringing in his ears. His words—he recalled them now—"You look a heap like Johnnie Bender. You don't happen to be kin of his, do you? It wouldn't be healthy for kin of Johnnie Bender's down yonder."

Kin of Johnnie Bender? Johnnie Bender, hell! He would yet show the inhuman lot who refused water to a man half-dead with thirst.

For himself—*Sangre de Cristo*! What mattered it? He had been treated thus before and shot his way through a cowardly crew. But if they had not attended to Rey del Rey—

By now the violence of his emotions had brought him upright, although the weakness from thirst kept him braced against the wall. His hand crept down to the butt of the forty-five that—strangely, now he thought of it—still hung in its holster. Probably because he had been so near gone when they had thrown him inside they had not so much as taken the precaution to disarm him.

He would show them—show her! The Mañana Kid, now that he was on his feet was far from gone. After all, he had asked so little, and that little had been refused. In the sudden clarity that had come to his brain he recalled his words when he had lurched around the corner of the ranchhouse to speak to the girl—and the fellow who sprawled on the steps beneath her.

"All I ask is water . . . for my horse." His words drummed in his ears. "Afterward, or not, as you care, I would drink. Yet I ask nothing for myself. *Chamaquita*, you cannot refuse water for my horse. For he has been hurt . . . water . . . water . . ."

He had appealed to her to return but a measure of the kindness he had shown her. He had appealed to her for Rey del Rey, that the gored, thirsty palomino might have aid and rest. Her answer to him had been—

His eyes darted around the darkened, suffocating storeroom. Had his lot, too, been the lot of Rey del Rey?

From Tijuana to Mexicala, from San Diego to Tucson there were many who knew him and quailed before the forty-five he now clenched tightly in his hand. Others had thought to kill the Mañana Kid; especially men of the type that had been with the girl there on the ranchhouse steps. He knew that breed; for years on the border he had slapped them aside with his cupped hand. Seldom had he used his gun with men like that. A well placed fist, a word of warning, always had sufficed. But that could wait. It was Rey del Rey of whom he thought. Rey del Rey, the golden palomino that had no equal in southern California. They had played fair with Rey del Rey or his gun would blaze death.

Even in his half-dazed condition the Kid was no fool. He slid the forty-five from its holster and broke the cylinder. Although it was too dark to see, he took each cartridge from its chamber, rolled the leaded end in his mouth. The chambers were full. No cartridge had been tampered with.

"Idiots!" The Kid spat as he replaced the cartridges, jammed the forty-five back into its holster. "Idiots, who would kill a man with thirst yet not understand that no man dies thus without a battle, especially if his gun . . ." Now the grim smile did succeed in settling on his lips, parched and swollen as they were. The cocksure fools had made no attempt to protect themselves if, by a miracle, he did survive. For his forty-five had been untouched. It carried a charge that held the power of life or death for six—or more!

Secure in the knowledge that he could meet the best, the Kid started across the storeroom. It was dark now—pitch dark. He tiptoed as best he could in his boots that set the floor to squeaking, seemed to shut off the blood that pulsed in his aching feet. Soon he would have rest. Off would come those boots. He would bathe those feet; himself have water. For if there was water on the rancho he would have it.

All the bitterness in his soul surged up against the girl—the girl who was to blame for this.

Presently his fumbling fingers found a door. It swung open at his touch. The cool of night struck him in the face. He sucked in his breath eagerly. That draught gave him strength. And somewhere out there under the myriad of stars that blinked down at his aching eyes was water. Somewhere out there was Rey del Rey, the one thing on earth that never had tricked him. He would find them both or die trying!

With cautious stride he left the storeroom, thankful for the darkness that concealed his movement until he could collect every faculty, coordinate every muscle that protested painfully his movements.

Just outside he stopped. The big ranchhouse was lighted at one end—the dull light of kerosene lamps. The outer wing was in utter darkness—sinister, foreboding, that wing struck him.

But the yard in which he found himself apparently was deserted. Far below he could make out the squat outline of the barn, could hear the nickering, the champing of feeding horses. Between him and that barn lay nothing save an open plot and a cooling breeze that gave him new life—a breeze that brought back his shoulders, whipped life into his face that felt paralyzed with heat. And out there somewhere was water.

For all his weakness he broke into an awkward trot. He was not challenged. Presently his ears, for all their drumming, caught the sound of water. That sound set him to running madly, running until he was staggering.

Then he had dropped to his knees beside a horse trough into which a pipe trickled cool water. But too long the Kid had known the desert to follow a wild impulse and throw himself headlong into the trough, drink his fill of its life-giving fluid. With a hand he scooped the cooling water to his lips, to bathe them. Then he let a few drops pass into his fevered throat. With all the strength he could command he kept from gulping the water, while he bathed his forehead, his face, his neck, his shoulders.

Presently he got up, his head dripping with the welcome moisture that trickled down across his shirt to wilt it even more than the perspiration that had plastered it to his body.

Time and again he bathed his parched lips, let the cooling flood envelop his head and shoulders. Then, when new life had surged into his aching body, he took a sip of the water, leaving off before his burning thirst was quenched.

His throat still ached but his head was clearer and his nerves far steadier. He pulled himself away from the trough, strode off across the yard toward the barn. A confident stride now—the stride of the Mañana Kid who had been given new life, who feared no one or no thing.

He slammed open the barn door, realizing the sound might be heard, hoping that it was. He had the butt of his forty-five clenched tightly in his hand. Further than that he cared not. He had cause to hate this spread. The girl . . . a consuming hatred against her welled up to increase his recklessness.

Inside the barn all was dark, save for the wan light of the stars through the open door. The nickering of ponies that lifted their noses from the mangers greeted him. Finding a match in the wilted trousers beneath his chaps, he lighted it, whistled softly. The whinny of Rey del Rey came back. He could hear the palomino straining on his halter, pawing in his stall. He moved forward cautiously.

Again he whistled to locate the horse. An answering nicker.

Then he found the brute, which nuzzled his

arm lovingly. He felt his way into the stall to the manger. It was heaped high with grain and hay. His hands stroked the palomino in the darkness, presently to seek out the gored shoulder. The wound had been salved and cared for. He placed an arm around the nickering brute's neck.

"Silence, *caballo mio*," he admonished in an ear that twitched—"Far better have they treated you than they did me. Because you are worth much to them. I . . . may cause them trouble. I only worried about you, *compañero*—worried for fear they had not attended to your shoulder and had cast you, too, aside to die. But you are well . . ." He kissed the horse lovingly on its jaw. ". . . and in shape to ride when we feel inclined—if we do so, *amigo mio*. Come morning we shall look this rancho over, *amigo*. As we have looked other ranchos and towns over. Just we two, *amigo*. For we trust no one else—especially women. We shall give them, perhaps, what we call the hell, *compañero*. Be on your guard. Listen for my whistle. For I may need you, *pronto*. After all, I may not be able to fight scores. . . . The grim smile was back on his lips. "Although we have done it before, and won, *caballo mio*."

His mood grew serious. "But the girl—the *chamaquita*—she worries me, *compañero*. For all she has done to me, still I cannot believe that she would order me cast into that storeroom to die of thirst. That we shall see, just you and I, as we always have done. Now my rig, *caballo* . . . I will find it here in the barn. For they yet have not had time to steal it as they intended to steal you."

Quitting the side of the pony, which nickered after him, he went to the wall of the barn where the saddles were suspended from pegs. With the cupped light of a match he located his. Letting the light die, he felt in the saddle pocket, found a strip of jerkie and a tortilla. He went back to pet the palomino while he ate.

When he had finished, he went outside to lie down along the horse trough and cool himself, taking occasional drafts of the cold water.

Now a dim light had flared up in a row of small buildings apart from the dull gleam in the wing of the big ranchhouse.

"The bunkhouse," the Kid decided as he peeled off every stitch and washed himself in the water. "The bunkhouse of vaqueros employed by men who would kill a traveler with thirst. Perhaps . . . and then, perhaps not, *lobos*." His body damp and cool, he dragged on his clothes, to stride away— the Mañana Kid of old, the grim smile bracing his lips.

"*Sangre de Cristo*!" he breathed. "What fools. To kill a man dying with thirst does not mean to throw him in a storeroom alongside of which almost, water is running. We shall see—and now for rest. Then to even the score with this girl."

CHAPTER ELEVEN

HORSE-BREAKING was in full swing at Rancho Diablo. Shortly after dawn a score of riders and vaqueros, with spur rowels hooked in the oak poles, were distributed along the top of a round corral, sucking on cigarettes and taunting sweating, swearing bronc-twisters struggling with the vicious brutes run into the enclosure.

No one noticed the arrival of the Mañana Kid. He slipped the bit from Rey del Rey's mouth and turned him loose to graze with bridle reins trailing. Then he sauntered over and joined the group. The air was thick with dust, dense clouds of which rolled skyward, powdering the clamorous crew and drifting away to sift in a dirty blanket over chaparral and mesquite. Oaths, snorts, bawls, the clatter of numberless hoofs combined in a deafening tumult.

Accustomed as the Kid was to the scene, entirely at home in the din and hubbub of a horse ranch, the bursts of raucous laughter and the curses of the riders inside the corral, fell on deaf ears. With a good night's rest behind him, food and water, he was his old self. And with

Rey del Rey beside him—his shoulder, on which daylight had shown only a superficial wound that had been properly treated—he was ready for anything. The same Mañana Kid who had ridden out from Guadalupe after defying a mob.

A hush of fearful expectancy settled down upon the crew and drew his attention to the pen into which a big, blood-bay gelding had been turned.

Head up, nostrils distended, its untrimmed tail almost touching the ground, it circled the enclosure, its legs moving with mechanical precision. Terror showed in the depths of eyes rolled back to the whites yet a defiance and unconquerable spirit that would test the mettle of any rider lurked in the steel muscles rippling beneath its sleek hide.

"Juan Lopez!" shouted the men on the fence. "Come on, you bronc-forker! Here's El Scorpion's brother. He's your meat. Ride him, Juan!"

The Kid looked around for this Juan for whom they were shouting. At that moment Toughy—the boy he had encountered on the mesa—rode up, dismounted and clumped across the yard to the side of a lanky rider sprawled on the ground, smoking. The fellow did not even glance at the boy who stood gazing at him with something akin to silent worship in his eyes. Toughy's penchant for flashy apparel was easily understood. Even to the swagger tilt of his battered hat he had attempted to imitate the dress of the man who, the Kid decided instantly, was Juan, the terror and the idol of Rancho Diablo.

The Kid sized him up from head to toe. A dark complexioned, hatchet-faced man with small, beady eyes. If his hard-lined countenance had one redeeming feature it was not discernible at a single glance. His chaps of soft brown leather, stamped with flowers, were fringed with strings of buckskin tied in glistening metal discs. A gaudy purple shirt, thrown open at the neck, flamed violently beneath a brilliant vest checker-boarded with vivid colors. A fancy cartridge-belt sagged under the weight of a big, pearl-handled forty-five slung well forward at his thigh. Silver spurs, with enormous rowels and adorned with bell-shaped danglers, completed the costume.

Of a sudden the Kid recognized him. He was the vaquero who had been sprawled on the steps at the ranchhouse, on his arrival. The vaquero who, no doubt, had carried out the girl's orders to deny him water and throw him half-dead with thirst into the storeroom. A slow hatred possessed the Kid. But he jerked his hand back from his half-drawn gun. They were talking, those two.

"Where'd you get that blood on your hand?" Lopez grunted.

Toughy glanced about wildly. His eyes met those of the Kid who nodded reassuringly.

"Fell down," he faltered.

"Where'd you get the rag? Let's see it?" Reaching out, Juan jerked the kerchief the Kid had given the boy from the wounded hand. Toughy winced with pain but did not reply.

"Where'd you get it?" Lopez repeated, arising and glaring down at the lad who shrank away from him.

"I found it."

"Don't lie to me," Lopez snarled. "You stole it somewheres. Who's been around here with them kind of trappings?"

"Honest, Juan, I found it," whimpered Toughy. "I—"

"Rattle your hocks, Lopez," shouted the men on the fence. "Lay off the kid; take a whirl at El Scorpion's brother."

Lopez reached out and seized Toughy. Holding him at arm's length he slapped him across the cheek. "Don't lie to me, you dirty little brat," he grated. "You stole this rag. I'll keep it just to learn you to tell the truth."

Pity for the forlorn child set the hot blood of anger pounding in the Kid's veins. His first impulse was to smash Lopez' hatchet face. He started to speak, to challenge this bronc-twister who had abused the sobbing boy, but cold caution tempered hasty judgment. With an effort he succeeded in getting a grip on himself.

"I'll get you for that, Juan," screamed Toughy. "You wait. You've busted me all you're going to."

"Keep the mouth closed," came a gruff order from behind. "You hombres turn that bay devil out. Already he has killed one crack vaquero and crippled another. Nobody will ride him if we did fork him down."

As the Kid wheeled to face the newcomer, a short, heavy-set man with the visage of an owl, he caught a fleeting look of relief on Lopez' face.

"That's the smartest thing you ever said, Mert Bradley," remarked Lopez, pushing the boy aside roughly and dropping back to the ground.

But the others were not to be denied the thrill of seeing the cock-sure Juan fork the outlaw.

"You're leary! You're leary!" they taunted. "Throw him back in the pasture with the milk cows. Juan wants none of him."

A dull flush spread over Lopez' face. Leaping up, he strode to the pole gate of the corral. Toughy was but a step behind.

"Let me hold your gun and belt, Juan?" he pleaded. "I'm not sore now. Will you, Juan, huh?"

"Get out of the way!" snarled Lopez, kicking the boy. "Some of these days I'm going to crack every bone in your body. I'll ride that bay," he told Bradley, sourly. "These damned railbird jaspers will have no chance to say I backed down for fear of any horse on earth."

Bradley shrugged. "I'm not ordering you to stay off him," he remarked carelessly. "I'm just warning you he has many of his brother's tricks and he'll tromp you to death if he throws you."

"He never will see the day he is as bad as El Scorpion," returned Lopez. "Besides, he isn't built right to throw me—no horse is. I'll take a whirl at him."

"If you've lost all interest in life, don't let me talk you out of it," Bradley chuckled nastily. "If you can top him we might be able to unload him in that bunch of remount stuff to the government." He turned away as Lopez crawled through the poles of the corral. The vaqueros roared their delight. Even Toughy, once more having swallowed his pride, was cheering at the top of his voice.

With everyone absorbed in the forthcoming contest, the Kid walked over to the enclosure and looked at the gelding which was causing the furore, wondering the while what sort of an outlaw this El Scorpion, Lopez had mentioned, must be if he was any worse than the man-killing brute inside.

Lopez started the horse running, then roped it around the forefeet. But it was not to be subdued without a battle. As the reata grew taut, it charged, mouth open, teeth clicking, ears laid back hatefully, biting, striking, squealing like a pig.

With easy grace, Lopez leaped aside—an almost effortless move that brought a salvo of cheers from the onlookers. The gelding crashed to the ground.

It lay stunned for a minute, making no fight against the gunnysack blind Lopez bound across its eyes. In spite of the dislike the fellow's personal appearance aroused within him, and the cold fury the treatment of the boy had kindled, the Kid could not but admire the skillful way in which he handled the outlaw. He was on the point of admitting to himself he had misjudged Lopez, had allowed his first unfavorable impression there on the steps of the ranchhouse to prejudice him. Perhaps, after all, it might have been the girl who, through fear that he might uncover her as the accomplice of the Guadalupe killer, had ordered him cast into the storeroom to die.

Again hatred blazed up within him against the girl. He would show her—wherever, whoever, she was. But where was she? He had found himself straining for a glimpse of her since daylight. She had not made an appearance.

He forgot her momentarily in the hot anger at sight of Lopez handling the horse. Instead of the hackamore that every good bronc-peeler used, Lopez had rigged up a war-bridle that was wrenching the blood from the bay's mouth.

The Kid loved horses even better than he loved men. Since childhood he had been in the saddle. Not once in that time had he ever seen a rider abuse even the most vicious outlaw with a war-bridle. The admonition of an old Texan who, in his day, had forked them as bad as they came, flew to his mind. "Be a sport when you're topping them, Kid. You've got all the best of it. A saddle to sit in, spurs to hang on with—and God gave you plenty of grip in your knees. War-bridles! Hell! Use a hackamore. You want them to pitch, don't you? Else why ride them?"

Fighting down the rage that set blood to pounding with a sluicing roar in his ears, the Kid glanced around. Apparently accustomed to the procedure, the riders thought nothing of it. He looked back to the corral. A second man had leaped inside, seized the rope pinioning the outlaw's front hoofs and braced himself with the hemp across his hip as the bay struggled to its feet. It stood trembling while Lopez eased the saddle into place, stooped with his back to the watchers to tighten his spur straps.

"The hombre is good even though he does resort to a war-bridle," the Kid mused. "It is too bad when a man such as he deliberately forces himself to be a brute. I wonder . . ."

At that moment Lopez slipped into the saddle. The helper flipped the throw-rope loose from the gelding's fetlocks. It hesitated for a moment, shaking violently, its swaying back threatening to give under the weight of the rider. Lopez' foot flew forward to dodge a kick that scraped stirrup leather, then back to escape the vicious snap the outlaw made at its own stifle joint. His spur rowels sank home with a force that brought a bawl of pain from the brute. A terrific wrench that threatened to dislocate its lower jaw, brought the blood gushing.

"Thataboy, Juan!" screamed Toughy shrilly. "You've got him going already."

The cry was caught up by the vaqueros strung about the corral. Bedlam broke loose. The outlaw threaded its nose between its front legs, straightened out, left the ground. Its belly curved in midair. It hit the 'dobe with a crash that rattled the poles.

The war-bridle tore at its mouth to turn it to a mass of bloody froth. Huge spur rowels had opened its hide from shoulder to rump. A wet buckskin quirt was slicing blood from its neck and ears.

Reared among men who knew how to handle horses, who themselves suffered many times rather than injure their mounts, who made companions of their animals on the long, silent trails, the Kid could not stifle the hot indignation that had taken violent hold upon him. Lopez' abuse of the bay, his brutality, fired him to a reckless fury, undermined his judgment. In spite of the warning of the old man of the cabana, in spite of the experience he already had undergone here on this rancho, fully aware that an outburst was foolhardy now when calm, cold reason should have governed every move, he sprang to the corral gate beside Toughy.

"Ride him clean if you can, hombre," he said in a voice chocking with coldness. "Ride him clean or take what any coward deserves—a beating."

Toughy stared speechless. "He'll—he'll kill you for that!" he whispered. "You better get going before Juan climbs down."

The Kid swept the faces about him in a single glance. "Kill me?" he lashed out. "One who abuses horses such as he kills nothing unless it is in darkness—and then only when he can stalk his quarry like a puma—from behind. I fear not men like him. They only vent their anger on *chamaco* such as you."

"Gosh, Kid," Toughy gasped. "We promised to be pards—back there on the trail. For that reason I can't let you down. I've got to warn you. That is Juan Lopez—the bad hombre I told you about back there on the . . . on the trail. Nobody who ever come into Rancho Diablo could talk to Juan like that."

"There is a beginning and an end to everything, *chamaco mio*," the Kid smiled grimly. "This Juan, as you term him, has much to learn both about horses and being a man, yes?" Leaving the boy gaping at him in wide-eyed wonder, he strode over to Bradley's side.

"You are the major-domo of this rancho, yes?" he demanded.

CHAPTER TWELVE

MERT BRADLEY stared. His jaw sagged. A slow pale shade blotted out the tan from his leathery cheeks.

"I reckon I am," he muttered in a hollow tone. "And you . . . where did you come from?"

Satisfied by the fellow's strange actions—which he could only attribute to fear—that in some way he had had a hand in throwing him into the storeroom to die of thirst, the Kid made no attempt to stifle a mounting anger.

"From the Pecos—and other points south, señor," he answered insolently, hoping the fellow would make something of it so he might vent the anger boiling within him.

Bradley's owlish countenance took on a pasty hue. But he only glanced about furtively. The smile he essayed was little more than a tightening of cracked lips across discolored teeth.

"Who—are—you?" he demanded.

The Kid smiled—a thin bracing of lips across even teeth. For all the seriousness of the thing he was enjoying the other's uneasiness as he tried to capture and hold the gaze that swept him from head to toe and back again. The fellow's eyes registered every emotion: greed at sight of the silver-bangled chaparejos, the silver and gold inlaid spurs with delicately wrought teardrop danglers; caution at sight of the forty-five notched away from its holster; a questioning fear when finally the eyes did come up to meet his. But only for a moment. Then back they went to their survey of the Kid; the careless manner in which the Colt was slung at his slender hip, the thumb of his right hand hooked in his cartridge belt,—fingers almost touching the well-oiled stock—suggested a cat-like speed. His easy grace and calm attitude told of reckless courage and confidence.

Bradley risked another glance at the Kid's eyes, cold and brittle for all their blackness, plainly capable of narrowing to flame-shot slits.

"Who are you?" Bradley got out again.

"What seems to trouble the señor?" the Kid returned politely. "From the way he looks one would think he had encountered a ghost, no?"

Bradley started violently.

"Ghost, hell!" he exploded in denial so quick it gave the lie to his words. "Why should I be afraid of a ghost? I'm only asking who you are. We have to be careful just who we're entertaining in this country of—of fugitives."

"Of a surety, señor," graciously—too graciously for the fire that suddenly gleamed in the Kid's steady eyes. "Always a man has the privilege of asking another's name, especially when that stranger happens to be on one's rancho. Also does one have the right to demand the history of one who travels and puts into a rancho. Therefore, I was born on the fifth day of . . ."

"I don't give a damn when you were born!" Bradley shouted. "I'm asking your name. To hell with your—"

The Kid was quick to notice his hesitation.

"As I was saying when you interrupted so rudely, señor . . . the name? That is so easy, and only courteous. As for other things, now that I think of them, if the one questioned does not care to tell, that is—well, one own's business, yes?"

Forgetting Lopez' abuse of the bay for a moment, the Kid gave speedy thought to the foreman's strange actions. Beyond doubt they were inspired by fear at sight of him after he had been thrown into the storeroom to die. But there seemed to be something else in the fellow's eyes—a vague light of recognition. Yet he was positive that never before had he seen this stranger. Perhaps . . . that was it. Bradley had mistaken him for someone else. But who?

Suddenly the remark Jim Brown, the old man of the cabana, had made, recurred. "You remind me a heap of Johnnie Bender," the old fellow had said. "You don't happen to be kin of his, do you?

It wouldn't be healthy for kin of Johnnie's down yonder."

If Jim Brown had noticed the resemblance, Bradley doubtless had done the same. The old fellow had said Johnnie Bender had died of a broken neck. That was no uncommon occurrence on a horse ranch. Then why should the unexpected appearance of someone who resembled Johnnie Bender—and he was convinced now that resemblance had something to do with the foreman's nervousness—upset Bradley? Unable to answer the perplexing question, he put it aside, determined, however, to find out before he left the rancho.

"They call me the Kid, señor," he said presently. "Whether I ride north, east, south or into the setting sun, it is always the same. Never do they show me the courtesy of calling me otherwise—always it is the Kid."

Something of a sigh of relief escaped Bradley. But question still loomed large in his eyes.

"What are you doing around here?" he asked sullenly.

"Having put in here—let us say recently—dying of thirst, leading a wounded horse . . . and having been treated so courteously, señor, I cannot but answer that question. It is so fair, and in its fairness requires an answer. Had I not been treated so fairly, I would hesitate. But now, señor, I can only answer, I thought I would accept

114

a position with your rancho." The Kid's eyes were smiling. But there was venom in his quiet words; stinging venom in the tone in which they were uttered. "Yet I hesitate—for never before have I accepted employment where a major-domo would stand by and allow a hombre, who plainly cannot ride, to tear a caballo to pieces with a war-bridle and slice him with a quirt. . . . As the major-domo now sees in his own corral. Of course, the señor will do something about that hombre abusing the bay, yes?"

Uncertainty and anger grew in the eyes with which Bradley regarded him. "You certainly are a stranger in these parts, fellow, or you wouldn't be sticking your neck out for trouble with Juan Lopez," he said meaningly. "It is always good sense for travelers to keep their mouths shut around this ranch. How did you get here, anyway?"

As though he didn't know, the Kid thought—as though he didn't know what had happened after his arrival, how he had been cast into the storeroom to die. Then in a flash it came to the Kid that in spite of Toughy's excuse for being on the mesa trail he had in reality been stationed there as a lookout. But the girl . . . Bradley's question itself was a dead give-away, there was something being done on Rancho Diablo that would not bear inspection. His own experience was proof of that. But what was it—and just how did the girl fit into it? He could scarcely imagine the trim little thing as a partner to these evil-looking vaqueros. Yet at Guadalupe—

For the moment he was tempted to disclose his meeting with Toughy to see what reaction it would bring. But the promise he had made the youngster flashed to his mind. Never yet had he violated a trust. Nor could he now. And, he noticed, Bradley shot a withering glance at the lad who stood trembling, his face chalky with fear.

"Didn't anybody try to stop you?" Bradley hurled at the Kid angrily.

"Had they attempted I should have come along just the same, señor. Unless there is something you must cover up on this rancho I see no reason why a stranger seeking only water should not ride within your gates, yes?" His lips were smiling again. But the dancing light in his black eyes had coalesced into a cold, set gleam. "And now that I am here—unfortunately, by the way you regard me—I have come to handle your caballos. For I am a caballero, señor—a real caballero who shall break to the gentleness of a baby the worst horse on your rancho."

"Oh, yeah?" Bradley sneered. "You've got to—"

"Had I not supreme confidence in my ability to do this, señor, then I would hesitate to make such a claim. But if yonder caballero cutting that

116

bay to pieces needlessly is a sample of men you employ, then, indeed, I ask no position with such a rancho. I treat horses fairly—as I do men—and as I know you do too, señor, yes?"

"My advice to you would be to whip a dally on that smooth tongue of yours," Bradley blurted out. "We aren't much stuck on strangers around here. Why should we be? We didn't invite you. But as long as you are here I just want to tip you off that I've got some tough hombres who aren't built right to take any of your lip."

"*Sangre de Cristo*, that I should offend—or even care what any of your vaqueros think, señor!" The Kid smiled. "Never yet have I been forced to take to my heels to avoid trouble. Advancing as I am in age, it would be foolishness to begin now, yes? Therefore, I say again, so loudly you cannot mistake my meaning, so loudly that all can hear—any lobo who will ride a caballo with a war-bridle and slash it thus with the rowels and beat it until it cannot pitch, . . . then I say he is unfit to work on any man's rancho. The señor, being equally as fair as myself, will agree with me, yes?"

Bradley's face was blank as he tried to fathom this stranger whose smiling lips gave the lie to every word he uttered. And while he pondered the thing in his dull mind the Kid's own mind was shuttling back and forth trying to find the cause for this recklessness that was driving him on, getting him deeper and deeper with the hard crew—with Bradley, who now was regarding him in open-mouthed amazement, with the vaqueros strung along the corral, even with the rider, Juan Lopez himself, whom he hoped could catch an occasional taunt above the pounding of the outlaw's hoofs.

Then, suddenly, he knew the reason. It was a girl. Bitterness toward her, suspicion of her, had fired him to a recklessness he never before had known, added to a cold fury at thought of how they had tried to murder him—a recklessness he could not seem to master. He wondered where the girl was now, hoped she could hear him challenging the whole crew which, in his mind, included her.

"The caballero who rides the bay rides in a cowardly fashion that should not be allowed. Further, he rides with locked rowels, señor," he found himself saying. "Such a one should not be allowed to ride any horse on any rancho. Only should he be allowed to fight with men whom he can curse and who will not fight back. Real men would first slap his face, señor. Then, should he display a desire to fight—a thing I doubt—should they strike him in the mouth with a fist. But never go for their gun. Against one so cowardly to horses, no real man should feel other than pity should they draw. For it would be murder, yes?"

The Kid's tone, which grew more deadly as he

spoke, ended in a sound like chipping ice, sent the foreman to edging off. He whipped a glance in the direction of the corral. Lopez' spurs, glinting in the sunlight, were locked and sunk like steel fangs into the bleeding sides of the bay.

"I'm running this rancho to suit myself—me and Ross Pearson," Bradley bellowed. "If you don't like it you can get out of here. Nobody asked you here. The quicker you get going the better. There are fast, gun-slinging hombres in my crew. Especially one—a caballero who takes nothing from anyone. My advice, hombre, is to lay off of Juan Lopez. He is bad medicine."

CHAPTER THIRTEEN

BAD MEDICINE, yes?"

The Mañana Kid's smile had frozen on lips that now skinned back like those of an enraged animal. His eyes shifted once—to lash Bradley from head to toe. Within he was chuckling, enjoying the tenseness that rubbed the nerves of other men raw. It was the Mañana Kid's way to defy men, laugh in their faces until anger forced them to go for their guns. But in this case it was different. For he had no fight with these vaqueros—at least with none he could single out. His fight was with the girl. He hoped . . . but damn the girl. He would settle with her later. But where was she. Why couldn't she be a witness to this crisis he was forcing—forcing because they had tried to kill him by thirst in that storeroom.

"Bad medicine, yes?" he repeated in a voice that grew softer as it grew more deadly. "Putrid is the word, señor, in case you lack verbal expression for your thoughts. Briefly, your caballero and the rest of your crew strung out there, stink. Pardon the word, señor. It is one that often roils me, too. I have been known to shoot because of its use.

But it is so apropos, yes?" He swung sidewise to Bradley, who was choking back his anger. "So the major-domo, or whatever position you occupy on this questionable rancho, will do nothing to protect your horses, no?" Tingling nerves told him that the show-down was near. And he longed for it—longed to make this hard lot realize that the Mañana Kid was not one to be tossed into a breathless storeroom to die with thirst. The girl—damn her—if she could only hear!

Suddenly the Kid lifted his voice.

"*Caballo mio*," he shouted to the bay. "Get that vaquero! Get him in such a way he will never come back. You out-think him, it is evident, *caballo*. Thus his need for locked rowels and abuse. Get that imitation rider, pronto."

Now that his love for horses and fair play—abetted by a cold smouldering anger at the way he had been treated—had driven him to challenge both Bradley and Lopez, the Kid's smile became grimmer. Many times before his rashness had backed him against the wall with no avenue of escape. And now . . .

He swept the evil faces of the vaqueros about him. Not one of them was friendly. There was still a bare trace of fairness on some. Others there were in the hard lot who, he knew, never would shoot unless the target was a man's back. More than one hand rested near the butt of a Colt. Yet they made no move to draw. That he possessed the courage to call Juan Lopez to account was enough to warn them to go slow. On the leering countenances the Kid read the fact that his words had struck home. They, too, were waiting for the show-down he had forced. His only regret was that the girl was not present to see it.

Toughy sidled close to his elbow.

"Give them hell, Kid," he whispered. "I haven't a gosh-blamed thing to fight with, but I'm against them—all but Juan. When you tie into him though, you've got me to whip."

The Kid raised a glance at the serious-eyed boy.

"Let me tell you, *chamaco*, no good hombre cuts a horse to pieces. Better that you become partner with one who fights for horses instead of against them."

His swift gaze caught Bradley's roving eyes for an instant. He read in them cowardice and brutality. Yet he knew Bradley would try for revenge, but never while an adversary was facing him.

"Prove to the hombre he cannot ride, *caballo*," he taunted. "For you against such a one that should be simple, yes?"

As though heeding his words the horse reared and hurled itself backwards. It rolled over on its side obscured by a choking cloud of dust, lurched to its feet, head buried between its fetlocks, bleeding nose scraping the ground. But Lopez was game. He had managed to escape the crushing saddle horn, vault aboard as the brute came up, his merciless, locked spurs sunk into its gory sides.

The action in the corral gave the Kid a moment's respite from his vigil. But with the horse up and pitching the tenseness increased. The very atmosphere of the place, which grated on his strumming nerves, hung heavy with portentousness. The group was taking heart from its numbers. The ugly glances cast in his direction warned him to speed the showdown while he had them all within range of his vision.

"Twenty dollars the hombre cannot so much as ride the caballo even with the war-bridle and locked rowels," he challenged loudly.

One by one the vaqueros eased themselves down off the poles, shifted to where they could move in toward him. No word was spoken but the Kid read their thoughts. Their expressions showed that not one of them could foresee the possibility of him winning his bet, but the wager and the defiance it carried were pregnant with possibility for gunplay which was to their liking.

They eyed him like hawks watching a nest. It was plain that he was not a man to be fooled with. But on the other hand, Juan Lopez' reckless courage was legendary in the Cuyamas.

"You're making fight talk, stranger," snarled Bradley, who again was peering at the Kid as though straining every faculty to recognize him. "Juan will scrap at the drop of a hat. That outlaw you are so tender-hearted about, has killed one hombre and crippled up another for life. I'm warning you, you'd better muzzle that loose tongue of yours. This crew isn't to be made suckers of. They'll get you."

"Twenty bucks he cannot ride the caballo whether he is tough or not," the Kid flashed back. "If the horse is the man-killer, then it is because you let some incompetent vaquero spoil him in the first place. No hombre who cuts a horse to pieces with locked rowels and uses a war-bridle will offer much fight only behind one's back on a dark night, señor."

Toughy had drawn away to stand glaring at the Kid through narrowed eyes, his face contorted with childish anger. But the speedy right arm, hooked by a thumb at the butt of the gun which never left its holster, warned him to silence. He shot a swift glance at the motionless men around him. It was the first time in the years he had been buffeted about Rancho Diablo, that he ever had known them to hang back when there was trouble. The mêlées on the ranch had been many. Always before, the boys had waded in and stuck together. Now it was different. Perhaps they recognized the stripe of this gunman, knew the forty-five at this young newcomer's hip spoke but once at any target.

But above the thud of the pounding hoofs and

the bawling of the enraged outlaw, Lopez heard the offer.

"You're on, *peregriño*," he panted. "Twenty bucks I top him slick, kick him down and make him like it. If I don't, I have five to one you cannot."

"It is a wager," the Kid shouted back. "Twenty dollars or more, as you wish, señor. You name the amount and I shall cover it. I measured your pocketbook only by your appearance when I set such a paltry sum. For not only does your apparel in its attempt to be elegant shriek of ill-breeding, but of poverty as well, señor. And as I watch, I see you as a rider who lacks much of being able to sit that caballo without tearing the leather from your saddlerig. And such a pity . . . for at least your rig is good."

A snarl from Lopez, a surly growl from the vaqueros stopped him. But only for a moment. He was facing them all now, had every man within range of his Colt.

"After I have won the twenty at even money, señor, then you offer five to one I cannot ride the caballo that will throw you? You are called in any amount to suit your purse. But I shall insist on cash. And now, *caballo mio*, go get yourself one badly beaten rider. It is only a matter of moments—I ask that you hurry the thing to show—"

He sauntered over to the corral poles, the least

perturbed of the entire group, fully aware that for the moment he was master of the situation. That he had dared challenge Lopez left the others speechless, plainly fearful to go for their guns. Always the Kid banked on the emotions of men—the emotions he read in their eyes. And there was fear in the eyes of those about him. There in Guadalupe he had faced the crowd crying for his life, had dared hurl the poster offering a reward for himself under their feet. He had defied that crowd—for there he had seen fear. Now he was defying these vaqueros for the same reason.

If he even noticed the hateful glances cast in his direction he gave no sign. He braced himself wearily against the corral. Apparently his gaze was focused on Lopez, who, at the moment, was the least of his adversaries to be reckoned with. But the vaqueros knew, and Bradley knew, that not a downward movement of a single hand would escape his sharp black eyes.

"Now, *caballo mio* . . . is the time," the Kid said quietly. "You have him off balance, for he knows not how to ride. The locked rowels are slipping. A little more effort . . . and there . . . he . . . *Gracias, caballo*. You have but proved my faith in horses."

The words were scarcely out of his mouth before the bay sun-fished the width of the enclosure, landed with the force of a stone-crusher, swapped ends and started bucking back over its course.

Careless, for the benefit of the vaqueros, Lopez had lost a stirrup. He was trying frantically to hook one locked rowel in the cinch. His flailing leg missed. The rowel that was to be driven home tore leather from his cantleboard. Lopez grabbed frantically for the horn. It swept past just out of reach. He lunged onto the brute's neck. There for a minute he whipped about uncertainly. The bay went into a spin. Lopez shot head first across the corral. For a moment he lay stunned. Then he came lurching to his feet, cursing. His furious roars, the rasping breath of the outlaw were the only sound.

"You dirty, lousy—" Lopez was screaming. "I'll—"

As though anticipating a hostile move, the brute, which had pitched away, came whirling back toward him. Up on its hind legs it reared, advanced, pawing the air. The Kid leaped inside. Bradley followed.

"It is no time to threaten after one has been defeated, señor," the Kid warned quietly, fingers bloodless on the cartridge-belt near the butt of his Colt. "For threats after one is so thoroughly beaten are but idle talk everyone scoffs at— the vain talk of cowards. You are, as I thought, hombre, a tinhorn—a gringo they should call you—a hombre who would tear the jaws off a horse with a war-bridle, lace him to pieces with locked rowels and then expect the dumb brute to love you and eat out of your hand. And now the señor . . ."—his taunting tone turned deadly; the words chipped from lips frozen across his teeth—". . . thinks to go for his gun. A man dies but once. If you feel this is time, then drop that hand lower. For, señor, I could let you pull that gun and still drop you in your tracks."

Lopez hesitated. The hand that had started for his Colt hung paralyzed before him.

The Kid's eyes seemed to be piercing those of the stunned rider. But even then he was prepared for the bay that charged down upon them. He leaped aside lightly. Lopez lurched back, shielding his face with his hands. A rope Bradley had seized up whistled out. It caught the crazed outlaw about the neck. From the corner of his eye the Kid saw a couple of vaqueros spring inside. The rope whined. The bay crashed to the ground, end-over-end.

CHAPTER FOURTEEN

EVER quick to seize upon an advantage, the Kid backed against the corral poles where he could command a view of the entire group. There he waited tense, thumb slung carelessly in his cartridge-belt beside the holstered forty-five. The moment was poignant, nerve-wracking. Bradley held the gelding, which had struggled to its feet. The vaqueros stood motionless. Lopez suddenly seemed to become aware of the brassy sun overhead which set the sweat trickling down across his face.

He was the first to break the silence.

"My bet rides, *peregriño*," he lashed out furiously. "Five to one up to one hundred dollars you cannot ride this outlaw clean. But should you happen to by some miracle, I have twenty to one with the sky the limit, you cannot ride his brother—El Scorpion."

The vaqueros blinked their amazement, exchanged furtive glances. That Juan Lopez had deliberately chosen to back down before this newcomer was beyond their comprehension. For Lopez did not seem unduly nervous. Rather his attitude was one of cool cunning that presaged swift and deadly action when the opportunity did arrive for him to call the turn. Rancho Diablo vaqueros knew Lopez—knew he never forgot and that somewhere, sometime, he would claim revenge.

Yet the hard lot cared not one way or another. Lopez or the stranger. What mattered it? But there was one among them who did—Toughy! The way Juan had backed down before the blazing eyes of the Kid caused something to snap in the heart of the youngster. An idol had been shattered. An idol, which he had worshipped for its bravery, had shown yellow before the quiet-voiced youth who thus far had stood the crowd at bay with only words and glances. Toughy's childish mind failed to grasp the thing. Never before had man set foot on Rancho Diablo to make so much as a gesture of unfriendliness that he was not shot down or gunned away. And now had come this Kid who had defied them all and gone unchallenged. But Juan, the abusive Juan, had represented everything that was brave and fearless. He even had attempted to emulate his garb with gaudy, childish trappings. Now Juan's hand had been called. At any cost, he must protect Juan from the taunts and jeers of the others.

He crawled into the corral, determined to seize the Kid's hand, which always rested so dangerously near the speedy forty-five. But his mission never was accomplished. He missed the barely perceptible nod that passed between Lopez and Bradley, started across the enclosure on a run.

"Leap! Leap! *Chamaco*!" It was the Kid's cry that burst upon him above a sudden thunder of hoofs. Toughy halted, wheeled. The bay outlaw was charging down upon him. He tried to heed the warning. Too late. Fear paralyzed him. The merciless hoofs were directly above him, had started to descend. He cringed away, threw his arms across his eyes to shut out the awful sight. He could only stand helpless, quivering.

He was only vaguely aware of being snatched from beneath the hoofs that tore up chunks of earth as they hit. Through fear-glazed eyes he saw the big bay rearing, going over backwards. Then tight, comforting arms were about him. From far, far away came a voice.

"Even so much as slacken that rope again for a single inch and I shall kill you." It was the Kid speaking, whipping out his words in a tone that seemed to crackle for all its quietness. "I warn you for the last time! You, Lopez! You, Bradley! You evil-eyed, man-whipped vaqueros without a mind that dares think for itself! That any of you should shoot causes me a laugh. For fear growls in your stomach to nauseate you all. Try, however, if you feel lucky. I make no move to draw. I only laugh at you—laugh at you and your whole cowardly rancho. Move if you dare. Go for your guns. Then shall I have some excuse for killing six of you before I pitch into this dust. I care not. But you . . . you are cowards. Cowardice is written on every face. You are afraid to die as you are afraid to fight."

Silence—silence broken only by the whine of the hot wind through the corral, the groans and rasping breath of the sprawling bay.

Then Toughy was aware that the Kid was whispering in his ear.

"*Chamaco*," the words came to him, "*chamaco mio*, it was a close one for you. Death or permanent injury nearly came to you. But never again, *chamaco*, shall this be when I am near. I pledge you, as I pledged your friendship back there on the . . ." The voice trailed off to be lost in the blood beating in the boy's ears.

"What—happened?" Toughy panted presently when he could collect his scattered wits.

"You and the outlaw—the caballo which threw the make-believe caballero—came near a collision which would have killed you, *chamaco*. I seized the rope, snatched you from under his hoofs barely in time to save you."

For all the fear that seemed to paralyze him, Toughy succeeded in opening his eyes which roved about as though in search of new horror. But the dust was thick, settling down in a choking blanket. Dimly he could make out

Bradley, sullen, scowling, fumbling with the rope that held the prostrate bay. And Lopez . . . he watched Juan as closely as he could through the dust curtain. For Juan was scheming. Taking advantage of the Kid's preoccupation his hand had found his Colt. Toughy tried to scream a warning. The Kid loosed his hold, lunged away with the speed of a cougar just as Juan's forty-five cracked. The bullet struck low. With a moan Toughy straightened out.

Uncertain from whence the shot had come, the Kid's eyes narrowed, flame-shot slits tried to pierce the dust. But his lips were smiling, braced back against his teeth in a smile that was almost a snarl. Before Juan could trigger his forty-five again the Kid was coming up. Half-way, it seemed to the staring crew, he stopped, threw himself to the ground to go sprawling on his back. As he went down his gun barked from its holster. Juan Lopez jerked. His second shot tore slivers from the top pole of the corrals. Again a gun cracked. And again The Mañana Kid's gun, lacing flame through the dust that made Juan only an outline. Consuming rage sent blood scalding into the Kid's temples. Lopez, the vaquero who had abused the *chamaco*, who had abused the bay horse, who had deliberately shot Toughy after he had risked his life to save him was still on his feet. Half the cartridges in his Colt were gone.

Now he was on his feet, backing away, his still

holstered Colt again sweeping the crew. Lopez had dropped his gun, was trying to stem the flow of blood from a wounded forearm. Of a sudden he pitched forward to measure his length in the dust.

The Kid saw Bradley let go the rope that held the bay, plunge across the corral. The Kid laughed. Bradley presented such a ludicrous figure, bear-legging on all fours, finally to belly down and wedge himself beneath the bottom pole where he stuck to kick and curse.

"It is now a fight, amigos," the Kid was challenging the group. "Perhaps among you are those who think they are tough. Me . . . I still know you only shoot in the back and cannot face one who shoots between the eyes. Three cartridges I have here, in my own Colt—a few more are left in the gun of Juan Lopez, which I shall secure. Still you have ceased firing, back off to eye me like a pack of wolves. *Sangre de Cristo*, did I ever see such cowards. Perhaps—this—may startle you out of your fear, set you to fighting." His gun spat from its holster. The bullet ripped slivers from a corral pole, which pelted the crew in their faces. Still not a man made a move for his gun.

"Bah!" The Kid gave up disgustedly. He picked up Lopez' gun, rammed it into his belt. Without so much as a glance at the crew, or Bradley— still wedged under the bottom pole of the corral and shouting for help—he lifted the inert form of Toughy and carried him outside the enclosure.

"I gave you a chance to fight, hombres," he challenged. "None of you possessed the guts. Now shall we look to the casualties? For always a flock like you wait for orders. Secure this Juan Lopez, who now stretches out there where the bay might trample him at any moment. Drag him outside, that we may look at him. Move swiftly," as the crew hesitated, "else I shall drill some of you. That bay might remember what Lopez has done and exact revenge."

The outlaw stood in a corner of the corral, snorting, slapping the earth savagely. The crack of guns, the screaming lead, the acrid smoke, the dust, the dodging men momentarily had stupefied it, for it hugged the poles, trembling.

Then it sighted the motionless form of Lopez. Throwing up its head, it sniffed the air, charged. The Kid, alone of the entire group in full possession of his faculties, sprang within. The flailing hoofs descended just as he dragged the lifeless figure of Lopez out of reach. The bay crowded back against the poles, tearing away chunks of earth with its striking, flashing hoofs to send up a new eruption of dust.

Throwing caution to the winds, but having little fear of the bewildered crew, the Kid dropped to his knees to examine the rider. Two bullets had opened the flesh in his arms. A third had struck in the leg, causing a nasty wound.

"Lopez is shot bad through the leg," he told the others, who moved up now that he had taken the lead. "Water, hombres. There is no use of either of them dying, although we might have to get a doctor for Juan."

Turning the unconscious vaquero over to Bradley, who had succeeded in extricating himself to get to his feet and stand shaking with nervousness, the Kid strode over to where Toughy lay, moaning piteously.

"Poor little *chamaco*," he muttered. "To think there is a hombre living mean enough to shoot you." His thoughts flashed back to the mesa—but after all his shot there when he had encountered the boy had been purposely wild. He had helped the youngster, tried to make amends. There was nothing like that here now. Once man or boy was wounded or helpless on Rancho Diablo, he decided grimly, he was left to die. Carefully he went over the lad. He found that Lopez' bullet had ripped a deep gash in the boy's forearm, but luckily had missed the bone. Toughy was suffering from shock and fright more than from the wound. Applying a tourniquet, improvised from a lariat, and scooping up clean sand which quickly congealed the blood and stopped the flow, the Kid waited. In a few moments the boy looked up at him.

"Did you get Juan?" he whispered weakly.

"Perhaps I did, *chamaco*," the Kid told him.

"No hombre ever shot a pardner of mine and got away with it."

A strange light flickered in Toughy's hazy eyes. He tried to move his arm. Pain drove the returning color from his cheeks. He smiled wanly.

"I'm sure off of Juan for good now, *compañero*. If you don't mind. I'll be like you—fight for horses instead of against them."

His childish words brought a lump into the Kid's throat. If he accomplished nothing else during his stay on Rancho Diablo at least he had started Toughy on the right track, was his thought. He turned away to the vaqueros, who, now the excitement was past, were hovering about, showing no inclination to renew the fight. The Kid could not suppress a smile at the deference they showed him. He had won his first tilt. But he made no attempt to fool himself into the belief that there would not be other flare-ups in which he might not come out the victor.

Juan Lopez writhed under the ministrations of the vaqueros attempting to check the blood gushing from his leg, moaned, opened his eyes. They came to rest on the Kid.

"You got me this time, *peregriño*, but I'll get you next," he ground between his teeth. The Kid could not help but admire the gameness of the fellow. Every word he uttered was an effort that brought beads of cold sweat to his forehead.

"And do not forget our bet," Juan gasped. "You fork that bay, or the vaqueros will gun you off the place for a damned coward."

"Threats are cheap, amigo," the Kid said. "Especially to a man who is down. For you know I am not the kind to shoot a cripple. Had I been the least bit fearful of you or what you could do with your gun, then I would not have dragged you out of the corral to keep the bay from trampling you. But as you wish, señor. The time and the place when you shall claim your imaginary revenge from me rests entirely with you. I am always at your service, señor."

Before Lopez could reply, Bradley found his voice. "I'm sick and tired of having that bay hellion around," he snarled. "Run him down in the pasture, vaqueros. Can't be topped, and raises hell in the herd all the time. He's getting worse than El Scorpion. Might as well get rid of him before he cripples somebody else."

"Allow me to ride him first, señor," the Kid urged, pondering the reference to El Scorpion. "You heard the wager of this hombre with me. I am not one of your vaqueros, so what difference does it make should I be injured?"

"You're damned right you aren't one of my hands," grated Bradley. "And you'll be lucky if you don't meet up with a fall before you shag it out of Rancho Diablo. You plugged the best vaquero I had just when I need him the most, and all because of a worthless brat you ought to have let that bay finish off. He's good for nothing around here."

The Kid's lips were braced in a thin, bloodless line across his teeth. "I have not had the honor yet to tell the señor what my thoughts are of him," he said. "But always shall I remember how you let that bay loose to trample myself and the *chamaco*. I tell you now straightly—as always I tell men. The boy Toughy has the making of a real man and I warn that you or no one else shall stop him. I shall leave your rancho when I choose to go. But while I am here I serve notice, no one—including yourself—shall further abuse this boy. Being fair, I only demand fairness for him—a thing you will grant I know, señor, yes?"

"You're liable to travel before you get ready," sneered Bradley. "There is such a thing as a sheriff in this country."

The Kid grinned good-naturedly. "A sheriff? The last thing you would want to see, I wager, señor, yes? If you seek to have a sheriff look me over, then shall I go get one and bring him in here." The threat might as well have remained unuttered for all the effect it had upon either the foreman or Lopez. Not until the words were out of his mouth did the Kid realize how absurdly childish and puerile they sounded. Juan only eased himself to a more comfortable sitting posture against a corral pole and gritted his teeth while an awkward-fingered rider finished washing and bandaging his wounds. A crooked smile twisted Bradley's lips.

The Kid changed the subject. "And now, shall I show this abuser of horses how one who knows how can ride?" he asked.

"No." Bradley was determined. "You can top his brother El Scorpion, any time you feel lucky. But I'm going to turn this bay brute out."

"The señor is as fearful I can ride him as is the wounded hombre?"

"Let him climb up," urged Juan who, although weak from the loss of blood, had resumed his cocksure manner. "Any hombre coming around Rancho Diablo telling us old hands how to fork broncs, when we have the reputation all over California for the class of stuff we handle, ought to get his neck kinked. Let him fork the bay— and top El Scorpion afterwards."

CHAPTER FIFTEEN

WHAT is your objection to letting him ride, Mert?" came a gruff voice from behind.

The group wheeled. A man of ponderous bulk had ridden up unobserved. The subservient attitude of both Lopez and Bradley, told the Kid instantly this newcomer was someone of importance.

The fellow cocked a big leg across the saddle-horn, looked down on Toughy.

"What's wrong with you?" he demanded before Bradley could answer the question that had been directed at him.

"Juan—shot me," the boy muttered.

"Juan shot you? What did you want to do that for, Lopez?" The newcomer chuckled as he shifted side-wise in his saddle to eye the caballero. For the first time he noticed the blood-stained chaps which had been cut away from Juan's leg. "What's the matter with you? Did Toughy shoot you, too?"

"Unfortunately, I was forced to shoot your caballero, señor," The Kid spoke, deep seriousness in his tone that might have been real or mockery. "Not fatally . . ." he offered hastily, ". . . that is—perhaps. The señor has but two or three bullet holes in him. The one in the leg—" he shrugged despairingly, "—may or may not prove . . . but even without complications— which are hard to avoid in such hot weather—the wound in the leg will inconvenience him for days to come."

"Juan Lopez shot?" the newcomer roared. "And you—"

"I repeat, señor . . ." The Kid faced him fearlessly, the smile again tugging at his slightly braced lips, ". . . much as I hated to wound one whose services are so valuable to you—one who can abuse a horse in such a manner as to ruin it forever—I was forced to. . . . But only after he had shot the *chamaco*, understand. I allowed him to continue his abuse of that horse without killing him. But never will I stand idly by when one attempts to abuse a child."

He started a survey of the giant—a lazy survey it appeared to the motionless vaqueros. But in reality the Kid's black eyes were everywhere, whipping up and down the huge frame. For from the brim of his sombrero to the tip of his well-polished boots the fellow was every inch a man—a man of enormous strength and vitality, who carried his bulk with surprising ease. Yet there was about his weather-pitted face a sinister heartlessness; the same coldness, but in a more marked degree, that was stamped on the countenances of Bradley and Lopez.

"You shot—Juan!" The fellow's great body jerked with muscular violence. But his anger was short-lived. The hot blood that sent a dull flush to his cheeks receded, leaving his face the color of wet leather. He swallowed hard, ran his fingers around the neckband of his shirt that suddenly seemed too tight.

"I'm Ross Pearson, owner of Rancho Diablo," he boomed. "Who the hell are you?"

If Bradley's strange actions had bewildered the Kid, Pearson's visible agitation dumfounded him. For like Bradley, Pearson evidently had mistaken him for someone else. Again he found himself wondering if it possibly could be the resemblance old Jim Brown said he bore to Johnnie Bender. But he had no time to waste in idle conjecture. What he read in the piercing eyes warned him that he now was pitted against a man of far different kidney than the other two.

Pearson, he saw instantly, was the brains of Rancho Diablo—a resourceful man who acted first and thought afterwards; a merciless brute who smashed his way through all obstacles, trampled down everyone who dared oppose him.

"I am termed—sometimes mockingly, señor, by those who laugh behind my back and far out of earshot—The Kid." Again his voice was brittle, his words chipping frozenly.

"The Kid!" Pearson roared. "Which Kid? There are hundreds of them—all fugitives from justice. There's the Puma Kid and the Cougar Kid and the . . . that Mañana Kid, who still scoffs at law and order. Some day they'll clean out all the gunslingers who hide behind the name of Kid. Now what's your real monicker? What Kid are you?"

"The Kid," quietly. "Only the Kid—the man who stands for no abuse to a horse; the Kid who shoots to protect a *chamaco*. I came here dying for water." He wondered as he spoke if this Pearson knew that he had been thrown into the storeroom to die of thirst. Perhaps . . . At least the girl knew. But damn the girl now. Later, he would attend to her. Now it was this Pearson, a hulking giant whose very size made men quail. There was no fooling with this fellow. Far different Bradley and Lopez—but this one—

"I'm asking where you came from?" Pearson was bawling. But, the Kid noticed, there was a strained note in his booming voice, a note of fear, perhaps.

"From the south, señor. Should I name the places I would only waste your time. For I have been everywhere, done everything. The present time—that is what you are interested in. Now that I am here I seek employment. You need riders badly, señor. That was made evident to me before you rode up. I have yet to see a rider on your rancho. I am offering to hire myself to you, señor, and will I guarantee to ride and break gentle as a kitten, anything you possess in the way of horseflesh."

He paused. Not because he was through talking. But to search the rancher's face. The Kid stood, legs wide apart, the thumb of his right hand still hooked in his cartridge-belt near the butt of the forty-five. That hand and arm seemed to hold a peculiar fascination for Pearson. Seldom did his eyes leave it long enough to meet the young man's steady gaze.

The Kid reasoned quickly. It was obvious that he had the advantage of steady nerves over the giant. For Pearson was laboring under great mental stress that had set him to trembling. Again the Kid seized on his advantage.

"You have the edge on most men by your size, señor," he purred. "But you do not frighten me. Never have I taken to my heels from man or beast. If you think to make an issue of me shooting your top rider, Lopez, then I suggest you reach for your gun. But expect no help from your crew, señor. They are but a pack of cowards, which I have proved."

The vaqueros hovering about heard this new challenge in utter amazement. That the stripling had bested Juan Lopez after goading him to fury surpassed their belief. That he had dared hurl defiance into the teeth of the merciless Ross Pearson staggered them. They waited for Pearson to fly into a rage, to riddle the youth with the bullets, trample him under his ponderous boots.

But Pearson suddenly appeared old and haggard. His shoulders drooped dejectedly. His right hand opened and closed near the butt of his forty-five. The same incomprehensible thing that filled them with wonder kept him from drawing. Playing his advantage for all it was worth, the Kid did a thing unheard of on Rancho Diablo. He deliberately laughed in the contorted face of Ross Pearson.

"If you know when you are well off, old man, you'll let that hombre alone," came the voice of Toughy. "He'll drop you before you get your gun half-way out."

The boy's words broke the tenseness. Pearson got hold of himself. Color flooded back into his cheeks.

"I reckon you figure you have pulled a hot one, coming in here and raising hell with us," he sneered. "But you'll get yours. Nobody ever got away with it before, although many have tried. Your name may be the Kid. But your face sure looks familiar to me. Are you right certain we never have met up before?"

Realizing that he had won the first bout with the big rancher, the Kid changed his tactics. It was plain that every man on the rancho, with the exception of Lopez, was in mortal terror of the owner. Now that he had challenged Pearson openly, without gunplay, he set about winning him over, believing that if he was successful the others would not dare start trouble.

"Not that I know of, señor," he returned, smiling. "Although many times men meet and forget names and faces—a thing to be deplored. Now, however, it takes but a glance to assure me you are a man who plays square. Sorry, indeed, I am that things at the outset should be hostile between us, but I wager on your fairness, señor— wager you will understand why I shot in defense of the *chamaco*."

Pearson expanded grandly under the cool flattery. "You damned know it," he boomed. "Nobody ever accused me of not being a square-shooter. You and me will get along swell, Kid. I could have shot hell out of you, but . . ." He stopped as though waiting for the youth to agree with him.

Chuckling inwardly, the Kid nodded.

"Sure, I could have," Pearson went on. "But I didn't want to. You are not much more than a kid yourself. The Kid! No wonder you call yourself that. And I want to congratulate you. You have a heap of nerve to stand up in front of me when I'm riled. Reckon I understand your feelings about seeing Toughy shot, although you don't know the brat like we do. He's no good. It's only a matter of time until we have to run him clean off the range." He shot a glance toward the corral. "And you were betting money with Juan you could ride that bay outlaw? Reckon you don't know he's killed one man and tromped all over another one. You say you are looking for work?"

"Not only has the bay tromped one fellow of whom I know not, but after throwing your finest caballero, he would have tromped on him too, señor, had I not snaked him out of there," the Kid said maliciously. "But should I ride him—a thing in which I have supreme confidence—what chance have I to secure employment?"

"You ride him and you are hired," Pearson said. "And if you do, you will be in line to take a whirl at El Scorpion, eh, Mert?"

"Yeah," Bradley smirked.

The Kid was on the point of asking about the mysterious El Scorpion. But what did it matter?

"While I am riding, of course, as gentlemen you will assure me there will be no back-shooting— no gun-play?" he said casually.

"I never heard of anyone getting shot in the back around here," Pearson returned in a nervous tone. "You are perfectly safe—while you're riding!"

The Kid waited for Lopez to speak. But the wounded rider only looked the other way. Nor did Bradley offer any assurances. Keeping close watch on the group he walked over to Toughy.

"How are you feeling, *chamaco*?" he asked in a kindly tone.

The boy looked at him for a moment, then climbed to his feet. "Finer than split frog's hair, *compañero*," he said brightly. "Mebbeso I'm kind of sickish in my innards, but I reckon all this ruckus is as much to blame as me getting plugged. But that damned Juan." His face twisted with hatred. "I'll get even with that lobo for this. You see if I don't. To think, he shot me when I didn't even have a gun."

Pearson guffawed. Bradley snorted. Lopez essayed a grin.

"I take it you are through with Lopez," the Kid observed.

"You're damned right I am—I'm off of that back-shooter for keeps," the boy cried. "I'll . . ."

"Perhaps I have done you some good turns today, *chamaco*, yes?" the Kid said. "If I have, then now you can return them."

Toughy studied him. "What are you driving at, *compañero*?" he demanded.

The Kid searched the boy's face. What he saw in the faithful eyes apparently satisfied him. For he stripped off his cartridge-belt, filled the empty chambers of his gun, rammed it back into the holster and buckled it around Toughy's waist. Lopez' gun he stuck into the front of his chaps.

"The Kid is about as popular on Rancho Diablo as a polecat, *chamaco*," he told the boy in an undertone. "Any one of these vaqueros would shoot me in a minute if they but get a single chance. On you—the one friend I have here—I am staking my life. Now you have a gun with which to fight. And in you have I placed my trust, *chamaco*. You shall drop the first one who shows hostility while I am up on that bay."

"You just tell a man I will, *compañero*," Toughy answered in a voice cracked with excitement. He dragged the big Colt from its holster, fondled it lovingly. "They've never gave me a gun for fear I would use it on them, I guess. Go on and make your ride. Top that bay slick to show 'em you can. Rest easy I've got the whole crew covered to give you a break—and it will be an even one, *compañero*. You can trust Toughy."

There was no mistaking the lad's sincerity. Thanking him, the Kid beckoned to one of the sullen men, crawled into the corral.

CHAPTER SIXTEEN

"PLEASE to upset him while I take off that war-bridle and put a hackamore on," the Kid ordered the vaquero. The fellow did as he was bid. The Kid worked over the brute easily. Then when the hackamore had been adjusted and the bay outlaw blinded again he turned to the helper.

"Let him up now," he said. "But without fright. Let him rise by himself when he discovers the rope is slack."

Going to where Rey del Rey was grazing, he stripped off his saddle and shouldered it to carry it back to the corral. Despite the gelding's mistrust he rigged it up with little difficulty, easing his own saddle onto the steaming back and tightening the cinch, careful however, to keep the group outside within range of his vision. But if the crew at Rancho Diablo had abused Toughy unarmed, it was apparent they had a wholesome respect for the lad with a loaded Colt in his hand. The youngster was bearing his pain stoically. The deadly glint in his eyes set the Kid to chuckling. There was little likelihood of any of them making a move toward their guns in the face of the forty-five Toughy clutched tightly against his hip.

Relying solely upon his steady nerves to pull him out of this predicament, into which his fiery temper had plunged him, the Kid centered his attention on the outlaw. "Easy, *caballo mio*," he crooned, "your day of mouth-wrenchings with war-bridles has passed. From now on you face only stern discipline and kindness."

The horse struck savagely at the voice. The Kid reached out and scratched its forelock. The bay snorted, lunged, struck savagely. Then intrigued by the unprecedented tenderness, it nosed forward. Cautiously the Kid worked with the brute, his soft voice inspiring confidence, his gentleness quickly quieting its nervous trembling. After a considerable time, during which he succeeded in breaking through the crust of the brute's suspicion, the Kid eased himself into the saddle, reached down and stripped off the blind.

"I shall take him now, señor," he told the vaquero, as he settled himself securely and began rubbing the gelding's ears.

The horse snorted, whirled to survey the group outside the enclosure. It shook its head impatiently at the soothing voice of the rider, stretched its neck gingerly to test out the wrenching war-bridle, discovered that its aching jaws were not clamped in the burning rope, and took a few mincing steps forward.

At a wink from Pearson, Bradley let out a

war whoop. A roar from Lopez—a bedlam of shouts from the vaqueros threw the bay into a panic. A real smile split the lips of the Mañana Kid. The horse went into the air. But the Kid's rowels scarcely moved. He made no attempt to rake the brute which, it was apparent, he could have done with ease. He seemed to loll in the saddle, his form whipping with the motion of the lunging bay, his body screwed down to the gorgeous silver-inlaid rig until he was a part of the plunging outlaw.

The Kid's ride that day became history on Rancho Diablo. Bawling like a terrified calf, blood streaming from its nose and lacerated jaws, the gelding uncorked its surest tricks, only to fail. Three times it reared and tried to hurl itself backwards. Each time the quirt which hung at the Kid's wrist brought it down, shaking its head savagely.

When it seemed that the foam-splattered animal was ready to surrender to the fearless rider bolted to the saddle, it bundled its iron muscles, pitched blindly into the cottonwood pole gate. A splintering crash! The corral swayed under the impact. The ragged edges of the logs tore at its legs. The outlaw broke through into open pasture. The howling of the riders, the guffaws of Pearson, who was doubled up with laughter, increased the brute's terror.

"Scratch him! Scratch him! You are such a

hellbender for forking bad horses," the pain-tortured Lopez drew himself up to shout.

The Kid heard him and smiled. For he was riding easily, his body a part of the heaving, twisting brute, his spur rowels now playing lightly up and down the brute's neck to meet behind the cantle.

"God A'mighty!" bellowed Pearson. "There is a hombre who really can ride. We want him, Bradley. Do you hear? We've got to have that bronc-peeling devil. He'll give Lopez cards and spades and teach him to ride. Look! He's raking that outlaw, and not even cutting him. He hasn't drawn blood and isn't trying to! Ride, you caballero, ride!"

Pearson missed the swift exchange of ugly looks that passed between Bradley and Lopez. He tossed his hat into the air and danced around wildly.

"He is raking the bay that can't be ridden—the outlaw every vaquero on Rancho Diablo has dodged," he roared. "Up and at him you hard riding vaquero from nowhere. Here, you hombres, haze him! Haze him! He's heading for bobwire!"

"Let him go," Lopez snarled. "He's too damned nosey to have around here. He has no business on Rancho Diablo."

"Let him get tangled up in the fence," echoed Bradley. "We've no room for him around here.

156

If he goes now it will just save us the trouble of putting him on El Scorpion. Damn that brat for—"

Pearson opened his mouth to countermand the order. Before he could speak, Toughy rammed the Kid's Colt into its holster, lurched up and threw himself aboard the nearest horse. Regardless of his painful bleeding arm, he raced out to cut the bay back from the wire. Inch by inch he crept up on the crazed gelding. Maneuvering carefully, he edged his mount between the outlaw and the glistening fence, crowded it away from the treacherous strands. Stirrups locked. Both horses went down. Dust swooped up in a choking blanket, obscuring everything. Pearson turned toward the house with a shrug.

"A couple of more busted necks," he said shortly. "They—"

A mighty shout. He whirled. Smiles froze on the face of Lopez and Bradley. The bay gelding had staggered to its feet, stood trembling like a new-born colt. The Kid, wiping the dirt from his mouth and eyes, was in the saddle.

Toughy arose shakily and helped his mount, badly slashed by the wire, to its feet.

"I'll be damned if they didn't pull through!" blurted out Bradley. "That hombre is tough, boss. We will have to do some tall figuring to get rid of him."

Pearson nodded.

"Keep him for a spell—until Lopez is able to ride again. Then take his smoking tobacco away from him and let him straddle El Scorpion."

Bradley started to speak. At that moment the Kid rode back, dismounted and stood rubbing the nose of the bay, which was now as docile as a work horse.

"And now, señor, have I won my five to one wager?" he smiled at Lopez. "Please to pay me."

Ungraciously, Lopez pulled out a roll of bills from his pocket and counted out the amount of the two wagers. "I'll pay off when I get my gun back," he bargained. Wheeling, the Kid strode over to Toughy. Buckling on his own cartridge belt and settling his gun at his hip, he returned to Lopez and extended the rider's gun, muzzle first.

Lopez snatched it, rammed it into his holster and passed over the bills. The Kid gathered up the money, turned back to Pearson. "And your word, señor?" he asked pointedly. "Of course it is good, yes?"

"Just as good as my bond," snapped the rancher. "Bradley will fix you out for a bunk. You're hired. Forty a month and found. You and Lopez fork all the bad ones when he gets able to ride again. Until that time, you'll do it alone. Now, some of you hombres, grab hold of Lopez and get him up to the house. We'll get a doctor for him."

The Kid stood by to watch as the vaqueros

lifted Lopez and carried him toward the house.

Then he unrigged the bay, carried his saddle back to where Rey del Rey was grazing. "We are not what one would call popular around here now that I have made my bluff stick, *caballo mio*," he told the horse as he stroked its neck. "And the señors will not hesitate to shoot me at the very first opportunity, yes?" He looked up quickly as a shadow fell across his path. Toughy stood before him.

"Reckon we're about even now, pard," whispered the boy hoarsely. "I—I—"

The words died in his throat. The Kid caught him as he crumpled to the ground.

"Poor little *chamaco*," he muttered, holding the slight figure in his arms and starting toward the barn. "You are possessed of more bravery than this whole pack of lobos who have been mistreating you."

CHAPTER
SEVENTEEN

A T THE horse trough the Kid laid Toughy down while he carefully washed the wound. The youngster bore the pain in stoic silence. Rey del Rey, who had followed along behind, looked on inquisitively, turning from time to time to drag his lower lip through the water, scooping up a mouthful only to let it trickle across his jaws as though reveling in the cooling draughts he had been so long denied on the blistering, waterless wastes.

When he had washed Toughy's wound clean of every particle of dust, the Kid straightened up to glance around. But apparently, for the time being, he had little to fear from the crew as they stood in attendance over the crippled Juan. The yard was deserted, although he could see several vaqueros squatted on their rowels near the ranchhouse.

"Had I something now with which to bandage it, *chamaco*," the Kid remarked. "For a bandage would keep out the dirt."

"Seems like you're always bandaging something about me," the boy smiled bravely. "I'd of still had that kerchief you gave me if Juan hadn't taken it away from me—the one you bound me up with on the mesa."

The mesa! The word whipped the Kid's mind back. Things had piled down upon him with such amazing swiftness for a time he had forgotten about the mesa; forgotten the brush with death in the storeroom, forgotten the left-handed gunman on whose trail he was supposed to have ridden; forgotten the girl herself. The others could wait for awhile. It was with her he would first settle the score. He would find out about her, find out about the many things that demanded an explanation: the killing in Guadalupe, her trickery on the mesa, the part she had played in the attempt on his life. Also would he find out who had been her companion that night when he had shared his water only to have her ride away. That companion would be the Guadalupe killer.

But her name, something about her, was the first step. She had refused to tell him because of fear, he was certain. Toughy would tell him. But he was reluctant to question the boy about it. After all, if she cared to keep it a secret what right had he to pry into her affairs? Yet the mystery of her intrigued him. Why had she not put in an appearance? Surely the gun-fire here at the corral, the shouts when he had ridden the bay, would have attracted her attention—at least to a point where she would have come to investigate. Still, it was possible that she, too, might be a victim of circumstance, forced to seek refuge at this ranch to encounter the deadly hostility with which he had been greeted. That was it—that was the reason for her fear.

"The kerchief Lopez took from you might do if we had it and it were sterilized, *chamaco*," he found himself telling the boy, although his words were no part of his thoughts. "But it must be properly bound. Perhaps the girl who lives here on the rancho would attend to it."

Toughy started. Fear flared into his eyes. He raised on his elbow and looked about the deserted yard. But he made no reply to the Kid who was watching him closely, wondering at the strange actions mention of the girl aroused.

"What frightens you, *chamaco*," he asked. "I only asked concerning the girl?"

"What girl do you mean?" Toughy whispered hoarsely.

"Why the girl at the ranchhouse. I met her first on the mesa. Her ankle was injured. Then, after I had bandaged it and while I sought to locate her horse in the darkness, she rode away—with some unknown companion."

The sharp glance Toughy gave him revealed nothing. Yet he was positive the youngster knew.

"Then when I struggled into the rancho half dead with thirst, I encountered her—"

"Who was she with?" Toughy demanded in a whisper.

"Now that I think of it," the Kid returned, "it was this Juan Lopez. But he did nothing to help me. The girl herself helped me to stay on my feet."

"And then what happened?" Toughy demanded.

"The next thing I knew I was sprawled in a storeroom, fighting to live against a thirst that seemed to burn me up."

You don't remember of going there—who took you?"

"No, but I can only believe that she must have had something to do with it. And I only asked for water."

"No!" Toughy said fiercely, his eyes sweeping the yard as though fearful a word would be overheard. "She didn't have anything to do with it, *compañero*."

"What makes you so positive, *chamaco*? After all, what am I to believe by the way she tricked me on the mesa, shortly after I met you. And then she rode away after I divided my precious water with her. There is something strange going on here. I shall find out what it is—find out who the companion was who rode away with her from the mesa. When I do—"

"You'll do what?" Toughy hung on breathlessly.

"If he is the one I believe, then I shall be forced to kill him, *chamaco*. But right now, of the girl if you please, that I may know what I am about instead of plunging into this thing blindly. What is her name?"

"Careful, *compañero*," Toughy whispered. "You don't know what you're getting into. Don't blame her for leaving you on the mesa. I know she didn't have anything to do with throwing you into that storeroom. When you've been here as long as I have nothing will surprise you."

"Nothing here makes sense, should you ask me, *chamaco*," the Kid said sourly. "But her name—something about her."

Toughy leaned closer. "Her name is . . ." He started to whisper.

"Shag a leg there, vaquero, if you're going to work here," the rough voice of Pearson boomed out to check the lad's words. "There are chores at the barn—work a-plenty. I'll have this kid looked after."

Startled by the voice of the fellow who had come up unnoticed from behind, the Kid whirled, his thumb hooked in his belt. But Pearson made no hostile move, although there was something in his voice that set the Kid's nerves to drumming again.

"I have cared for the *chamaco*," he said quietly. "Unless perhaps for a bandage on his wound. It would be well to have the lady of the house care for it."

"Lady of the house!" Pearson boomed. "What are you talking about? There is no woman on Rancho Diablo. The heat must of affected your brain. You tend to the chores. The vaqueros will show you your duties. Later, I shall have Bradley take you in hand. Come on, Toughy—get going!" he ordered the boy.

The youngster stood up shakily to cringe away. The Kid caught the movement, would have protested. But he also caught the look Toughy gave him. The boy was pleading mutely for him to be wary. Without a word the youngster turned toward the ranchhouse. Pearson started away behind him.

"One moment, señor," the Kid said. "I once appealed to your fairness. That I am an outsider here I well understand; that I should snoop or pry is beneath me. Strange things seem to be afoot—things I make no attempt to understand. But one thing you shall understand, señor— and understand briefly—I shall countenance no harm to the *chamaco*. Who harms him dies. You have seen my gun in action. I make no threats, I simply tell you, señor—the *chamaco* is my friend and as such commands the protection I can and shall give him."

Without another word he spun about, placed an arm around Rey del Rey, and sauntered away toward the barn, the palomino nuzzling him as they went.

Pearson stood watching after him. Then he too turned and strode off to the house behind Toughy.

CHAPTER EIGHTEEN

THE TRIANGLE call for supper found the Kid hanging back until the others had washed at the tin basins outside the cook shanty and trooped into the ranchhouse. Having looked again to Rey del Rey's shoulder, which now required but a slight application of grease to ward off the flies, he too went to the house, tidied himself up and strode within.

Ever fastidious, the Kid made even more of his toilet than usual, thinking perhaps now to encounter the girl who would surely appear for the meal.

His entrance apparently went unnoticed. For the vaqueros, strung out at a long oil-cloth covered table, were wolfing the food piled on platters. Pearson, he saw at a glance was not present. But oftentime ranchers did not eat with the men, so he thought little of it. Bradley too, was missing—and—

A feeling of disappointment he was at a loss to explain came to him. The girl had not put in an appearance. The fact that he had not laid eyes on her since he had first arrived, together with

Pearson's denial that there was a woman on the place, only increased the mystery of the thing. On the other hand, Toughy had been about to name her when Pearson had interrupted.

Toughy? The boy was not at the table.

"Where is the *chamaco*?" he demanded of the man alongside of him.

The fellow only glanced at him, but said nothing.

Making no inquiry as to the condition of Lopez, who he was certain would be laid up for many days, he finished his meal quickly, arose and went outside into the lowering light of evening that set the shadows creeping up the sides of the bluffs and in the brush.

Failure of either Toughy or the girl to put in an appearance at the table worried him. That Pearson had ignored his warning that no harm should come to the boy, he did not believe. Still, Pearson had many men here on Rancho Diablo, any one of whom could ambush him and cut him down with no one being the wiser. In an open fight he feared them not. From cover he stood little chance.

He was satisfied that the girl was on the rancho. Pearson's denial was offset by what Toughy had started to tell him. He wished the youngster could have finished. Things would have been made much easier—for foolhardy as it appeared, he was determined to find that girl. Why, he did not know. While the memory of her actions rankled within him, he had no desire to find her only to accuse her and make her suffer. He had thought that at first. Now he knew differently. He wanted to find her because . . . there was no answer to the question that framed in his mind. But find her he would!

Dusk fell over the Cuyamas to envelop the valley of Santa Ynez—darkness save for a red-glowing horizon that long disputed the creeping advance of the purple gloom. With time on his hands, among the vaqueros who made no attempt at conversation, the Kid prowled about trying to keep each man within range of his vision while also keeping a sharp lookout for Pearson or Bradley, who, as far as he knew, had not yet put in an appearance.

As night advanced the sinister aspect of the place grew more menacing. Still he prowled about, watching the ranchhouse for a light. Surely the girl, if she were there, would have a light. And Toughy—the youngster was wounded. He would require attention. But aside from the dull light of coal-oil lamps in the dining room and mess shanty, there was nothing to indicate that any other person was in the ranchhouse.

He had stumped about in his high-heeled boots until his legs and feet ached, and his whole body cried for rest. Twice he had gone to the barn to reassure himself that Rey del Rey and his silver-mounted saddle-rig were safe. For he found himself trusting no one on the place—unless perhaps it was Toughy. Long since the vaqueros had headed for the row of squat 'dobe bunkhouses below. He could hear them talking among themselves, their voices drifting out from the lighted doorway to come beating back in eerie whispers from the canyon walls. Apparently they were playing cards, for an occasional explosive curse volleyed into the night.

Again the Kid made his way to the barn to stand for a time stroking the neck of Rey del Rey. The palomino was deep in its feed, although it turned to nuzzle him briefly and go back to its manger.

At last he could stand the weariness no longer. He moved outside to look around, determined to take Rey del Rey from his feed, saddle him and move off a distance where he could keep the ranch under surveillance and still get rest.

"The señor said you should sleep in the bunkhouse," came a voice from his elbow that startled the Kid and brought him whirling around. Behind him stood a vaquero, a half-breed, who he doubted not, had followed his every move since he had quit the ranchhouse after supper.

"And you please to tell the señor—whoever he may be on this rancho accursed—that for many years I have slept out under the stars and am used to no roof over my head," the Kid replied evenly. "Therefore, not now shall I break a lifelong

170

habit." He tensed, hoping the fellow would make something of it, cursing his nerves that seemed to have tightened until he was hostile to every man.

"As the señor pleases," the vaquero said, moving out from the shadows of the barn until he could distinguish his outline clearly. "I only repeat my orders. If the señor chooses to disobey them . . ." He faded into the darkness. ". . . then I can only say it is the señor's own funeral."

The Kid waited for him to continue. When he did not, he listened for the sound of his retreating footsteps. But apparently the man who had watched him was barefoot. He had vanished completely in the shadows. No sound came to the Kid's straining ears.

He stood motionless for a moment, nerves keyed to a point he never before had known. The rancho was truly named Rancho Diablo—ranch of the devil. For even the men who stood guard over him made no sound as they slunk about to watch every move.

The Mañana Kid braced himself. Hand on his gun he went back into the barn. A glance, as he entered, still showed no light from the ranch-house. The girl—but damn the girl now. It was his life against the lives of those—and he doubted not they were many—who watched him through the gloom.

"Come, *caballo mio*," he told the palomino, striding alongside and stripping off the brute's halter. "We sleep far better and more secure in the open."

Rey del Rey free, he went over to where he knew his saddle-rig hung on the wall. Taking it down he succeeded in saddling the waiting palomino in the darkness.

When he had rigged up the brute, the Kid knotted the reins, tossed them over the horn and led Rey del Rey—reluctant and nickering his disappointment at leaving his food—to the door.

Kicking it open, the Kid went outside, the horse, its golden coat gleaming dully in the darkness, at his heels. A short distance and the Kid stopped.

"Rey del Rey," he told the palomino, "everywhere on this accursed rancho are we under the muzzle of a gun. No one dares face me— no one dares face any man who fights as fair men fight. Therefore, as we move across this clearing, lighted only by the stars, the guns of cowards are trained upon us. But we have been there before, *caballo mio*—been where cowards dare not show their faces. Now my gun sweeps the crew, *caballo mio*. We shall cross this yard. And out of the darkness may come bullets. How we laugh at them . . . as I laughed at their bullets today, *amigo*. But should one hit you, forever and through hell shall I hunt that coward down—and kill him. We sleep outside as we have always slept, and no man stops us only in death. For only do cowards lurk in shadows to obey a coward's command."

He swung up into the saddle. Shoulders squared, gun half drawn from its holster, he rode across the yard. No shot came from the darkness, although his quick ear caught the sound of footsteps hurrying back toward the bunkhouse.

Rey del Rey stopped short before a gate. The Kid got down, dropped it, led the palomino through, replaced the wire, remounted. Now the vaqueros were coming from the bunkhouse, heading on a run toward the barn.

"Should he escape our lives will be the forfeit," he heard a panting voice. "Saddle your horses and spread out, men—it is the primero's orders."

The Kid chuckled as he rode away in the darkness. The pounding of hoofs presently came to his ears. But the sound was from the opposite direction. He waited until it had died to a throb on the night air that now had become cool and restful after the heat of the day. Before he dipped down into an arroyo, he looked back at the ranchhouse. Somewhere there was the girl. And Toughy. He had pledged his protection for the *chamaco*. As for the girl. If he could prevent it no girl would suffer while he rode the valley of the Santa Ynez deep here in the heart of the Cuyamas. But how to prevent it was the one query now in his mind.

After a time he got down in an arroyo. Long since had every sound ceased on the night air save that of insects, the distant croaking of bull-frogs, the small thin whisper of crickets.

"Again we ride, *caballo mio*," the Kid told the palomino as he stretched lazily, then turned to start stripping off his saddle-rig that glinted even in the dull light. "The Mañana Kid—and his palomino, Rey del Rey—known from one end of the border to the other. Some day they may shoot us down in the darkness. But never shall we two be parted, only by a bullet some coward who dares not face us sends out of the night."

He hobbled the palomino with the leathern hobbles he took from the saddle, straightened the blanket on the ground.

"Here I shall rest, *amigo*, while you forage for your food. The one friend I have. Should they come, I know you will sound the warning as you have done many times before."

He threw himself on the blanket. "*Buenos noches, amigo*," he told the palomino, who waited just above him. "Find your food—that you may have strength. As for me, I sleep and dream of the chamaquita to whom I owe nothing, the chamaquita who owes me much—her life perhaps. And as I dream I think of the left-handed gunman there at Guadalupe—the gunman who cut down the youth in the prime of life—I dream of Toughy. Also I must have unpleasant dreams, so . . . I dream of Pearson and Bradley and Juan Lopez. And as I dream I laugh, *caballo mio*. For never yet has the Mañana Kid failed in his purpose. That purpose now is to find out the mystery of Rancho Diablo. In that you shall help me, *caballo mio*, for on your speed and your endurance dare I stake my life. The one thing— no the two, *caballo*, is first the girl and then the *chamaco*, Toughy." His voice trailed off as he sprawled out on the saddle blanket. Rey del Rey came closer, nuzzled his prone form.

"The girl—we shall find her, *caballo mio*," came softly from his lips. "We shall accuse her. But shall we? Do we care who killed the youth at Guadalupe? Do we care who is the left-handed gunman? Do we care, *amigo*, save for that sweet-faced chamaquita who, of all women we have seen, the Mañana Kid could love?"

Again Rey del Rey nuzzled the suddenly quiet form. But it did not respond. It lay limp, movable under his nose. Rey del Rey raised his head. All was quiet. And about him was feed. Not the feed in the manger from which he had been taken so reluctantly, but feed, nevertheless. He moved off from the still form, dropped his head and went to grazing.

CHAPTER
NINETEEN

THE DAYS that followed were busy ones for the Mañana Kid. With Lopez—who he later learned had been taken to town for medical treatment—temporarily out of commission, he not only was called upon to do the work Bradley heaped upon him—which in itself was enough to tax the best efforts of any man—but that of Lopez as well. From the morning he had ridden back into Rancho Diablo after the night spent out under the stars with Rey del Rey, it was apparent the primero had set out to deal the Kid enough misery in an underhand way to force him to admit defeat.

But the Mañana Kid had yet to learn of that word—defeat. Bradley's purpose was so obvious, his efforts at cunning so bunglesome, the Kid could scarcely repress a chuckle when some order sent him at a job usually reserved for the lowest helper on the rancho. Determined to see the thing through until, at least, he could get a line on Toughy and the girl, he made no complaint. He went about the task of riding the Rancho Diablo outlaws quietly, making no advances for friendship, receiving none; enduring the muttered threats and jibes of the jealous, hostile crew and suffering the clumsy thrusts of Bradley—who always followed up with a sneering laugh—in silence.

Occasionally, when the vaqueros had out-done themselves in rounding up some wild-eyed horse they were positive he could not ride, he mastered the brute with comparative ease and smiled in their faces as he turned it over to Bradley with all the fight kicked out of it. Whatever the ugly crew thought of him, not one of them could deny that he was a rider of championship caliber, a rider capable of mastering horses they themselves gave wide berth.

Pearson had disappeared, as had the girl and Toughy. Relying to some extent on the rancher in the showdown he knew must come, the Kid swallowed his disappointment and became even more vigilant. In the days following, Pearson returned from time to time with strangers who, it was noised about, were horse buyers. During these visits the Kid was spared the nagging of Bradley who went with the owner while he showed the buyers over the ranch.

Shortly after these trips Bradley would return to the rancho and the strangers would disappear. The Kid never knew when nor how they left. But one thing he did notice. They seldom, if ever, bought any horses. He finally decided that the chief business of Rancho Diablo was unloading outlaws, which had been ridden once, as thoroughly broken mounts—probably for cavalry service.

The longer he stayed the more firmly convinced he became that something was wrong about the whole outfit. Even the atmosphere of the rancho keyed his nerves to the highest pitch. The owl-faced Bradley was laboring under some great mental stress which sent him about muttering to himself. The vaqueros slunk around the rancho as though they were always on their guard against something. What it was, the Kid did not know—and in his few contacts with the surly, untalkative crew he had little chance of finding out. But he stuck on doggedly, determined to learn.

Spring lengthened into summer—blistering days that set the wild region dancing like a mirage in the heat waves that rose from the griddle-hot earth, dried the Santa Ynez river, which ran just below the rancho, to a chain of pools. Cattle, bellowing thirstily, prowled the arroyos. The Kid wondered at that. He had seen no cattle on Rancho Diablo; yet, apparently, the outfit ran both cattle and horses. Vividly he recalled his encounter with the bull back at the foot of the *peñasco* the day he had staggered into the rancho half dead for water only to be cast into the stifling storeroom to die. It took but a look at the scar on the shoulder of Rey del Rey to recall the experience. For he kept the palomino with his gorgeous saddle rig always near at hand, ready to ride after the showdown.

The Guadalupe posse he had forgotten. It was evident those on Rancho Diablo maintained no contact with the village from which he had ridden the night of the murder in Cantina El Paseo. A thing for which he was thankful; at least it spared him a constant vigil in that direction.

As for the left-handed gunman, in the press of work he had given him little if any thought. For recollection of that Guadalupe murder always set his mind whirling back to wonder what had become of the girl. But this, too, seemed a mystery that as time went on he began to admit he never would be able to solve.

Then one day in late August, when the evening breezes whining up the Santa Ynez had begun to carry the cool whip of fall, Toughy appeared. The youngster strode out among the crew. The Kid sighted him instantly, made for him.

"*Chamaco mio,*" he said eagerly, while the vaqueros about him only looked on with their customary sullenness. "Glad I am to see you again. Your wounds? They are now completely healed, yes?"

"Partner!" Toughy took his hand and clung to it in a fearful way. "I'm glad to see you, too. I've been . . ."

Bradley put in an appearance at that moment

to cut short what Toughy was about to say—as Pearson's appearance had stopped the boy weeks before at the moment he had started to tell the Kid of the girl. Toughy cringed away, turned and started for the barn. The Kid squared off. But Bradley apparently had no intention of precipitating a showdown for he only sauntered on toward the ranchhouse.

Time and again during the next few days the Kid attempted to talk with the boy. But Bradley, sensing their friendship, was careful to keep them apart and always found some excuse for separating them when they chanced to meet.

When not working, the Kid stole away from the rancho and spent his time on the mesa with the white stallion he had encountered the day he arrived in the Cuyamas. On his first trip back after the encounter with the outlaw, the brute had shown fight, but by filling his pockets with sugar which he filched from the mess shanty, the Kid quickly won its complete confidence.

Within a week the horse was following him around like a dog. Within a month he had saddled and ridden it, the only observer Rey del Rey who, hobbled and stripped of his saddle and bridle, looked on reproachfully as the white minced away making no effort to pitch. After he had broken the stallion to the gentleness of a cowpony, he decided to make Pearson an offer for it, presuming of course that the brute belonged to Rancho Diablo. Each time he was on the point of bringing up the subject Pearson was either away from the rancho or preparing to go, with the result that the offer never was made.

Although he kept a sharp lookout for the notorious horse, El Scorpion, to which Bradley and the vaqueros referred constantly, he never succeeded in catching sight of the animal. Had it not been for the stark dread in which the brute was held by every man on the place, as time passed he would have decided that El Scorpion, like many man-killing outlaws around horse ranches, was a phantom animal conceived in the mind of some joker and held as a constant threat over all top-riders.

Came early September. A broiling sun hung like a scourge over the Cuyamas. Dog-tired, the Kid climbed down from a rangey sorrel that had hammered his muscles until they ached, and made his way to the bunkhouse, into which after several nights in the arroyas, he had moved a bedroll. At the door he met Toughy who appeared to be greatly excited. The boy had discarded his home-made chaps for overalls, thrown away his collection of conchas and rosettes and had dropped much of Lopez' talk. It was obvious the hero-worshipper had swapped idols.

"Juan is coming back to work tomorrow," he whispered hoarsely as he passed the Kid. "They are aiming to give you your walking papers—and they are framing to get you, partner. Keep your eyes peeled."

Bradley, who always seemed just at hand when he encountered Toughy, sauntered up at the moment. Toughy hurried on. The Kid went into the bunkhouse to which utter weariness had driven him, and threw himself on his bedroll, pondering the warning. Now that Lopez was able to ride again, he was not surprised that he was to be let out. In fact, he had expected it. But in view of the unconcealed hatred both Bradley and Lopez bore him, he often had wondered if they would allow him to depart without first attempting to get revenge. And from his angle there was always the girl to consider. For he was not yet convinced she was not on Rancho Diablo, although he never had laid eyes on her. If only Toughy could tell him. But the youngster was never given a chance to talk to him for more than a few moments at a time.

Before he answered the cook's call to supper, he carefully oiled his gun and looked to the cartridges. After he had eaten with the surly vaqueros who ignored him, he returned to his bedroll, Toughy's warning still ringing in his ears.

Morning came. At breakfast the Kid was aware of an unusual stir. Lopez, apparently no worse for his wound, strode up beside him as he left the mess shanty.

"I'll take over the bad ones from now on, *peregriño*," the fellow remarked, carelessly.

"So?" The Kid made no further comment, choosing to let Lopez reveal his hand.

"The day you came here," the rider went on hatefully, "you bet me you could ride that bay."

"No one has disputed that I did not make good my word—and win my wager." The Kid shrugged.

"You won good money off of me, sure. I'll admit that you are—well—a square-shooter. But no one ever won twice from Juan Lopez."

"Never have I been accused of back-shooting, señor—or trying to kill a helpless *chamaco*, as did you, if that is what you want to know."

Lopez flushed darkly. "And you still think you are some rider, don't you?"

The Kid halted. "What is the señor trying to say in this round-about manner?" he demanded coldly. "When one talks one should speak what one thinks."

Lopez twisted a cigarette and inhaled deeply before he replied. "If you will recklect when you forked that bay, I offered you twenty to one odds that you couldn't top his brother, El Scorpion. They ran him in yesterday, hombre. Have you got any money now that says you can fork him—or are you yellow when it comes to a show-down?"

At last the Kid knew what Toughy had meant.

184

This El Scorpion was the way Lopez and Bradley had calculated to get revenge.

For no apparent reason Jim Brown's remark back at the cabana flashed to his mind. "Seems like it's the out neck-breakin'est place in southern California," the old fellow had said. The Kid stared hard at Lopez trying to read the fellow's mind.

"Getting cold feet, are you?" Lopez sneered.

The Kid smiled. "You ask me that after I send you to the doctor to be laid up for weeks! Never fear. Always shall I have your number, Lopez—even though I am fair and you are . . . a cowardly—lobo. Always I call for a showdown of any hand such as you hold. I sabe not the present frame-up. But convinced I am that it is one. For only by trickery do men of your caliber win anything. Now, I call your hand. Of a certainty I shall take you on. The wager rides as you made it. Twenty to one I can fork him. I have one hundred dollars of money that says I can. You would cover it?" His teeth clicked grimly. He had heard of man-killing horses possessed of tricks that unseated the best bronc-peelers, but he never had encountered one. El Scorpion undoubtedly was an outlaw capable of testing the mettle of any rider, yet he resolved to die rather than give either Bradley or Lopez the satisfaction of seeing him back down.

He stared at the roll of bills Lopez dragged

from his pocket. "One hundred bucks at twenty to one is . . . two thousand dollars I'm putting up, isn't it?" leered Lopez. "Now let me see your hundred."

The Kid produced the money but did not hand it over.

"Are you going to bet?" demanded Lopez, reaching for it.

"Of a certainty I shall. I'll put it up when I am satisfied I shall have at least a chance of having it returned, señor," the Kid said pointedly.

Lopez caught hold of himself, to keep from flying into a rage. "El Scorpion is over in the corral waiting, *peregriño*," he sneered. "All the vaqueros are taking time off to see you kick him down. You have made your brags about how good you are. Now is your last chance to prove it." Making a flash with the bills, which he still held in his hand, he turned on his heel and sauntered away. The Kid followed him with his eyes.

Toughy edged up. "Don't get on that horse, partner," he cautioned under his breath. "They've framed you. That's the dangest man-killer in these parts. Used to be Bradley's . . . but he beat it so's he can't get anywhere near it any more. That's—"

"What's eating on you, brat?" demanded Lopez, coming back to push in between the two. The boy slunk away. The Kid bristled. But he held his tongue. Fully aware that the insolent

Lopez was intent upon forcing trouble, he hung on to his smouldering anger. Anxious to catch a glimpse of this El Scorpion, notorious killer, he made his way to the corral.

Toughy's words had given him an idea which he determined quickly to follow up. He looked through the poles at the brute; stood stock still for a minute, surveying it critically. Then he wheeled on Lopez, who had joined Bradley and was coming toward him.

"A bad-looking caballo," he admitted. "But still I play the hunch I can ride him with little or no effort—the confidence is so great I should like to wager a little more money, Lopez." He dragged from his own pocket a roll of bills. "One thousand dollars, Lopez, at twenty to one I ride that horse, get down and have him follow me from the corral as does Rey del Rey."

"Twenty thousand dollars!" Bradley blurted out. "Lopez you can't—"

"Lopez can!" Juan stopped him angrily. "You are called *peregriño*—called for twenty thousand dollars."

"And the señor's money—if he possesses that much—of course he carries such a sum on his person?"

"Ride El Scorpion," Lopez snarled. "Should you win you will be paid. But you will not win."

"And should I . . . you are prepared to pay—promptly as I should demand payment?"

"Lopez, you can't . . ." Bradley began.

"The hell I can't," Lopez bawled to silence him. "I shall collect that amount from Rancho Diablo—for what I know. Bradley, do you get that straight?"

CHAPTER TWENTY

"AND NOW perhaps the señor who bets so bravely would care to go even further," the Kid suggested. "Of course, I understand not the reference you just made of collecting from Rancho Diablo for what you know. Nor care I what it is. The wager alone concerns me."

"I'm calling you," Lopez shouted wildly. "I told you I was calling you!"

"But I offer you even greater chances to win," the Kid said smoothly. "Rey del Rey, for instance. That palomino of mine is worth his weight in gold. Many times have I refused for him a thousand dollars. And the saddle gear I ride—alone the saddle cost five hundred—not to mention the spurs, the bridle, the martingale. . . . My chaparejos are worth more than a hundred. They were all made especially to my order in Juarez, by an excellent leather worker whom I shall recommend to you, señor. Now is your chance, vaquero, to possess such a rig as you shall never have an opportunity to possess again. Everything on Rancho Diablo that is mine save my gun and cartridge belt—easily worth two thousand or more they are, señor. I wager them at even money."

"You're called again!" Lopez blurted out, his eyes snapping over the men who had moved up to stare open-mouthed. "Twenty-two thousand dollars against everything you own but your gun and cartridge-belt that you cannot ride El Scorpion."

"The señor figured well," the Kid mocked in a voice that was amazingly gentle. "And now that the wager is placed, we have overlooked one important detail. Not that I doubt your honesty, understand, señor. Never can it be said that I mistrusted, for so much as an instant, a fellow-man . . . and surely not such as yourself. But you shall sign a paper—a note, señor. For I am sure your note is good—a note that I shall receive when I win the wager."

"I'll sign nothing," Lopez bawled furiously.

"By that statement you admit you have no intention of paying should you lose, señor. You have shown me little in the way of money to cover such an enormous wager. Twenty-two thousand dollars, my dear señor, is a sum comparable to a King's ransom. A wager is a wager, hombre. The money in sight or your note to cover it, yes?"

"You're not trying to insinuate . . ." Lopez began hotly, backing off.

"The señor continues to resolve the demand for a straightforward business deal into a personal affront. I insinuate nothing. Never do I insinuate. Always I speak plainly and to the point. And I say now, señor, plainly that all may hear. You do not possess twenty-two thousand dollars. The threat you employed just now in the hearing of Bradley will avail you nothing. From what I have seen of Rancho Diablo, señor, they pay not in coin; they have other ways here to collect and silence protests."

"What do you mean by that?" Bradley roared.

The Kid bowed courteously. "Exactly what I said, señor. I say, that you may get the full import of my meaning, that it is my personal opinion that on all Rancho Diablo there could not be raised twenty-two thousand dollars. Further am I convinced that for a tenth of that sum—or even a hundredth, señor, every man who wears the brand of this rancho would slit his closest friend's throat. If you like not my talk, then there is one way to stop it—or attempt to."

He was braced back on his heels now, the Mañana Kid, his thumb hooked in his cartridge belt, his light-shafted eyes whipping the growling vaqueros. But no man made a move.

Finally the Kid's gaze came to a focus on Lopez. The vaquero was licking his lips savagely, but making no move toward his gun.

"Does the señor sign the note?" the Kid asked.

"I'll go to the house and fix it up." Lopez snarled. He whirled and started away.

"And while you are absent, señor," the Kid said, the mocking tone again in his voice, "I shall wait in the barn. For there four walls protect me from those who would, I have little doubt, knife me or shoot me between the shoulder blades. Never between the eyes, señor. For such is the brand of men I see about me." He deliberately turned his back on the crew. "But remember, señor," he threw over his shoulder, "dead, I am worth nothing to you. Alive . . . perhaps I may be worth twenty-two thousand dollars."

"Get the hell out of here and back to your work, you vaqueros!" Lopez exploded. "What are you being paid for around here? The first man who makes a crooked move for his gun I'll attend to."

The Kid went on to the barn, chuckling. Bradley stood as though transfixed. Lopez strode to the ranchhouse. The vaqueros fanned out to fall to some sort of task.

When he sighted Lopez returning, the Kid left off petting Rey del Rey and went outside to meet him. From the corner of his eye he saw the vaqueros again closing in.

"Here's my note," Lopez said grandly. "Made out to you if you win this ride."

"And backed by what, señor?" the Kid inquired politely.

"My word!" Lopez thundered. "No man lives who—"

"Now we speak like gentlemen instead of grooms," the Kid smiled graciously. "When one relies on one's word then has one pledged his fairness—if he possesses such. Therefore, I accept your note. Now only one thing remains to be settled. I claim the right to choose the stake-holder. You understand, yes?"

Lopez shrugged. "As you want. For no man leaves Rancho Diablo alive with that note and money, if you lose. And your stake-holder?"

The Kid beckoned Toughy to him. The youngster came up fearfully. "Behold my stake-holder, señors," the Kid said dramatically throwing an arm about the boy's trembling shoulders.

"That damned brat," Lopez sneered. "Why he hasn't sense enough to hold that much money. I'll get one of the vaqueros—or what's the matter with Bradley?"

"The *chamaco* holds the stakes or I do not ride," the Kid said. "As for the sense he possesses, from my observation it is far greater than any I have seen about me. Here, *chamaco*, you understand this money and this note belongs to me?"

"The hell it does," Lopez flared. "Not until you've won, it doesn't. Don't try any funny business."

"Your mistrust hurts me at times, señor," the Kid mocked. "For I shall win your money. And you, *chamaco*, guard it with your life." Unstrapping his cartridge-belt, he buckled it around the boy's lean waist. "And listen, *chamaco mio*," he said in the youngster's ear in a tone too low for the others to hear, "this is where you and the Kid make the grand clean-up together. Never for a moment let one of those hombres approach you. You wanted a gun with which to fight. Now you have one, *chamaco*, my gun—the gun of the Kid that never yet has missed its mark." He pressed the Colt into Toughy's hand. "Now you can fight for me as I shall fight for you, always."

"Nobody but Juan or Mert will try to double-cross you," the boy whispered shakily.

"I shall care for Bradley," the Kid said. "Understand that, *chamaco*."

"Sure, *compañero*," Toughy choked. "But don't try to ride El Scorpion. He is the one who—"

"I have the hunch at what you are driving, *chamaco*. But do not worry. He is . . ."

"Well, the brat's got the money," Lopez cut in. "We're waiting for you to get your neck broken so I can collect."

"One minute more, señor." Still the Kid stalled mockingly. "That caballo in there is bad—the worst of its kind. I can tell by the way you hombres fear it. But ride him I shall, so do not go to spending this *dinero* in your mind. But our wager did not say where I was to ride him, so I choose to ride him in the open instead of in that round corral."

Bradley's face took on a deathlike pallor. "He'll

kill you out here in all this bobwire," he managed to gasp.

"That is what the señor is calculating on him doing to me in the corral, is it not?" the Kid smiled. "As though you care if he kills me, yes? I simply repeat—I shall ride this caballo in the open." He captured Bradley's shifting gaze. "I have good reason to believe he must once have belonged to you. If such should be the case the Señor Bradley will frighten him less than another. Therefore you shall drop the corral gate-poles after I mount him."

"I—I—" stammered Bradley. The Kid laughed. The idea Toughy had given him had worked. It was plain that the foreman was in mortal terror of the horse.

Lopez attempted to cover up Bradley's fright. "You just climb aboard. He will drop the gate-poles as you wish, *pelado*."

The Kid turned smiling eyes on Toughy. "You heard what Lopez said, *chamaco*? Lopez is a man of his word. Thus, we believe him, yes?"

"Yes." Toughy attempted to grin but it froze on his white lips.

"The Señor Bradley is going to do it, as I say— he shall not double-cross?"

"He will drop those poles just like you are telling him to, *compañero*, or I shall drop him," Toughy replied grimly. "You don't have to worry none, partner."

The Kid secured his saddle and started for the corrals. "I trust you, *chamaco*, as ever one friend should trust another. And you, Señor Lopez, you think this El Scorpion is a bad horse?"

"No horse ever lived who was worse," Lopez said.

"And . . . should I ride him slick here in the open, the señor will admit I am the greatest rider ever to put in an appearance at Rancho Diablo?"

"Not only the greatest, but the nerviest," Lopez winked at Bradley who had not moved, but stood with face colorless, twisted with fear—deathly fear, the Kid thought.

"Now, señors," the Kid smiled. "I shall show all cowardly hombres on Rancho Diablo how I—a *pelado*, a *peregriño*, as you have termed me—learned to master horses. So this is El Scorpion—the horse who strikes terror to your hearts?" He crawled into the corral. "Come, *diablo blanco*!" he cried. "Come . . . meet your master!"

Backed against the poles at the far side of the enclosure the outlaw pricked up its ears, reared, struck savagely at the air a couple of times, then walked, head down, across the corral and laid its muzzle on the Kid's shoulder.

Lopez turned livid with rage. Bradley choked. Toughy howled with delight. The vaqueros stared in blank amazement. The Kid only grinned and stroked the horse's neck. For El Scorpion was the white stallion that he had encountered the day he had ridden onto the mesa—the stallion which for weeks he had worked to tame.

Without even roping the white, he hoisted his saddle onto its back, slipped a hackamore over its ears and climbed up. The outlaw strained on the rope but made no effort to pitch. Cursing loudly, tearing up earth in his bare hands, like an infuriated bull, Lopez seemed to lose his reason. Bradley, too, went berserk.

"Just a minute, Mert," Toughy reminded in cool tones. "You're going to open that gate—that's what the Kid said—that was the agreement."

Bradley stopped. "Go to hell, you brat!" he snarled. "I'm not going to do anything of the kind."

The white stallion heard Bradley's voice. Up went its head and tail. A whistling snort tore through distended nostrils. Like a thunderbolt it hurled itself against the gate. Insecurely patched after the bay had splintered it, the poles gave way with a deafening crash. Bradley started at top speed for the barn. In a dozen terrific leaps El Scorpion was pounding at his heels, teeth grinding, forefeet slapping the earth. Despite the Kid's frantic efforts to turn him the white tore on.

Bradley wheeled, flung up his arms to protect himself. A blood-curdling scream! The striking hoofs descended like a ton of steel.

When he finally succeeded in quieting the

crazed brute, the Kid rode back and dismounted to wipe beads of perspiration from his forehead. Uncinching the saddle, he pulled off the hackamore, turned loose the still nervous white.

"It is best that you vaqueros carry Bradley up to the house," he said quietly to the gaping riders. "One of you had better find Señor Pearson. Tell the señor to get a coroner—but there is no hurry now."

Sickened, the Kid turned away. Snorting defiance at the group, El Scorpion stood still for a minute. Then he spied Lopez. With a bawl of rage he charged. Juan made the mess shanty as the stallion thundered up. A spurt of flame leaped from the door. The horse went down, end over end, kicked convulsively, then straightened out.

The Kid's face went white. He sprang toward Toughy. "My gun, *chamaco*," he lashed out. "The lobo—the—he has killed El Scorpion. I—"

The words died in his throat, became a rasping gurgle. He took a faltering step, spun around dizzily, pitched to the ground.

Juan Lopez, blue smoke from his Colt wreathing about his head, stepped from the mess shanty and started toward Toughy.

CHAPTER
TWENTY-ONE

T HE MAÑANA KID groped back to consciousness. When he was able he opened his aching
eyes and stared about groggily. Again his head
was throbbing; his body afire with fever as it
had been when he had recovered his senses that
day in the storeroom. He attempted to ease his
cramped muscles but they failed to respond. He
dropped back to the ground with a groan, trying
to bring order out of his chaotic mind.

Slowly the events at the corral came back to
him. The vivid memory of the white stallion
trampling the helpless Bradley sickened him.
Then there had been Lopez. The wager . . . his
lips braced grimly. Anger gave him strength.

After several futile attempts he succeeded in
getting to his feet to stand and stare bewildered.
A terrifying glow bathed everything with a stain
of blood. Hazily he strove to get his bearings.
As near as he could determine by the weird
light flickering on the dirt walls he was in an
abandoned dugout.

He felt for his gun. With sinking heart he
recalled that he had not had time to seize it from

Toughy's hand before Lopez shot him. A fear that Juan had killed the boy assailed him.

He sat flat down on the dirt floor to think. He wondered where he was and how he had gotten there. The throbbing in his head nauseated him, left him spent and dizzy. He rubbed his temple. A big lump where Lopez's bullet had creased him was clotted with blood. But to his surprise he discovered the wound had been bandaged.

Tightening his grip on unstrung nerves, he climbed to his feet again and fell to staggering about. By now his burning eyes had become somewhat used to the eerie red glow. His groping fingers came in contact with a door. He tried to open it. It was blocked with mud and debris and defied his efforts. Dropping to his knees, he clawed away the dirt with his fingers. Arising, he pulled. The door shifted slightly on rusty hinges. Squeezing through the crack, he went outside. The strange, unearthly light lay all about him.

At first, believing it a fancy of his feverish brain, he rubbed his eyes and looked again. He was completely surrounded by great fingers of flame that leaped into a moonless sky. The inert air was heavy with the acrid fumes of burning sulphur.

Fear of the unknown, of these tentacles of fire, gripped him. Mustering his courage, he took a few cautious steps ahead. A tall column of white smoke burst from a rift in his path. The baked earth crumbled beneath his feet as he recoiled. The pungent odor of sulphur stung his nostrils. Through the clefts he could see the lurid glow of subterranean fires with here and there tongues of blue and cherry-colored flame dancing to the surface.

The Mañana Kid made no pretense at trying to convince himself he was not afraid. Never had he feared man or beast, but now he was trembling from head to foot, partly through weakness and the fever sapping his strength, partly because of a horrible dread he could not overcome. He sat down again. Even the earth was warm. Minutes dragged by. Still he waited, struggling to get hold of himself and feel more secure as he became accustomed to the inferno.

Presently he heard a step. At first a crackling of the parched ground, then the soft tread of cautious footsteps. Rising, he slunk back to the side of the dugout and crouched in the shadows.

A lone figure hove in sight. The Kid fought to quiet the breath that was rasping through his dry throat in labored gasps. The figure stood outlined against one of the tongues of flame. It was Toughy!

More relieved than he would even admit to himself, the Kid stepped into the light.

"Gosh dang, you scared me!" stammered Toughy, leaping back fearfully. "I didn't just figure to find you prowling around yet. I'm sure glad of it though. Kind of hoped you would come to in the daylight so this here hell-hole wouldn't throw the fear of God into you like it did me the first time I ever saw it."

"What is it? Where am I?" the Kid demanded. "How long have I been here?"

"A couple of days," Toughy said. "You are about three miles south of Rancho Diablo. This here is the edge of the desert. The fires are burning coal beds. They keep catching somehow. They been burning ever since I can remember. They call them the Pillars of Hell back at the rancho. Bradley and Pearson used to bring me in here when I was a little shaver and make me stay all alone. I sort of got used to it thataway, although it sure scared the stuffing out of me at first."

"I do not wonder at that, *chamaco*." The Kid shuddered and glanced around nervously. "But how, please, did I get here?"

"Lopez and the old man brought you. This is where they bring the horse buyers."

"The horse buyers?" the Kid repeated blankly.

"The horse buyers who come to the ranch with the old man. He stakes them to El Scorpion—"

"And El Scorpion throws them and breaks their necks?" The Kid finished breathlessly, giving voice to a suspicion that had become a practical certainty in his mind.

"That's it," answered Toughy, matter-of-factly.

"El Scorpion turns somersets with them and busts their necks. Then the old man and Juan and Mert steal their money, divvy it, and snake their bodies in here. Once in awhile, when El Scorpion doesn't finish the job, Juan has to. I came danged nigh giving him away on one killing he didn't know I saw—that first day I met you up on the mesa." The Kid recalled the boy's slip which had puzzled him, but made no comment. Toughy went on. "It's no trick to get rid of them in here with all this fire."

"So that is it?" mused the Kid, suddenly understanding why he never knew when and how the buyers left the ranch. "And El Scorpion is the way all this neck-breaking occurs, *chamaco*?"

"Do you wonder now I tried to tip you off not to go near that killer?" Toughy said. "I don't know yet how you handled that outlaw. No one else ever did. How did you—"

"Some other time, *chamaco*. Then we shall make a good story of it and both laugh. But right now—tell me more about Rancho Diablo, about the horse buyers and Lopez."

"I'm not supposed to know." The boy's voice dropped. He glanced around fearfully. "But I'm wise to a lot of their stuff they don't know about. I've been keeping my eyes and ears open ever since I was a little bit of a cuss. Why, I can even remember when Juan came here. Mert and the old man were here before that. When Juan came they hid him out for a long time and used to beat me if I nosed around to see what he was doing. Gosh, I wasn't much more than knee-high to a cricket. But I remember a sheriff and a deputy came in here one time hunting for Juan, and Mert and the old man staked them to El Scorpion and kinked their necks."

"How long you been here, *chamaco*?" the Kid asked.

"I don't know." The boy shook his head. "I don't even know how old I am. I can't recall of ever being any place else."

"Does the *chamaco* remember ever hearing of a hombre by the name of Johnnie Bender?" the Kid questioned, suddenly recalling the reference the old man of the cabana had made to this Bender and to the striking resemblance he bore him.

"Sure thing," was Toughy's answer. "And I've heard Mert and the old man talk about him lots. That was before Juan's time. He used to be foreman down here. Must have been a square-shooter too, from what I've heard them say. He got his neck busted. I heard the old man raving about it after Juan told him you had forked El Scorpion. He said you were the only hombre who ever did it besides Johnnie. It seems funny to me that El Scorpion would bust Johnnie's neck if he rode him, doesn't it? How did you handle that outlaw so easy, partner?"

"It is scarcely time for that now, *chamaco*, as

there are other things more vital. But you ask it, so . . ." Quickly he recounted how he had worked with the white stallion for weeks, little dreaming that he was the notorious El Scorpion. When he had finished the tale, he picked up the broken thread of conversation.

"As you remarked, *chamaco*, it is odd that this Johnnie Bender got his neck broken if he rode El Scorpion," he mused aloud. "What else does the *chamaco* know?"

"I'm scared to go on," the boy admitted. "There might be somebody listening. Juan and Pearson would kill me if they knew I'd told you this much. The old man rode in after Juan shot you from under cover and thinking you were dead, they threw you across a horse and brought you out here. I knew where they were coming, so as soon as it got dark I sneaked out. I thought you were dead too. But I fixed up that crease on your temple the best I could. And I've been bringing you water and trying to take care of you ever since. This would be a hell of a place to die, wouldn't it, partner?"

The Kid could not suppress a smile at the lad's awesome tone. "It matters little where one dies, *chamaco*. But, as you say, this would scarcely be the setting in which one would . . . say, enjoy dying. Thanks to you, however, I did not die. But why did you take the risk of helping me? You owe me nothing."

"I guess not," returned the boy. "You're not the hombre who didn't kill me when I held you up with a pipe, I guess? You didn't keep that bay from tromping me? You aren't the hombre who plugged Lopez for shooting me, huh? And partner . . ." He burst into tears. ". . . I—lost—your—money."

"How?"

"I dropped your gun trying to hand it to you. Before I could get hold of it, Juan shot you and had me covered. Then he kicked me all over the lot, took your forty-five and stole the stakes."

"It is too small a thing over which to worry, *chamaco*," the Kid consoled the sobbing lad. "There was little of cash, much of worthless paper signed by Lopez. We shall recover it, never fear. Then shall we two go somewhere and set up a little rancho of our own, yes, *chamaco*?"

"Do you really mean that, partner?" exclaimed the boy, joyfully.

"Of a certainty."

"And you won't hold losing that money against me?"

"Never for a moment. None of us can do more than our best. Many times our best does not suffice, as in this case. But you did all you could, so now forget it, yes?"

"Gosh, I'm glad. Here, I brought you some water."

He produced a bottle of water. It was cool, and

allayed the throbbing pain in the Kid's parched throat.

"And now for a cigarette would I give much," the Kid sighed when he had drunk his fill.

"I've got your making," the boy said. "Juan searched you and took everything you had, but I stole your tobacco and papers back. I tried to get your gun too, but they were watching too close. And here is some grub I brought. It isn't much, but it's all I could sneak away without them getting wise."

The food he pulled from his pocket was little more than scraps. But the Kid ate it with relish. When he had finished he twisted a cigarette and lighted it. After he had taken a couple of comforting drags he felt better.

"No friend could ever do more for me than you have, *chamaco*, and the Kid appreciates it and will not forget."

"Forget what?"

"The bravery of you, *chamaco*—how you risked everything to bring help to me."

"You have been good to me, partner. The only hombre who ever was. Besides, I'm off of Juan Lopez for life. I'm going to be like you."

"Why?"

"Because you are a man instead of a coward. And I'm going to tell you something else— because now that I have helped you, you're going to help me—us!"

"Us?" the Kid asked. "And who is us?"

"Me and . . ." He broke off, listening. From out of the Pillars of Hell came the muffled beat of horses' hoofs.

"Quick!" he whispered. "This way—lay low."

"Who will that be?" the Kid asked.

"Juan and the old man. They'll kill me if they catch me here. And we haven't a gun to fight with. I'll sneak back to the rancho the way I came. *Adios, compañero*. I'll see you tomorrow night."

He vanished in the darkness. After the Kid's quick ears had lost the faint tread of retreating footsteps, he sprawled out on his belly waiting for the horsemen to approach. But, strangely, they did not come near the dugout. And suddenly the hoof-beats ceased. Worming his way forward, he pulled up on the rim of a rise and peered below into a shallow basin almost walled in by columns of flame. Seated within arm's length, their backs to him, were Juan Lopez and Ross Pearson. Off to one side he could hear several vaqueros cursing a bunch of horses that snorted and tried to bolt at sight of the fingers of flame.

CHAPTER TWENTY-TWO

L OPEZ was speaking.

"It's damned lucky you run on to this U-Bar bunch just when we were getting short on stuff to fill that remount order, Ross." The rider chuckled. "We won't even have to go to the trouble of working that brand. We'll just re-run it into a smeary Pitchfork and let it go at that."

The words gave the Kid his first inkling as to the reason for Pearson's prolonged absences from Rancho Diablo. The rancher was a horse thief who rode the range constantly, spotting herds which later were picked up, re-branded and sold. And, he decided, it was during these trips that Pearson induced strangers to return with him on the pretext of selling them horses, only to murder them.

"It is lucky," agreed the ranch owner, without enthusiasm. "But I'm not thinking about horses right now. That damned Kid worries me. I'd feel a heap easier if I knew he was done for. Hadn't we better go over to the dugout and toss him down one of these fissures?"

"He's done for, all right," Lopez sneered. "He was dead, or so near it when I snaked him there, I didn't take the trouble to throw him in. What's eating on you? You're getting more nervous than a colt lately."

"I'm going over there and make sure, just the same," Pearson announced decisively. "He's Johnnie Bender's kid, sure as hell. And I want to be certain he's where he can't cause me any more trouble."

"You act like a scared old woman," Lopez snorted disgustedly. "You're losing your nerve. What makes you think he's Bender's kid?"

"I'm not losing my nerve," Pearson denied angrily. "But he's a dead ringer for Johnnie. I noticed it the first time I laid eyes on him. I thought I'd seen a ghost. Bradley felt the same way. I know Johnnie had a kid, because he was born right here on Rancho Diablo. After his wife died, Johnnie took the brat down along the border for some friends to raise."

"Reckon there are a lot of kids along the border who aren't Benders," Juan scoffed.

The Kid lay scarcely breathing. Knowing nothing of his antecedents he could not but agree with Lopez. Still, the old man of the cabana had mentioned the resemblance he bore to Johnnie Bender. And Pearson had just admitted that this same resemblance had been the cause of his fear the day they met. There was no other way to explain Bradley's terror. Yet the thing was so utterly improbable.

"Maybe so," came Pearson's voice dubiously. "But did you notice this Kid always kept the thumb of his right hand hooked in his cartridge-belt?"

"That was so he could get at his gun quick," Lopez remarked carelessly.

"Could he drag his gun all right?" Pearson demanded.

"He didn't drag it at all," Lopez said. "He shot from his holster."

"He didn't drag it because he couldn't," Pearson blurted out nervously. "His arm was stiff at the elbow. It didn't bother him only when he tried to bring his gun up."

Still Lopez was not convinced. "That doesn't make him Johnnie Bender's kid by a long ways," he snorted.

"The hell it doesn't," Pearson exploded. "I recklect when Johnnie's kid was just creeping around, he fell against a hot stove and burned his right arm bad—clear to the bone. The doctor said then that his arm would be stiff at the elbow."

Lopez came to his feet with an oath. "Well, what if he was Bender's kid?" he snarled. "What are you scared of him now for?"

"I'm not scared," Pearson blustered. "But I have cause to keep my eyes peeled. I don't reckon you know why. But it was me who plugged

Johnnie Bender while he was riding El Scorpion slick. Johnnie's neck was broken all right, but it never would have been if we had of waited for El Scorpion to do it. Why wouldn't I be nervous with that reckless brat of his snooping around?"

The Kid caught his breath for an instant, fearful that the two below heard the whistling sigh that escaped his tight-set lips. He moved his gun arm slightly. For the first time in his life he knew the reason for the stiffness in his elbow that had started him shooting from his holster. Pearson was right. It never bothered him except when he drew a gun. Few noticed it. Few had time to notice when his gun started blazing from its holster.

In fact, he had hooked his thumb in his cartridge-belt so long now that he rarely thought of it himself. Yet it had not escaped the sharp eyes of Pearson. The old man of the cabana, he knew, had detected it. But then old Jim Brown seemed to let nothing pass unobserved, and had given him an insight into the affairs of Rancho Diablo with uncanny precision. It was old Jim who first had noticed his resemblance to Johnnie Bender. He had set it down for inquisitiveness then. But now he was convinced beyond the shadow of a doubt that he was Johnnie Bender's son.

And Ross Pearson had killed his father. That explained Toughy's wonder at how Bender's neck had been broken if he had ridden El Scorpion.

His father had been murdered. Forgotten was the fever sending chills up and down his spine. A cold, numbing fury laid violent hold on him. Unarmed though he was, he struggled desperately to keep from obeying a wild impulse to face the two and call them to account.

"Well, he won't bother you any more," Lopez' voice cut in on his seething thoughts. "It doesn't make any difference now whose brat he was. He's done for, I tell you. And besides, there are two of us against him if he does happen to pull through. He couldn't hurt us any before he is mowed down."

But Pearson could not overcome his uneasiness. He fell to pacing back and forth nervously. "But there's Toughy," he said, halting abruptly in front of Lopez. "That little devil knows things. And he thinks this here fellow, the Kid, is the real article. If the nosy fool should be alive, and gets away from us, those two might get their heads together and figure out that Toughy is Pedro Rodriguez' boy."

If the startling discovery of his own identity had dumfounded the Kid, this new admission by Pearson staggered him. Toughy was Pedro Rodriguez' boy—the son of the late owner of Rancho Diablo, of whom the old man of the cabana had told him. As many times before in the past weeks, Jim Brown's words again flashed to his mind. "Pedro Rodriguez had a kid," the old man had said. "He was only two when his pop got busted ten year ago. He hasn't been seen since. But the boy would own Rancho Diablo if he was alive today, wouldn't he?"

The Kid only had time to marvel at the cunning Pearson had employed in allowing Toughy to remain on the rancho without knowing he was the rightful owner, when Lopez spoke.

"Supposing they did get together and figure it out?" the rider queried. "How would they prove it? And don't forget, we were smart enough to block any such move when I took that eight thousand dollar mortgage on the place a few years back. The brat would play hell raising eight thousand and getting hold of the place before he disappeared, wouldn't he?"

Until now the note Lopez had put up to cover the wager had meant little to the Kid. He had only accepted it on the spur of the moment, thinking perhaps some time it might come in handy. In the face of what Lopez had just said, that note represented the rancho for Toughy. With it in his possession he could force Lopez to hand over the mortgage. That he would recover it, along with his own money, he had little doubt. But he had no time to think of it. Lopez was speaking again.

"With that damned nosy Ortega Garcia out of the way . . ." The Kid heard this new name with little interest. It meant nothing to him, yet it would be well to remember it—Ortega Garcia.

". . . and the girl," Lopez was saying.

The girl! The Kid jerked until he was fearful of detection. He strained to hear more.

"Never mind her," Pearson put in. "It's Toughy and this Kid we have to worry about. The way the Kid threw a scare into that man-killing El Scorpion makes me think him and his old man both had charmed lives. You thought you had the Kid nailed after you lied to the girl and tossed him into that storeroom, dying of thirst. But the minute I rode back to the rancho here he was, plenty alive, fighting like hell and making you all like it."

The Kid struggled to master his rage. So it was Lopez who had thrown him into the storeroom to die? As Toughy had said, the girl had no hand in it. Lopez had lied to her. It was but another thing for which Lopez would be called to account. But Pearson was speaking.

"And poor old Mert Bradley . . ."

"Bradley got what was coming to him," Lopez growled. "I didn't have any intention of opening that corral gate. I knew the white stallion would kill Bradley if he ever got out in the open. And I have a hunch the Kid knew it too. I tried to keep Mert going. But he would have to stop to chew the rag with the brat."

"Toughy had him covered, you said?"

"What is a rattle-brained brat with a gun worth?" Lopez snorted. "I took it and the money away from him and gave him a beating he'll remember to his dying day. Bradley could have done the same thing. Forget it now and let's get this stuff branded."

"I suppose we had better get busy," Pearson agreed wearily. "We'll clean up on this deal, then I'm going to get out of the country. Things aren't breaking right—they haven't since that damned Kid stuck his nose into Rancho Diablo. Here, you *pelados*!" he shouted to the vaqueros. "If you have those horses corraled you can ride on back to the rancho and turn in. Juan and I will handle them now."

The Kid heard the horsemen gallop away. He listened until the hoof-beats had died to a throb in the distant dark, although his gaze never left the pair below who were standing now, silhouetted against the fingers of flame.

"Now that Bradley is gone I'll just collect his share," Lopez announced shortly. "You own the place. It's only fair that we go partners and split even. You say after this deal you're pulling out . . ."

"That will leave the girl, won't it?" Pearson sneered. "You've always wanted her. Now you can have her, provided you'll take her so far away Rancho Diablo never will hear of her again. But I'm not turning over Bradley's split."

The listening Kid hung onto himself with an effort, until sane reason got the better of reckless judgment. To leap down there would only mean death. Now that he knew something of the girl, he determined to play safe until he could find out more. But before she should be bartered like a common chattel to Lopez, he would—

"I say again that from this moment on we are partners," Lopez snarled.

"Like hell we are!" Pearson's raw nerves seemed to snap in explosive denial.

"Perhaps you can figure it another way," Lopez sneered. "But I happen to hold the mortgage on the rancho. As you say, things are not running so smoothly. The matter of the girl settled, there is nothing more save a division of the rancho. You brought the girl back, did you?"

The Kid found himself scarcely breathing while he waited Pearson's answer. Then the girl really had been away. She had not been, as he feared, a prisoner in the ranchhouse.

"She came back yesterday," Pearson said sullenly, "and started to raise hell again about the Kid—wanted to know where he was, if he had been treated well."

"I suppose you told her that he was our most honored guest, that his absence was only temporary?" Lopez laughed.

"I didn't tell her anything. I'm tired of explaining. That's why I'm giving her to you. You handle her from now on. She's made life miserable for me for years."

"No longer shall she deal you misery," Lopez smirked. "From this moment on you can consider her as Mrs. Juan Lopez, wife of the new half-owner of Rancho Diablo."

"The girl you can have—gladly. But half the rancho . . . no!"

"There are many who would like to know Johnnie Bender didn't die from a broken neck, that he was shot—in the back," Lopez taunted. "The sheriff, for instance, would like to know that."

"And he also would like to know where the Kid is," Pearson flared hotly. "And of Ortega Garcia. You're lucky I haven't handed you over to the law long ago, Lopez."

"You're a fine one to talk about turning anybody over to the sheriff, aren't you?" Juan jeered in a voice that now trembled with anger. "Now I demand a half-interest in Rancho Diablo."

"You demand nothing from me," warned Pearson. "Don't forget the reward is still good for Blackie Ware. I hid you from the law once, you damned murderer, but now . . ."

A violent oath escaped Lopez. He leaped back, to become only a vague outline to the watching Kid. "I warned you years ago never to speak that name," he ground between clenched teeth. "It is not too late for you and I to—"

Pearson drew. Juan's gun spat flame. The big rancher's shot went wild as he threw up his arms, lurched backwards and sprawled to the ground, dead. His Colt fell not more than a foot from where the Kid lay. Unable to see Lopez' menacing gun he dared not move.

He waited, tense, breathless. He heard Lopez turn and stalk deeper into the darkness. But not until he had ridden away did the Kid move. Then cautiously he secured Pearson's gun and got to his feet. It took but a look to tell him Pearson was dead. But he felt little pity for the sprawling form. Pearson had suffered the fate, there in the Pillars of Hell, intended for him.

The Kid spent no time in idle thought. His mind was whipping lightning fast. The girl of mystery had returned to the rancho. By Pearson's own admission she had asked concerning him. She had had no hand in attempts on his life. Toughy had defended her, tried to tell him of her, always to be interrupted. The things of which he had accused her in his mind vanished. She was in danger—danger of Lopez, who even now was riding to the rancho.

He leaped away into the darkness, forgetful of his throbbing head, forgetful of the fever that had sapped his strength. Suddenly he realized that since the moment he had laid eyes on the girl in red at Cantina El Paseo he had given her more thought than he had given all the others. For all the bitterness he felt at times toward her, in his heart he still believed her as honest and frank as her eyes had seemed back there in the dance-hall. But who was she? Why had Pearson—

He was moving away swiftly through the darkness. Toughy had said the rancho was about three miles below. How he wished for Rey del Rey, who would cover that distance like a golden meteor. But for once Rey del Rey was not at hand. And his head again had set up its awful throbbing. He was hot and cold by turns. His knees threatened to give way as he trotted along over the rough ground in his high-heeled boots.

Farther and farther into the night he plunged, now running, now slowing down to fight for the breath that rasped in his aching throat.

After what seemed an infinity of time, he lurched up out of an arroyo to peer into the gloom. But no rancho lay ahead. Again his sense of direction seemed to have deserted him. He was positive he had come toward the Pole Star that hung brightly in the Heavens. He was just as positive he had come more than three miles. But no outline of buildings greeted his straining eyes.

He threw himself on the ground. Again, as on the mesa, the wild country had tricked him. There was nothing to do but wait until dawn. In the meantime Lopez would have reached the rancho. The girl . . .

"You act like one possessed," he berated himself aloud. "Should you find the rancho you have not the strength to face Lopez. You will find him a mad killer, who already tonight has sent one man to his death. Better that you rest, Kid. Then with the first light of dawn you shall have gained strength. You can secure Rey del Rey. . . ." He was conscious that his words were coming thickly, rushing out like gibberish. The pain in his temple was crashing with sickening regularity. It threatened momentarily to overcome him. Stretching out, the Mañana Kid fought weakly against the black mantle of insensibility that presently enveloped him.

CHAPTER TWENTY-THREE

GLARING light that seemed to sear his eyeballs pulled the Mañana Kid back to consciousness. He started up only to fall back, his violently aching head whirling. For the moment he thought himself again in the stifling storeroom where he had so narrowly escaped death. His sensations were the same as then. He was conscious of blistering heat that wilted the clothes to his body, turned sweat-soaked chaparejos and boots to leaden weights. But now, at least, he could breathe, although the breath he sucked greedily rattled in his parched throat.

With an effort that shot pains through every muscle, he rolled over on his side. He felt easier with the blinding glare shut out from his burning eyes. He passed a hand across his face only to set the wound on his temple pounding.

Then suddenly he remembered. He had stretched out on the ground to await the coming of dawn that he might locate Rancho Diablo, had fallen into the deep sleep of insensibility. Now, as his faculties cleared, everything came back to him with a rush—the scene there in the awful light of the Pillars of Hell when Lopez' flaming Colt had snuffed out Pearson's life, his own mad attempt to reach the rancho to aid the girl and Toughy.

Thought of her brought him to a sitting posture, holding his head to ease the infernal hammering. Pearson had given this girl of mystery to Lopez as though she was a common chattel to be disposed of at will. And with both Pearson and Bradley dead Lopez was master of Rancho Diablo—a ruthless, lust-mad brute whose word would be law, unchallenged by any of the subservient vaqueros—a blackguard whose claims would go undisputed.

The Kid managed to open his eyes, which he shielded with a hand until they became accustomed to the glare. Beside Lopez, only he now knew the secret of Rancho Diablo—the gamut of crime and lust that had been run within its wide acres. And Lopez believed him dead—believed himself safely beyond reach of justice or retribution. That belief, which would make the vaquero careless, greatly increased his chances of aiding the girl and Toughy.

When he was able the Kid looked around groggily. The Pillars of Hell had vanished. About him was a wild region of arroyos and barrancas spiked with heat-glazed boulders. The young day he had expected to greet had extended into midafternoon. All night and most of the day he had stretched there on the fringe of the desert, sleeping the sleep of utter oblivion. But throb as his head did, he felt stronger for the rest. Muscles protesting, he climbed to his feet to stand clutching his head until it had ceased its crazy spinning. When, presently, he felt secure on his feet, he made a careful survey in every direction. Then, as he turned to the north—

"*Sangre de Cristo*, Kid!" he burst out violently, "should you give yourself up and atone for your sins. For no longer are you fit to fight the battle of the desert. Even Rey del Rey would be ashamed of you now—you who have so long prided yourself on being a man of the border, a riding hombre that ever knows where he travels."

Clenching his teeth because of the throbbing pain in his temple, he rubbed his eyes again. For there, but a few hundred rods ahead, the buildings of Rancho Diablo danced and shimmered in the glaring sun.

The Kid shrugged. Something of his old assurance was in that shrug.

"At least, hombre, whom I like not greatly," he muttered to himself, "you have not, as I feared, lost all sense of direction. You came to Rancho Diablo in the dark, your only fault that you underestimated the distance." He was striding along now, taking strength with motion that seemed to drive the pain from muscles long cramped on the hard earth. "Four things have you to do, Kid—you who once prided yourself as being the phantom gunman of the border. Four things . . ." His step grew steadier under the rhythmic throb in his temple—grew steadier as he walked and talked aloud. ". . . four things. First, Rey del Rey—to assure yourself the palomino is safe and, from this point on, always waiting for your whistle."

He stumbled on the rough ground, went sprawling. He lay for a moment stunned. Then he dragged himself up, strode off again with step measured to the monotonous sound of his own voice that seemed to drift from far, far away to ears that sputtered and whined.

"Second . . ." He was talking aloud. He was positive of it. But the voice was not his. ". . . second—you shall assure yourself that Toughy is safe."

For all the short way to the rancho he seemed to be getting no nearer. For now, with the deceptiveness of distance on the desert, the buildings had almost vanished. Yet he knew they were there. He marched on.

"Third . . ." The word rang in his ears like a challenge. ". . . third—you shall assure yourself that the chamaquita is all right. The chamaquita . . ." his voice died in bitterness. And his mind took up where the voice left off.

Why should he care about the girl? He did not so much as know her name. For months now he had watched for her the while he risked his life on Rancho Diablo. Many times he could have ridden for it, laughed back at the clumsy crew from the shadows of the night as he had at others before. Not until now did he know why he stayed on. And he cursed himself for that sudden knowledge. He had stayed because of her—because of that girl in red from Cantina El Paseo, hoping that in some way he might help her, hoping that there on Rancho Diablo they might meet and she would tell him of herself. She had asked concerning him, Pearson had said, and she had had no part in the attempt to kill him in the storeroom.

His step grew firmer as he marched along. Bradley? He had given the primero scarcely a thought. Always his thoughts had been of the girl. He was sorry that Bradley had been killed. After all, it was not the way of the Mañana Kid to turn a man-killing stallion loose to trample a human to death.

A man-killing stallion! El Scorpion. A smile braced his thin, dry lips. Even now he could chuckle at the manner in which he had beaten them at their own game. The luck of the Mañana Kid was what it had been. For not once again in a lifetime would a vaquero encounter such a horse as El Scorpion on the open mesas, take weeks to win the brute's affection and confidence only to discover, at last, that he had conquered the mightiest man-killer in the region. But no longer would El Scorpion kill men. Lopez' Colt had seen to that—the same Colt that had silenced Pearson forever.

Pearson! Now the going was rougher under foot. Always he seemed to be dipping down over the edge of an arroyo or climbing back up the other side. But the rancho was getting nearer and his strength was increasing. Even the pain in his head was not so intense. His muscles were responding as of old.

Pearson! Always he had hated to see a man killed. But Pearson deserved it. Not at the hand of one so unworthy as Lopez. But Pearson, too, had been a killer—the killer of his father, the man who had plotted his own death. Still, he had much for which to thank Pearson. The revelations the fellow had made out there in the Pillars of Hell before the bullet from Lopez' gun cut him down had supplied him with the evidence he needed. And Pearson's loudly-voiced fear had cleared up his own background. So he was Johnnie Bender's son? Often had he wondered at the stiff arm that would not let him draw his gun. Now he knew. But something else he knew: the shots he had learned to fire from his holster were the fastest ever seen on the border. He had to fear no man in gunplay.

But Johnnie Bender—his father? He wished he had known him, the only other man to master El Scorpion. Apparently Johnnie Bender had ridden the great white brute without the advantage of weeks of effort winning his confidence. A champion rider, Johnnie Bender must have been—a rider of which any other rancho would have been proud.

So his father had been killed on Rancho Diablo? Murdered according to Pearson's own admission! Pearson no longer could pay for that crime. But Pearson's revelations had doubled his determination to clean out this rancho of the devil—this rancho where murder and crime were rampant, where men boasted of their killings as other men boasted of simple things.

Now the barn was swaying just before his hazy eyes. But his knees were weakening again. He couldn't fail now. There was too much at stake. He had things to do. His hand crept down to the butt of Pearson's gun rammed in the waistband of his chaparejos. There were many things he must do. He couldn't just remember how many, because a mantle of haze seemed suddenly to have clogged his brain. There was one, he remembered—see Rey del Rey. There was two—see that Toughy was all right. And three—that was the girl, the mystery girl in red from Cantina El Paseo. Still there was another. . . .

Four! He clutched out for the gate that blocked the way. Just ahead was the yard of Rancho Diablo. There was no one around. Probably at supper, for now that he noticed, the sun had dropped behind the walls of the canyon and shadows were creeping across the dun-colored earth. Strange how that glowing horizon, which seemed to heat cherry-hot during the day, so long defied the cooling purple of evening.

Four! He dropped the gate, started to reach down for it. But his head was swimming too badly. He let it lie, marched on toward the barn. But now his movements were more cautious, tense fingers gripped the butt of the forty-five. There was the horse trough. He dared not run, although his throat ached at thought of the cooling water. But too many times he had seen an unheard shadow glide out of the gloom of this accursed Rancho to challenge him.

Four! Now he was at the horse trough. After a careful survey he wetted his lips, bathed his temples and burning eyes. The cool water gave him new life. He dropped to his knees, running the water through his hair and letting it trickle down across his face. And always his ears were tuned for the first footfall, the first alien sound.

Presently he got up. Strong blood began to hammer through his veins, although its pulsing in his temple still sickened him. Now for the barn and Rey del Rey. After that . . .

He was opening the barn door. He whistled softly. A nicker came out of the gloom within. The Kid's heart leaped. The palomino was lunging back on the halter rope, pawing in the stall.

"Quiet, *caballo mio*," he warned. "One would think my return pleases you the way you carry on." Then he was beside the brute, had both arms around its arched neck, while it whinnied and curveted with joy. "You have missed me too, *caballo mio*?" he whispered in a twitching ear. "But no more than I have missed you. Never again shall we part. I pledge you that—only in death. Rest I must for a moment. Here on your back, *amigo*, shall I wait for darkness." He climbed wearily onto the palomino's back. The brute stood perfectly still. And there the Kid stretched out full length, his booted feet, toes down, across the animal's rump.

"There was another number, *caballo mio*," he said, thickly, after a long period of silence during which the palomino scarcely moved. He stroked Rey del Rey's cheek, which still shone golden in the swift falling gloom. "Another number among the duties I must perform. I counted only to three. And there were four—four—four. . . .

"*Sangre de Cristo, amigo*—I have it!" He bolted upright to slide to the ground and stand straining into the shadows. "That fourth duty was to—kill—Juan—Lopez! Await me, *caballo mio*. For this time when I shoot, I shoot . . . to . . . kill. And again we may ride for it." He threw back his head and laughed softly. "Ride for it—the Mañana Kid, *caballo mio*, and Rey del Rey. They know us not on this rancho. They know not what my golden meteor can do streaking away in the dark. Neither yet have they tasted the lead I can throw. But they shall, I pledge you. I go now—to find Toughy and the girl. But first I saddle you in readiness, that you stand by and wait my whistle. Then shall I be safe should I be forced to retreat."

He lurched across the barn, felt about in the gloom until he located his saddle-rig where he hoped it would be. He dragged it over, hoisted it weakly onto the palomino's back. When he had rigged up the brute, he led it forth into the yard. It was dark out there now. And still there was no one in sight. Apparently the vaqueros had not yet finished supper. For a dim light shone out of the mess shanty.

"We shall wait," the Kid said, swinging into the saddle. "On your way, *caballo mio*, while I rest."

He slumped down to close his eyes. Reins flapping loose, Rey del Rey took the trail up which he had just come.

CHAPTER TWENTY-FOUR

Hours later, it seemed, the Mañana Kid awoke with a start. But no longer with the start of unexpected surroundings. He was in motion—motion he knew so well, for beneath him Rey del Rey picked his way along carefully.

The night he looked out upon was stygian in its blackness, lighted only by countless stars that now were but pinpoints high in the spangled void. He found the reins, pulled up sharply.

"You take me only on a merry-go-'round, *amigo*," he chided the palomino, which stopped to paw the ground impatiently and strain on the bit. "And now by your eagerness to be gone you only succeed in increasing my own anxiety lest we too long be delayed by the duties I have yet to perform. For it is high time we were started somewhere, *caballo mio*. I care not which direction, nor do you, yes? But too long, far too long, have we been in this one spot when our souls cry out for freedom and our hearts for new places. However, *amigo*, there may be another who some day will ride with us—a girl in red, *caballo*. For much time now have I slept here on your back and dreamed things out. No longer do I feel the least bit of bitterness toward her. She has nowise been to blame. Pearson told me that, although he knew not I was listening."

He cocked a leg across the saddle horn, found in his wilted clothes the "makings" Toughy had brought him, rolled a cigarette and lighted it between cupped hands that carefully shielded the flare of the match. He dragged on it deeply, let the smoke trickle out through his nose.

"What a pleasure is a smoke, *caballo mio*. Almost it is as pleasant as this girl. And truly as dangerous when one's enemies fill the night and need but the red glow of a *patillo* in the darkness for a target, yes? But who am I to tell you of her? You know her as well as do I. For we rode behind her out of Guadalupe—out of Guadalupe when you stretched those golden legs to show mere horses ridden by possemen how golden legs can stretch to blast earth into the faces of horses that are fit only for peons, not kings. She was the girl, you recall, *caballo mio*, we served as boot jack for there on the mesa that night which now seems years ago. And it was she . . ." He leaned forward to tickle Rey del Rey's twitching ears until he had the palomino throwing his head angrily. ". . . who begged us to trust her while she tricked us and rode away in the darkness with another hombre."

He jerked up straight, slapped the palomino

across the neck, which arched proudly. "Again she is in trouble. We have yet to see a woman in trouble if we can lend our aid. We are gentlemen, *caballo mio*, yes? And as gentlemen no lady in distress suffers." He gave the reins a flip. "Then back to the rancho, *amigo*. Now knowing she has returned there I shall search until I find her. Should she be gone, then we two shall ride forever—on the trail of Juan Lopez."

The palomino reared its length, pivoted on hind hoofs, hit the ground with a resounding thud and started in the opposite direction, one ear laid back along its head to catch the Kid's words, the other cocked forward for any sound out of the darkness ahead.

Now the Kid felt better, stronger. When, presently, the buildings of the rancho grew into an outline before his eyes, he felt fit for anything save to combat the gnawing hunger that growled within him.

At the barn he got down. Now the vaqueros were back at the bunkhouses, for he could hear them at their cards, hear the occasional curses that volleyed into the night from the open door. No need for fear from that direction. His fear was of Lopez, who might be anywhere.

Ahead lay the ranchhouse shrouded in gloom save for the dim light flickering from the cook shanty. But somewhere there—unless Lopez had spirited her away—was the girl. At any cost he was determined to find out. He would search that ranchhouse from top to bottom. If she were there he would find her. If she were not, then . . .

Well behind the corrals he dropped the reins of Rey del Rey, who, with the optimism of desert horses, immediately set to sniping at the sparse stalks of cured grass. The Kid rounded the corrals, made his way cautiously toward the ranchhouse, moving from shadow to shadow, ever keeping his eyes whipping the yard and his ears straining.

Of a sudden he stopped. One room above, he noted as he drew nearer, was lighted—dimly lighted as though by the rays of a single candle.

Never before had he seen that light there, although he had watched for weeks. It could only come from the room of the girl.

Elated by his discovery but more than ever ready for a sudden and unexpected challenge from Lopez, he moved up to the porch. There he stopped to remove his boots, sweating and panting over the process until he was fearful he would be heard. Finally he succeeded in dragging them off to feel the cool of the night on his aching feet. He stood for a moment reveling in it. Then cautiously he climbed the porch rail, started out across rickety flooring that squeaked with every sound.

He cursed himself for an idiot as he crept along—cursed himself that he would thus risk his life for a girl whose name he did not even know. Death blazing out of the darkness would be his lot if he were detected. If he found her, then what? But once started, the Mañana Kid never yet had turned back. Now he was started. There was no turning back.

Stealthily he opened the door into the dining room, keeping a sharp lookout behind as the knob turned. But the vaqueros were engrossed in their cards. And apparently Lopez had set no guard, for he had yet to be challenged or hear a suspicious sound.

Then he was inside, had pulled the door shut softly behind him. Thus far he knew his way. Never had he entered this room where the vaqueros ate that he had not studied it. He knew the exact location of the two windows on his right, the single pane beside the door on his left. Through them wan starlight filtered to make them a little lighter than the side walls.

A door opening into some unknown part of the ranchhouse just ahead had intrigued him from the first—a door which for weeks he had watched, hoping the girl would appear. But she had not. Now perhaps he would open it to meet Lopez. The Kid shrugged. He was ready, hoping now to encounter the vaquero!

Tiptoeing across the dining room, he tried the knob. It grated loudly on his taut nerves. He waited with bated breath. From the mess shanty came the clatter of dishes, the voices of the cooks always maudlin with drink by this time. Still no threatening sound from outside.

Taking heart in the silence, he put more pressure on the knob. The door unlatched, but still it did not open. He was forced to put his weight on it to swing it wide enough to enter, muffling the sound with his body. Again he listened. Then he passed through, pulled it to behind him but did not risk relatching it. He stood stock still until his eyes could pierce the gloom of the room in which he found himself. After a time, by the dull light through two windows, he looked about.

He was in a great living room that ran the width of the ranchhouse. The room had the smell of unused places and was typical of the main room of many haciendas where people spent but few hours indoors and those in the dining room.

Although he could see it only indistinctly, the Kid could almost picture the furnishings in his mind. One end—the opposite to where he stood—contained a great rough stone fireplace, he knew. Above it would hang the mounted antlers of a deer some vaquero had prized above all else. Beneath the windows would be the customary sofa, gaudily upholstered. The pictures would be chromos, mostly of border scenes and vaqueros, while probably, some favorite horse would stare out from a golden frame. The floor beneath his feet was polished and slick, covered with rugs he knew to be of Indian weave.

But the room or its furnishings held no interest for him only as it offered a way into the interior of the house. Moving cautiously lest one of the rugs slide on the slick floor and send him crashing, he presently located another door. He found the knob, tried it. Again the latch yielded raspingly to the pressure of his hand. But the door swung soundlessly. A cool draught struck him in the face. He opened the door the width of his body, squeezed through.

Now he found himself in a hallway. He felt rather than saw the smallness of the place even before his eyes became accustomed to this new and deeper gloom. His groping fingers came in contact with another door, which by its location, he decided, would open onto the porch. He tried this one too. It was locked, but the key was in the latch. A slight grating was the only sound as the key turned and the latch yielded to his touch. It would be an avenue of escape if the vaqueros should come. Leaving the door slightly ajar he looked about. By the dull light through a transom he discovered he was standing at the foot of a flight of stairs that disappeared in the gloom above. Up there somewhere was the small light he had seen from without.

He started up the stairs, moving now with extreme caution, placing each foot carefully, testing out each creaking step before he let it bear his full weight. Inch by inch he advanced—up, up in the darkness, eyes trying to pierce the stygian void, ears straining for any sound. The excitement of the moment had driven away the throb in his temple. Never had his hearing been so acute. Never had his eyes seemed to cleave the darkness with such unerring clearness.

After an endless period of stealthy climbing that keyed his nerves to the highest pitch and speeded his breathing—which only seemed to become more audible as he strove to control it,—he gained the top of the stairs, was moving down a carpeted hallway, facing a small window through which came starlight—pale, wan light that was little help in the thick darkness.

As he moved along his hands groped over the side wall. A few steps and he stopped. His fingers had encountered the panels of a door. He waited until his breath had evened to place an ear against the panel. No sound came from within—no sound save the pounding of his own heart that seemed to boom in his ears.

Satisfied, however, that no one was behind that panel, he went on, slowly, stealthily, making no sound that could be heard above the chirping of crickets, the zoom of an occasional bullbat or other sounds of the night.

Presently his groping hands encountered

another door. Again he plastered his ear to the panels. And again no sound came from within.

Now he was at the end of the hallway, beneath a small window through which stars were visible. A breeze stirred through an open door nearby but, familiar with California haciendas, he knew that door would lead to the ramada or patio, which would prove a certain trap in case of flight. He eased about. Apparently his stealthy movements had not been detected, for his quick ear caught no sound.

Crossing the hallway he found another door on the opposite side. Again an ear was plastered to the panel. And again without result. He halted for a moment. Two doors he had found on the other side through which he had heard nothing, seen no ray of escaping light. One door panel on this side had produced no sound. There could only be one other room. The one at the head of the stairs must be lighted by the candle. He crept forward. He had seen a light up here somewhere—unless it had been extinguished.

Then he was at the door of that last room. He laid his ear against it. His muscles tensed. From within came the sound of labored breathing. A low moaning. He strained closer. The sound was of someone panting, writhing on a bed, he decided. He waited, every nerve on edge. Still nothing moved in the hallway. A wild impulse seized him, throttled his judgment.

"*Chamaquita*," he whispered. "Is it you, *chamaquita*? You need help, yes?"

Hell broke loose about him—roaring, blazing hell that shattered the stillness and sent hot lead whining around his ears. In a flash the Kid was down flat on his belly, worming his way to the stairs. Suddenly in answer to the gunfire came the sound of running boots—men tumbling out of the bunkhouse. They would come through the dining room, he reasoned. The shots had come from the door leading to the patio. His one avenue of escape was the door he had left ajar at the foot of the stairs.

Now he had reached the end of the carpet. Bullets were splintering about him. He found himself wondering why, in the light of flaming lead, the gunman could not find his target. A poor marksman, he thought. But not Lopez—for Lopez would be bellowing and cursing. Probably a guard, who had stolen into the ramada to doze only to be awakened by the whisper for which he cursed himself. But even in this perilous predicament the Kid smiled. What asses some men who tried to handle a gun—who tried to down a low-moving target by shooting at the roof!

Then he had bellied down the stairs head first, sliding all the way to the bottom and coming up like a youngster on a coasting hill.

Boots were pounding now in the dining room.

Outside lantern lights had flared up, were bobbing and flickering across the yard. The vaqueros were coming, cursing and growling. The Kid squeezed through the door he had left ajar, pulled it shut behind him just as the vaqueros burst into the hallway. He flattened himself against the side wall of the porch, stood for a moment chuckling. Then he moved off into the shadows to wait.

He heard the vaqueros clumping up the stairs, heard muttered oaths, startled exclamations. Then there were excited voices just above. But he could not catch the words. He moved off the porch and around the corner of the house. The dimly lighted window was just above. It was unscreened, he noted, and the window was slightly raised. But to reach it. He had no time to search for a ladder. Moving any object high enough to stand on would be too risky. Rey del Rey? His whistle for the palomino would betray him. He felt about in the darkness. His hands encountered the projecting end of a log. Logs were dovetailed up the corner of the 'dobe building and afforded an easy way to within reach of the candle-lighted window.

The Kid started to climb. A few clinging moments and he was above the lighted window. Taking a firm hold, he stretched across. His chin was on a level with the sill. It was but a short drop to the ground. Clutching the sill, he let go of the logs, swung over to look through the slightly open window, the lower frame of which concealed his head from those within.

CHAPTER TWENTY-FIVE

W HAT the Mañana Kid saw at Rancho Diablo hacienda that night numbed him with cold fury, all but made him lose his precarious grip on the window-frame. The vaqueros had burst into the room. By the dim light of a candle he could see them grouped around a bed on which stretched a form, writhing and twisting in fetters, trying desperately to speak through a tightly bound kerchief that made the sounds of words inarticulate.

It took but a glance to tell the Kid the bound figure was that of the *chamaquita*—the girl of the red dress from Cantina El Paseo—the mystery girl of Rancho Diablo whom he last had seen on the day he had collapsed in her arms from thirst. She had tricked him, but had done him no harm. She had tried to help him, Pearson had disclosed. And in return he now grimly dedicated his life to aiding her. The muttering of the excited vaqueros gave him hope.

"Where is Lopez?" one demanded. "He will kill us if he ever finds out someone attempted to enter this room."

"It was not my fault," came a whining voice. "I only went into the ramada for a breath of air. Then I heard someone whisper. I opened fire."

"And the one who whispered evaporated into the air," a vaquero scoffed. "The whispering you heard, *amigo*, probably was the gurgle of the tequila from the bottle you have cached in the ramada."

"I took but a small drink," whined the man—apparently the guard who had sent the bullets crashing down around him, the Kid decided. "I shot at only a voice for a target—and everything was dark. I heard no sound afterwards."

"You couldn't have heard anything for minutes because of the bombardment you laid down in the hallway," someone sneered. "The lantern shows the walls riddled with lead. No human could have escaped. You'd better throw away that bottle before Lopez hears of this. One who shoots at whispers in the darkness is a danger to every man within gunshot."

"I tell you there was someone," the guard persisted.

"Then where did he go? No more than a minute elapsed from your first shot until we were coming up the stairs. Human beings do not fly, *pelado*. Neither do they vanish." The vaquero's voice hardened. "As for me, *amigos*, I have no fight with women. Who are we to stand by and see this girl bound so she can scarcely move, let alone

246

escape? We no longer have Bradley to fear. . . ."

"But Lopez," one whispered fearfully.

"Lopez may think to master women thus," the voice came back. "But by the Mother, I shall be no party to keeping this girl a prisoner here."

A low chorus of growls met the announcement.

"But what of the one who attempted to enter her room?" came the guard's whine.

"*Sangre de Cristo*! No one tried to enter. It was but a notion gulped from the neck of your tequila bottle. No girl deserves this, vaqueros. Come, let us give her air." He strode over to the window, slammed up the sash.

The Kid barely had time to let go and drop to the ground to escape detection. The banging of the window drowned the thud of the fall that left his feet tingling painfully.

Of a sudden he remembered his boots. Should the crew by chance make a search at the urging of the tipsy guard, they would come upon them and recognize them. For there were none other as fine on Rancho Diablo. He had ample time, for he had no fear that the girl would be harmed. Going back to the porch he secured his boots, pushed them far back beneath the floor. After a quick survey, again he climbed the logs and swung over to the window.

"I for one would turn her loose," the heavy-voiced vaquero was saying. The Kid tried to place the fellow, but he had paid so little attention

247

to them he could not. Yet here, of all the hard lot on Rancho Diablo, was one who, at least, showed something of manhood.

"Your death would be the forfeit," the guard whimpered. "By the Cross, I swear someone whispered. If anything happens to this girl Lopez set me to guard over, then many of us will die. Somewhere on this rancho is the one who spoke softly just outside her door. Lopez will go mad when he hears of this. If we do not find the one who whispered—"

"You are right, *amigo*," one of the crew said. "I, too, revolt at seeing this girl held prisoner. But— the one who spoke outside the door could not have been Lopez himself?" he asked the guard.

"He was in a fit of rage when he left," the guard said. "Had he returned in that state he would have kicked the door down, not whispered like a love-sick boy. It was not Lopez."

"Was it Toughy? Where is the boy?"

"He has not been around since suppertime. But it was not Toughy. He would have made known who he was after the first shot."

"The Kid?" a vaquero suggested.

"The Kid," another snorted. "When we saw him killed before our eyes and carried away to his burial."

"But we also have seen him dodge death other times when other men would have perished," the vaquero argued.

"But even if the Kid has returned to haunt Rancho Diablo he could scarcely disappear in a minute. . . ."

"Unless he went out the front door onto the porch as you were coming through the dining room," the guard exclaimed.

"*Sangre de Cristo*! That is a thought. Perhaps the whisper came not from the tequila bottle after all. Come on, *amigos*. If the one who came to this girl's door is on the rancho we must find him."

Still the vaquero who had raised the window and so nearly caught the watching Kid hung back.

"I'll go," he snarled. "But if you hombres will back me up we will force Lopez to release this girl. Lopez is not the primero. Now that Bradley is dead, Pearson will hear our demands."

Silence met the fellow's challenge. Led by the guard, the vaqueros quit the room. The Kid heard the key turn in the lock, heard heavy steps descending the stairs.

Momentarily the peril of his predicament increased. Before they reached the bottom and had fanned out to search for him he could gain the corral, throw himself aboard Rey del Rey and ride for it. But the girl . . . he could not leave her behind, bound, helplessly waiting the fate the brutal Lopez would impose on her.

"As I told you," came a shout. "The door at

the foot of the stairs is unlocked. The one who whispered escaped by way of it."

No time for flight across the yard now. His boots were safely hidden. The hard-packed ground beneath the window would not betray his tracks. There was only one way out.

Already the light of the lanterns was piercing the deep shadows of the yard. Boots were clumping about on the porch. The angry growls of the searching men assailed his ears.

Giving silent thanks to the vaquero who had dared throw up the window, the Kid moved an arm cautiously across the sill, gripped the inside frame. Then with his sock feet braced against the 'dobe side wall he pulled himself over and into the room.

The voices came off the porch, moved around to rise from below the window. Curses of disappointment, vile curses hurled at the guard who again they had begun to accuse of shooting at a fancy. The Kid smiled. The suspicion they voiced diverted attention from that window.

Once within, he stretched flat on the floor, bellied his way across the room to the side of the bed. From below came the sound of retreating footsteps—the men fanning out across the yard toward the barns and bunkhouses. He was safe for the moment. And he knew Rey del Rey would not betray him. At first sight of the lanterns the palomino would move far back to escape the rays. Long since the brute had learned to dodge any light that stabbed the darkness unless a tight rein held him toward it.

The Kid heard the door at the foot of the stairs slam, heard the key grate in the lock and the guard clumping back up the steps, muttering to himself.

He stretched out, slid beneath the bed. But the guard stopped only for a moment outside the door, where the Kid could hear his hoarse breathing and growls.

"*Sangre de Cristo*," the fellow muttered. "Truly is this called the rancho of the devil. Someone was there, I can swear. Yet it could have been no human. Well indeed it is that one has tequila— for only with tequila could I master these jumpy nerves that cry for me to flee this place of spirits which defy bullets and vanish in the dark."

The Kid choked back a chuckle as he heard the fellow tiptoe away down the hall and out the door to the ramada, where, he pictured him, again pulling at his bottle.

Waiting until he had controlled his own breathing, he slid out from under the bed and raised up slowly. He placed his hand over the girl's mouth to stifle any outcry that terror might force through the kerchief, bringing the crew down upon them with blazing guns.

"*Chamaquita*," he whispered. "It is I—the Kid. You need help, *chamaquita*, yes?"

Stark terror gleamed in the eyes she raised to him as his figure came out of the semi-darkness beside her. He felt her choke back the scream that rose to her bandaged lips. After the first start she quieted, eyes pleading, head nodding affirmatively in answer to his question.

With fingers that suddenly became awkward, he found the knot of the kerchief behind her head, and untied the gag. Then he leaned closer.

"They have mistreated you, *chamaquita*?"

"No," she managed to get out. "But undo the bonds. They have hurt until I feel numb. Quickly or the men will be returning."

Warning her to caution with a finger on her lips, he fumbled about until he had undone the strips of cloth that bound her hands behind her back and her ankles close together. She stretched thankfully, lay lax for a moment.

"Never was an angel more welcome," she whispered. "But they said . . . they said you were dead. . . ."

"Perhaps I return as an angel to help you, *chamaquita*," he said. "But quick now—if we are to get out . . ." He lifted her to her feet, pulling her to one side to avoid being seen from the open window.

"The risk you take," her voice quivered in his ear. "They will kill you. . . ."

"Not only will they not kill me, but now their first suspicion has proved groundless they will not so much as suspect me," he assured her. "For, as they said in your presence, *chamaquita*, I am dead."

"Dead?" With misgivings he heard her startled voice rise to an audible whisper. "They have—"

"Come quickly," he warned. "My ear catches the footfall of the guard coming back from his drink in the ramada. Now he is brave enough to watch over you even though spirits threaten. I will tell you later. Then we shall laugh together— out where the shadows of the night offer us protection for our talk. You want to go, yes?"

She laid a hand on his arm. "Yes?"

"But, again we must take off the boots, *chamaquita*," he said. "Again I must be the bootjack—but quickly and quietly."

She sat down on the edge of the bed. And again the scene on the mesa was re-enacted as he pulled off her boots between his legs. Again he touched the silken ankles, thrilled to their slender loveliness. Gone now was all recollection of the ordeal in the Pillars of Hell, gone all trace of fever that had racked him. He was strong— the old Mañana Kid. He was armed. And at last he was fighting for the girl for whom he had watched for weeks.

Without a word, he stuck her boot-tops in his belt, lifted her from the bed and carried her to the window.

"I must lower you, *chamaquita*," he whispered.

"It is only a few feet. See, I let you down as far as I can. Then you must drop. My gun shall cover every move. So be not fearful."

She offered no protest. Helping her over the sill, he seized both her hands and with every ounce of his strength leaned far out and lowered her. Then when he was fearful that the added weight would topple him head first to the ground, he let go. A momentary fear that she would hurt herself assailed him as he pictured her dropping through the darkness. A dull sound told him she had landed.

Without an instant's delay, he slid over the sill, lowered himself full length and let go.

"You are unhurt, *chamaquita*?" he demanded, coming up beside her.

She did not answer. But a hand on his arm reassured him. At that moment a group of the vaqueros gathered near the barn to speak excitedly. He drew her deeper into the shadows, flattened himself against the wall.

"To the left!" It was her whisper in his ear. "There are some caves in the bluffs. We will be safe over there."

"Hug the wall, *chamaquita*, and go on," he told her, his lips close to her cheek. "I shall secure my boots. Off where our footsteps can no longer be heard, we will put them on to protect our feet, yes?"

She moved away in the darkness until he

could only make out her dim form against the 'dobe wall. Going quickly to the porch, he found his boots, dodged away barely in time to escape detection in the ray of a lantern moving back toward the bunkhouse. All the vaqueros were coming in now, cursing the guard for his stupidity and swearing vengeance on him for so rudely interrupting their game to follow the trail of a phantom.

Around the corner of the hacienda he glided. Presently the form of the girl rose up darkly before him. "Lead the way, *chamaquita*," he whispered. "I shall be but a step behind you."

CHAPTER
TWENTY-SIX

O NCE out from the sheltering shadows of the hacienda they picked their way along in the dim starlight that turned the valley floor to a sea of black, obscuring cacti, brush and arroyo, and made travel difficult. The girl moved ahead, a blurred form, the Kid behind keeping a sharp watch on the yard, deserted now and quiet as a grave. Off there somewhere in the gloom was Rey del Rey—who, he had little doubt, had kept from reach of the searchers' lantern beams—waiting his whistle to come to him. But he dared not call the faithful palomino. The thunder of his hoofs would have brought the vaqueros pouring from the bunkhouse to investigate. Alone he would not have hesitated. With his gun covering the crew, and Rey del Rey galloping up, he could have vaulted aboard and streaked into the night as he had many times before to laugh back at them.

But no longer was he alone. Now there was the girl to consider. She needed the protection he could give her, if for no other reason than that she was a helpless woman among a group of lawless men. That she wanted his help was evidenced by the fact that she now crept through the night before him, leading him to a place where they could talk—where she could tell her story. For now, he doubted not, she would tell him the things he long had wanted to hear—of herself, of her fears, perhaps explain why she had fled from Guadalupe that night of the murder.

A stifled cry brought him quickly to her side. Unconsciously he placed an arm about her.

"The *chamaquita* is in pain, yes?" he whispered solicitously.

"I am sorry," she told him in a low, husky voice as he held her so close it set his heart pounding. "I guess—I guess I was so terrified I wasted my strength straining on those bonds. I was there so long. And I was so afraid. . . ."

The Kid scarcely realized his arm had tightened, that she was lying against him, shivering. His other arm crept around her.

"Now shall the *chamaquita* cease her fear, yes?" he whispered. "For never again need she be terrified—never so long as this gun I possess can speak."

She drew away from him. "I am not so afraid now," she said through chattering teeth. "But— but in my stocking feet I have stepped into cacti. Can't we put on our boots? It is quite a way to the caves."

"Of a surety, *chamaquita*. But one moment

first. Here shall I find a place for you to sit." Down on his hands and knees he went, scraping about with his fingers until he found a spot bare of brush or thorn. He straightened up. "Señorita, allow me," he said, a note of banter in his voice. "Please sit where I—where I maneuver you."

He thrilled to her brave little laugh. Then his arms were about her. He lifted her clear, placed a hand beneath her knees, and lowered her flat to the ground. She sighed gratefully as she stretched out.

"Were it not for the cacti in my foot I could enjoy the rest . . . Kid," she said softly.

"One who ever plays bootjack to a lady should also extract cacti," he returned lightly, wishing he could see her face in the darkness. "The foot, *chamaquita*—it could not by chance be the injured one I bandaged there on the mesa. Always when we meet I seem to hold your foot."

"No, the other, *caballero*," she returned, almost gaily, he thought.

Again he held a silken-clad foot in his hand. He bent to his task, rubbing a finger carefully across its side.

"There!" She started. "There they are! Perhaps you can extract some of them—if you would be so kind."

"From injured ankles to cacti," he said. "From murders to . . ." She caught her breath sharply. He stopped, ashamed. His searching fingers found the cacti. One by one he plucked them out, then continued to rub the foot over in search of more.

"That is all that pains me," she told him presently. "Again I thank you. Now please, my boots . . . Kid."

He liked the way she drawled that Kid—soft, musical, husky—a tone that reminded him of a deep-toned reed he had heard blown by the natives on the border.

Pulling her boots from his belt where he had carried them, he slipped them on. Then he straightened up to stand above her.

"The cacti—they hurt you not now, *chamaquita*?" he asked.

"I guess you got all of them," she returned. "Now, shall we go on?"

He slipped on his own boots, then helped her up and moved back waiting for her to take the lead.

"I know not your caves, *chamaquita*," he apologized. "Therefore must I trail behind, yes?"

"And with me as your guide if you fear getting lost," she mocked, "I give you my hand, señor—I shall lead you."

He thrilled to the touch of the hand she extended back to him in the darkness, purposely feigned difficulty in walking that he might feel it occasionally tighten on his own.

In silence they crossed the wide valley. Great

as was the distance it seemed only moments to the Kid until she stopped.

"We must climb now," she told him over her shoulder. "We are at the base of the bluffs. I know the way, if you will follow."

"To the end of the earth, *chamaquita*," he said gallantly. "You have but to lead on." But he was sorry then. For she did not offer to take his hand again.

Then they were climbing up the bluff in loose, sliding dirt. Somehow it reminded the Kid of that climb he had made out of the box-canyon the day he had outdistanced the Guadalupe posse. And it was the same girl there ahead of him now who had managed to stay ahead of Rey del Rey through that night of the murder only to be encountered among the boulders with an injured ankle.

Now she had stopped. He scrambled up beside her, turned to look back toward the rancho. But the outline of the buildings had vanished. No sound came out of the darkness in that direction.

They had come onto a wide, dirt ledge in the bluffs that pitched down into the valley. Wan as it was the starlight on the 'dobe gave them light. And just behind he could see the dark outline of the mouth of a great cave.

"Here we are, safe, and we can rest," she sighed. "The sound of our voices will not carry down to the rancho."

"One is never safe on this accursed Rancho Diablo," he said bitterly. "Rest, yes, for you need it badly." He felt about on the ground. "Again have I chosen a spot free of snakes, *chamaquita*—a spot for you to rest."

She offered no protest as he pressed her down. She stretched out full length, arms under her head, the cool night breeze whipping her dimly outlined face. "This is glorious—Kid," she whispered. "And again I thank you from the bottom of my heart?"

"For what, *chamaquita*?" he asked, dropping down beside her, conscious of her nearness—too conscious for comfort.

"First, for aiding me there on the mesa when the pain in my ankle left me helpless, sickened."

"You mean there on the mesa where you tricked me into looking for your horse in the darkness, *chamaquita*?" He would have bitten back the words. But it was too late. "Where you rode away with another companion, yes?"

"I hated to do it—Kid. Worse than ever before I had hated to do anything. But there was no other way. I had to protect him." She had taken a hand from beneath her head, laid it on his arm. The contact tightened his nerves. His fingers crept over hers. Somehow it seemed to give him a sense of companionship he never before had known— except for Rey del Rey. But that was different. "And—I was—afraid of you," she finished.

"You were fearful from the moment I laid eyes on you in Cantina El Paseo, *chamaquita*."

"I have always been afraid. I am afraid now even though your hand, your nearness, gives me confidence."

"Do you care to tell me why, *chamaquita*? Do you care to tell me the companion you rode away with there on the mesa, leaving me hunting the horse you rode in the dark."

Her face was close to his now, her eyes veiled in the darkness.

"Yes, I care to tell you—Kid. Everything. I asked you there on the mesa to trust me. Had you known the story, it would have been different—easier. But you were a stranger—a stranger I had seen only once before at Cantina El Paseo. Therefore I could not tell you; it would have taken so long. I could only say, trust me . . . and some time—"

The pressure of his fingers tightened on her hand that lay limp in his grasp. She made no effort to withdraw it. He thought once that she was returning the pressure. It set him to trembling. He cursed himself for his momentary weakness, straightened up to drop her hand. She looked up at him, a hurt look. Again his fingers found hers caressingly.

"But the stranger with whom you rode off the mesa?" he demanded. "Was he the killer from Cantina El Paseo?"

She shrunk away from him, covering her eyes with her hands. He could hear her sobbing.

"I am sorry, *chamaquita*," he said contritely. "But one who knows nothing cannot so much as question you intelligently. When you please, tell me of this hombre with whom you rode off the mesa, leaving me there after I had shared the last of my water to relieve your injured ankle. It was because of that I . . ."

"I'm so sorry!" She bolted up now alongside of him, again to lay a hand on his arm. Her face was wet with tears. She was so close he could breathe the sweetness of her. "I knew I was taking your last water. I hoped you would follow me. I tried by every way I knew to show you, to tell you I was leaving. And still I was fearful that you should follow me—fearful that you were a posseman, riding out from Guadalupe to drag me back."

"The *chamaquita* picks not her men well," he said, stroking her arm and trembling with the contact. "I resemble nothing that rides in a posse. I ride not like a posseman—I can ride well. And I ride a horse no posseman ever can hope to possess."

"Then it was you who started out after me in the night there at Guadalupe—you, astride the fastest, most gorgeous palomino I have ever seen. I tried to outrace you. I could not. So I took to the arroyos—hid myself while you raced past."

"It is Rey del Rey of whom you speak," the Kid said. "The wounded palomino which I led half dead, into Rancho Diablo that day to plead with you for water."

"And you got it, señor." She was clinging to him now, her low voice grown even huskier with her tears.

"Of that later, *chamaquita*," he said softly. "Still I ask who the companion was who left the mesa with you?"

She was looking him squarely in the eye.

"Toughy was my companion—I was afraid for Toughy. That is the reason I left you, tricked you, if you will, into searching for my horse in the darkness—my horse which was close at hand."

"Toughy!" he exclaimed. "What has Toughy . . ."

"We were trying to escape Rancho Diablo together, Toughy and myself. You stopped us, else today we would be free of this."

"So it was Toughy who was your companion there on the mesa? He tried to tell me. But . . ." He broke off shortly. ". . . where is the *chamaco* now?"

"Just before Lopez seized me and tied me in that room, Toughy told me he was going for you—going to the Pillars of Hell, where he knew he would find you. He told me you would come to save us both . . . And when you appeared I thought—"

"Where is Lopez?" he demanded.

"He rode to Guadalupe after a priest—to wed us."

"To wed you?" slowly. "And you, do you want this—wedding?"

"No! I will die first."

"You do not want to wed Lopez!" he mused aloud, jerkily. "That is as it should be. But Toughy—the *chamaco* is searching for me in the Pillars of Hell. And Toughy was your companion on the mesa? And Lopez is after a priest to wed you. Come, *chamaquita*. We have work to do." He seized her hand, almost jerked her to her feet. She winced at the pressure. But he did not notice. He was standing upright, straining out into the darkness toward Rancho Diablo.

"Glad I am, *chamaquita*, that I have found you—that I could help you—glad indeed. But now Toughy, the *chamaco*, needs me. I am going to him."

He started away. She seized hold of him.

"Toughy will be all right if he does not return to the rancho," she pleaded. "And he promised me never to return unless he could find you."

"*Sangre de Cristo*!" The Kid sat flat down to scratch nervously in the earth while the girl stood above him. "Ever am I faithful to a duty. I owe one now to you, *chamaquita*. Another to the *chamaco*. Both of you I shall take from here. The *chamaco* is safe, I know. For he is smart. So he risked his life to seek me again in the

Pillars of Hell where he left me, yes? If he does not find me, he will not return?"

"He will not return," she assured him, "until he has found you. You, señor are his idol—his life."

CHAPTER TWENTY-SEVEN

"S O IT was the *chamaco* with whom you rode away from the mesa, *chamaquita*?" the Kid mused aloud presently as though trying to convince himself her words were true.

"We were attempting to run away from Rancho Diablo," she said in a low voice. "We saw you coming, so we separated. You encountered Toughy. I was terrified when you shot. I heard everything you said—and you were so kind. When you started away I turned my ankle trying to escape your gaze. But . . ."

"I found you anyway," the Kid put in softly. "Only to lose you. Why were you trying to flee Rancho Diablo?"

"To get away from Lopez. He has hounded me for months. Bradley was not so bad, because he feared Pearson, but Lopez—"

"You have been away for many weeks, *chamaquita*, yes?" he observed as she stopped.

"You noticed?" Her voice throbbed with an emotion she herself could not understand. For again his fingers had found hers in the darkness, closed over them. And again she offered no resistance.

"Each day, *chamaquita*. Thinking you needed help I have kept constant vigil. There were so many things to learn—things of which I know not yet."

"And so many things to tell, now that I have found someone whom I can trust," she whispered.

"But first, your name, *chamaquita*," he urged gently. "After all these weeks have I yet to hear it."

"Does my name mean so much?" she asked, and he thought the pressure of her grip on his hand increased. "Once I told you—back on the mesa, so long, long ago, now it seems—that you must trust me."

"Have I not trusted you?" he demanded. "Would man risk his life for any woman thus if he did not see something in her that merited his trust? Your name, señorita?"

"*Chamaquita*," she whispered. "For that is the name you have given me—a pretty name by which I always shall be known to myself—and you."

"*Chamaquita* it shall be then," he said. "*Chamaquita mia*, yes?"

She looked long at him in the darkness. Once he started to bend over her, search out her lips, but caught himself quickly.

"Tell me of the things that led up to your—your being held prisoner in that room," he urged shakily.

"I had just returned to the rancho," she said, "with an Indian woman who held me almost prisoner. Pearson took me to a camp far down the valley; there I was treated well, but allowed no freedom. And I was so fearful for Toughy." She stopped, but he did not speak, waiting for her to go on.

"Then Pearson came and brought me back to the rancho, and rode away. Last night Lopez came to the rancho in a rage. He struck Toughy, sent the child screaming into the night. When I attempted to interfere, he struck me, and warned me he would force me to marry him. When I refused and defied him, he carried me into the room where you found me, bound me fast. He left, swearing to return in a few hours with a priest. I lived through endless hours of torment, hoping, praying that some help would come. And help did come—through you, the one in whom I have placed my trust since the moment I saw you there in Cantina El Paseo. But you—you scarcely looked at me."

She fell silent to sit with downcast eyes. Again and again he was on the point of taking her in his arms, attempting to comfort her, but he was fearful of frightening her. And he wanted to hear her story; wanted to get clear in his mind the many things he had heard and seen but which yet did not seem to make sense.

"Tell me, *chamaquita*," he urged presently, "that I may know how to proceed. For there is so much that needs explanation here on this accursed rancho of the devil. You, for instance—even though I know not your name—how came you here?"

"Never have I lived in another place that I recall," she told him. "My earliest recollection is of this rancho. Then it was owned by a man named Rodriguez."

"Pedro Rodriguez?" he supplied.

"Then you know?" she looked up at him, surprised.

"I knew him not personally. But of him I have heard. The *chamaquita* will go on, yes?"

"I grew up here on the rancho where there were great herds of cattle. I rode with the men, a vaquero among them even as a child. And always was I treated with great respect and courtesy."

"But how did you come here?" he asked.

"I am Pedro Rodriguez' niece."

"Then you are Toughy's cousin," he announced quietly.

"Toughy's cousin?" she gasped out, an incredulous light flashing into her eyes. "Toughy's cousin . . . do you mean that Toughy is Pedro Rodriguez' son?"

"None other, *chamaquita*. But of those things later. Now I can understand perhaps the close comradeship of yourself and Toughy—understand why you two were trying to escape—understand why he defended you."

"They abuse him terribly," she said fiercely. "Many times would I have killed them had I been able—especially Lopez."

"Toughy has tried to tell me, *chamaquita*, only to be interrupted. But never again shall we be interrupted. No one shall come between us."

"I am so glad," she murmured, her fingers again finding his in the darkness. "Long have I prayed for such deliverance."

"But of yourself, *chamaquita*?"

"An old Mexican *madre* raised myself and my brother on this rancho. For I never knew my mother. Then, when I was but a child, one day there came word that my uncle, Pedro Rodriguez, was dead. I recall how the old *madre* gathered my brother and myself to her and told us many things. But I was too young to get their meaning."

"She told you what, *chamaquita*?" He was conscious of the sudden pulsing of blood in the arm he slipped across her shoulders. The contact seemed to ease her fear for she went on.

"She told us that from then on our trust should be in the major-domo of Rancho Diablo. That we should trust none other than he. For he too, was a father, who knew and loved children, although his son was separated from him."

"That major-domo was Johnnie Bender, *chamaquita*?"

"How did you know?" Again she pulled away to stare at him. "You frighten me with what you know. Perhaps back there on the mesa you knew more than I did myself."

"Not on the mesa, *chamaquita*—but since I have arrived on Rancho Diablo. Truly is this accursed place well named. And to think, for all these years you have been here. But proceed!"

"After my uncle's death, Johnnie Bender took us in charge, my brother and myself. And he brought Toughy here from somewhere. Never did man lavish affection on a boy as he lavished it on Toughy. He quickly became the major-domo of the rancho, although he was only a tiny fellow. Why, almost before he walked well, Johnnie had taught him to ride about the rancho."

"Now you know why, *chamaquita*."

"Never have I known until you told me. I only knew that I loved him—that we seemed near and dear to one another. Almost as dear as my own brother. Now that you have told me that he is my cousin, I can understand."

"You are learning much tonight, *chamaquita*—as am I," he said hoarsely, hoping she would find no double meaning in his words. "Now I can realize why you and Toughy were trying to escape this accursed place. Once I had thought—"

"What?" she asked, as he hesitated.

"Thought perhaps it was the gunman who shot

down the youth in Cantina El Paseo with whom you were riding there on the mesa. For you left the cantina at the time of the . . . the shooting—rode into the night. I too, left. . . ."

"For you were the Mañana Kid," she accused. "I saw you there, trembled to believe what you would think of me in that short red skirt, my brazen attitude in that . . ." She stopped, shivering. "For I did not belong there. It was the first time in my life I had gone there or to any other such place."

"That I surmised," he assured her. "For honesty and truth were stamped upon your features. And you recognized me as the Mañana Kid, yes? But how?"

"Because you sat in the line of my vision with the reward notice posted just above your head. One does well, Señor Mañana Kid, not to sit beneath posters offering rewards when one's own likeness—and a true likeness—is just above one's head."

"Again you are right, as always, *chamaquita mia*. But I noticed it not. My eyes were all for you—as you looked then in that velvet skirt. Pretty you were, *chamaquita*, pretty as a picture, shapely . . ."

She placed a finger over his lips, a cool finger that silenced him.

"It shames me yet to think of it," she said softly. "I had only come dressed thus to mingle with those—those . . ." Her voice broke. She buried her flaming face in her hands.

"And they allowed you to leave the rancho?"

"They did not know it unless Toughy and I started out together. Occasionally I could escape for a few hours. The red skirt, the *madre* once told me, belonged to my mother. I dressed myself in it and stole away from the rancho while Toughy remained behind to keep them from becoming suspicious."

"And you went to Guadalupe, to Cantina El Paseo to—" he began, only to check himself. "The youth who was shot down, *chamaquita*. You—you loved him? He was perhaps your—your—"

She seemed to anticipate what he was attempting to say, anticipate the word that somehow he could not force to leave his lips.

"He was my brother," she whispered. "I went to Cantina El Paseo to save my brother. They had arranged that trip for him here at Rancho Diablo, had invited him to Guadalupe. For months they had made so much over him here it sickened me. They taught him to drink and gamble. They plied him with liquor, provided him with too much money. It was ruining him. The praise they heaped upon him went to his head. He had become a swaggering braggart. I knew back of it was some motive but never could I understand their purpose."

"It is simple, *chamaquita*," he said. "Your brother knew something he should not have known—too much, perhaps. They took this course to . . . but please go on. They arranged this party in Guadalupe for your brother, yes?"

"I pleaded with him not to go." She fell to sobbing. "For the first time he became angry with me, told me it no longer was my affair what he chose to do. He left me in tears. Then, when he had ridden away from the rancho with men I had never seen before, I became more and more fearful. So I dressed myself in that red dress to conceal my identity and shame and followed. I entered that . . ."

So close now had she drawn to him the Kid could feel her body trembling. Again his arm went around her shoulder. But he was so conscious of the contact his arm felt big and awkward and out of place. But apparently she did not notice.

". . . that resort to be near him and protect him, dressed so I would seem one of them, determined to be as shameless as the worst if necessary to save my brother. And then—"

"*Chamaquita mia,*" he said softly, "never did you think I fired that shot as did the others?"

"No, señor. For I was looking directly at you when that shot was fired. In fact," she confessed in a voice so low it was scarcely audible, "I had divided my glances equally between yourself and my brother. I had eyes for no one else. The others sickened me. I was fearful of them, fearful they would . . . Only two there were in that resort for me, one my brother whom I wanted to save, the other . . ." Her voice trailed off as though her thoughts had taken up the thing she was about to voice.

She roused herself. Her voice came clearer. "Stark terror drove me to flight—terror for my own life when I found, there in the cantina, vaqueros of Rancho Diablo—our own vaqueros who in their drunken bravado might recognize me and accost me. I hated myself for my flight— for leaving my brother. But there was nothing I could do now that he was gone. I had tried so hard to dissuade him, but he had not listened. Now Toughy needed me more than he." She broke down to bury her face in her hands and sob. He patted her shoulder awkwardly.

She looked up presently, the tears glistening in her eyes. "There is little more to tell. I fled like a coward into the night, toward the rancho, there to shed the red dress that made me feel so—so immodest."

"And I followed you instead of the real killer, yes?" he offered.

"Do you know who killed my brother, señor?" she demanded suddenly.

"Not of a surety, *chamaquita*. But I have my suspicion, yes?"

"And you will find him for me, bring him to justice?"

"When I can find a certain hombre—but when liars talk one can be sure of little. Therefore, that I make no mistake, I bide my time, choosing my own method to gain my ends. When the time comes, *chamaquita*, and I assure you it will not now be long delayed, then shall I turn the slayer of your brother over to the justice you ask. Perhaps—by then—"

"What do you mean?" she asked fearfully.

"As I said, perhaps by then there will be no need for justice."

"You will not kill him. Promise me. I have seen so much of violence I awake in the night crying. Promise me!"

"The *chamaquita* was telling me of Johnnie Bender." He changed the subject quickly. "She said that Johnnie Bender was her friend?"

"A strange note creeps into your voice, Señor Kid," she said. "Almost for a moment it makes me fear you." A reassuring but awkward pat on her shoulder silenced her. He could not understand the awkwardness of that hand which was so swift with a gun. Yet now even his fingers felt large and bruising to the slight shoulder beneath their touch.

She essayed a wan smile.

"Johnnie Bender was the finest man I ever have known. Always he took Toughy and brother and myself around the rancho. It was grand. I remember the old Mexican *madre* beamed whenever Johnnie Bender came near. For after Uncle Pedro died we knew no other father. And then one day—"

"Johnnie Bender, too, was killed."

"Yes," brokenly. "He was thrown by El Scorpion. His neck was broken. You will hear and see much of El Scorpion, señor."

"I have," he said grimly, but offered no explanation.

"Why they do not destroy that vicious animal I cannot understand. Since I can remember he has killed men on this rancho."

"They did not destroy El Scorpion because that caballo was one in a million, *chamaquita*," he told her. "A horse who fought men as men fight men."

"I do not know what you mean. But the name El Scorpion has been a nightmare to me for many years. I was too young to realize when Pedro Rodriguez was killed. But when Johnnie was—"

"Murdered!" He snapped out with a sudden venom that startled her. "But never again need you have fear of El Scorpion, *chamaquita*. El Scorpion is dead!"

"Dead?" she whispered. She asked no detail, apparently satisfied to take his word without question. "And Johnnie—was—murdered?

How—how do you know that?" The words came through teeth chattering with fear.

"Because I am Johnnie Bender's son," he said.

CHAPTER TWENTY-EIGHT

"JOHNNIE BENDER'S son?" The girl stared at him in the darkness. "Johnnie Bender's son! I knew there was reason I should trust you. I knew there was reason why I risked everything, poured out my soul to you, knowing that I could trust you. You—the Mañana Kid—Johnnie Bender's son!" In the excitement of the moment she had thrown her arms about him, was clinging to him. The contact made him tingle. But he did not want it thus. Her gesture was only prompted by excitement. Much as he hated to, he disengaged her arms, took her hand in his. "You can prove this, Señor Kid?" she whispered.

"The *chamaquita* needs proof, yes?" he said. "After all, you said Johnnie Bender was your greatest friend. But of this later. Tell me about Johnnie Bender's death, how you heard—"

"That's all I know. When Johnnie died they said around the rancho that El Scorpion had killed another man."

"And who brought you the word, *chamaquita*, please?"

"Ross Pearson."

"And this Pearson . . ."

"Until then he had been but a vaquero on the rancho. But he had been kind to me at times for all his rough ways. And he did not abuse Toughy within my sight as did the others. But I never felt secure when he was near. Always he seemed to be watching me, scheming something."

"And this Bradley," he prompted.

"He always seemed to take orders from Pearson. Bradley was underhanded and sneaking with everything, but he had little to say. His fear of Pearson was the talk of the rancho."

"And after Bender died—"

"My brother took charge of things," she said. "But he was very little older than myself— not yet twenty. He was no match for Pearson and Bradley. They quickly made a fool of him, dressed him in gaudy clothes, furnished him with money to turn the head of any youth."

"You knew from whence that money came, *chamaquita*?"

"No. I pleaded with him. To no avail. Pearson and Bradley had done their work well, had succeeded in getting my brother within their power. Only once did I hear him lift his voice against them. That was one time when they had cursed Toughy and beaten him until we feared for the *chamaco*'s life."

"That was after Johnnie Bender's murder?" the Kid said, as she hesitated.

"Murdered?" she gasped again. "Was Johnnie Bender really murdered?"

"The Señor Pearson shot him in the back," the Kid returned grimly. "I heard his own confession. But proceed, please. Of those things we can talk later. About Lopez?"

"It was not such a great while after Johnnie—died, that Lopez came. I hated him from the moment I laid eyes on him, for always he had a leering look. Always was he following me around, attempting to lay his coarse hands on me. When he stared at me I felt—felt—I hated him!" she whispered fiercely. "Many times Ross Pearson drove him away from the ranchhouse, ordering him never to return. Bradley was different. Therefore I lived in dread during the days Pearson would be gone from the rancho. I locked myself in a room and did not even come forth to eat. For Bradley was as bad as Lopez. But never would he do anything in the open. But Pearson— of him I can say he protected me against Lopez."

"That, perhaps, will be the one bright mark for him above," the Kid said.

"You mean . . ." she faltered.

"Ross Pearson is dead!"

"Dead!" She clapped a hand over her lips to stifle the half scream. "How?" she whispered.

"Lopez killed him out in the Pillars of Hell— out there where they threw me thinking I, too, was dead."

"I do not understand," she got out.

"Do not try," he told her. "Later, we will check each detail with care. But now—"

"Ross Pearson, dead," she repeated dully. "Then only Lopez and Bradley are to be feared."

"No fear need the *chamaquita* have of Bradley," the Kid said. "For Bradley, too, is dead."

"Did Lopez . . ." she began fearfully.

"Bradley died the victim of El Scorpion—the horse he had abused so many times, the horse in a million, who remembered a voice and took his revenge."

"This is terrible," she whispered. "Señor Kid, please take me away. It seems as though I've been afraid so long I'll—I'll die of terror. Please . . ." He placed a comforting arm around her. And now she came close to him to bury her face on his chest and sob.

"Pearson—Bradley—gone," she murmured over and over again. "Yet I feel no sorrow, only terror. Pearson was good to me. But Bradley . . . Still I have to fear the one who torments me the most—Juan Lopez. How I hate him. Always he follows me around. The only respite I have had was when Pearson took me to the camp. There for weeks I was free of Lopez' advances."

"Only too well did I realize it was weeks, *chamaquita*," the Kid put in. "For those weeks were long with waiting and watching for you— heavy with fears that you had disappeared after

286

I had found you." The arm about her tightened. With a little sigh she snuggled closer. He could feel her heart pounding against his own.

Thus they sat in silence, she trying to quiet her fears, the Kid staring out across the deep black that was the valley floor. Still from the rancho had come no sound. Apparently the vaqueros had given up the search and turned in. For only the small sounds of the night greeted his ears that never for a moment had ceased their straining vigil.

"Now should the *chamaquita* quiet her fears," the Kid said after a time, reluctant to break the spell, fearful that the girl would pull away. But she made no move to do so and his arm only drew her closer.

"I have no fear of the future," she whispered. "Yet fears of the past will not die in a moment. Do they know on the rancho that you are Johnnie Bender's boy?"

"They know nothing. They believe I am dead," he told her.

"You did not tell me about that?"

Quickly he told her of the scene at the corral when Lopez had shot El Scorpion, then wounded him, and of waking in the Pillars of Hell.

"Toughy told me you were there," she said. "But he only had a moment before we were interrupted. And they really left you there to die—the brutes!"

"They have paid, *chamaquita*," he said. "And those who have not, shall. Now must we think of the *chamaco*. We have remained here long."

His words seemed to rouse all her fears again within her. "I had forgotten," she whispered. "I have learned so much, and you have relieved me so greatly. But must we . . . I can't—I won't go back to the rancho."

"Never shall you return to that rancho, *chamaquita*," he assured her. "Not until—"

"Until what?" she asked fearfully.

"Until that time comes when I shall ride among them to assert your claims—your claims and Toughy's."

"But I have no claims that I would press on that place." She shuddered. "Once away I never want to lay eyes on it again. Please, Señor Kid—please promise me, that you will not take me back."

"No need to fear, *chamaquita*," he whispered. "But there is work to be done. A great horse rancho cannot be cast aside when it rightfully belongs to Toughy and yourself."

"That is something I have always wondered about," she said thoughtfully. "Rancho Diablo is not a horse ranch. It is a cattle rancho. The horses have been brought in here since Pearson and Bradley and Lopez have been in charge. Once Pedro Rodriguez had cattle—great herds of cattle that stretched almost to the border, I have heard brother say. Now we have none. What became of the cattle, Señor Kid?"

"I only surmise," he said. "But to prove my suspicion we shall some day ride and find out. I think every one of those cattle have been rustled from Rancho Diablo."

"But how?" she asked. "Never have we known rustlers in this country. Never have I heard such a thing talked, even by the vaqueros."

"There are always ways when smart men like Pearson and Bradley get their heads together and compare their evil thoughts," he said. "But no longer will we be forced to pit ourselves against their treacherous scheming. Only now have we Lopez to reckon with."

"And I fear him most of all." She shuddered. "For it is Lopez who even now is in search of a priest." As though all her fears had suddenly centered in one moment, she tore herself away from the Kid and sprang to her feet. "Rather than to go back and marry Lopez I will—I will—"

He got up to stand beside her. With a temerity that surprised himself he reached out and gathered her into his arms. She lay sobbing against him.

"Never, I have told you, *chamaquita*," he whispered, "will you marry Lopez."

"But what shall we do? We must eat. We must have water. We are miles from another rancho. And Toughy."

"Problems only magnify as one tries to solve them in one's mind, *chamaquita*," he reasoned aloud. "Therefore let us take them one at a time. Man who is armed can ever find food. Water—that is different. For one cannot force water from the desert floor. But of those things later. Now I must find the *chamaco*. After that . . ."

"But what of me?" she whispered.

"One does not pull plans out of thin air, *chamaquita*. We must reason our course, weigh it carefully and then proceed. Rey del Rey awaits me out there somewhere in the darkness. How far I know not. But *caballo mio* will come if he is within range of hearing."

"What are you going to do?" she demanded. "Any sound will be heard."

"And in such darkness we may walk for hours without finding Rey del Rey. Once astride him, even double, nothing on Rancho Diablo can overtake us. I shall summon Rey del Rey. Then we shall find Toughy. After you two are safely away, I shall return and . . ." He broke off to whistle. He listened as the shrill note beat to a whisper across the valley. No sound came out of the darkness. He whistled again, again waited breathlessly for the sudden clatter of hoofs that would be his answer. But again only silence met his ears.

"It is strange, *chamaquita*," he said with a

note of grimness that was deadly in his voice. "*Caballo mio* does not answer."

"Perhaps he has strayed away—out of hearing," she suggested.

"One does not know Rey del Rey who reasons thus," he said. "For if he is within sound of my whistle he will come. But wait. . . ." Again he whistled. And again and again. And then, out of the gloom came the pounding of hoofs.

"*Caballo mio*," the Kid breathed. "Never did man have such a friend. See, *chamaquita*, the breaks now are with us. For here out of the darkness comes the one who alone in all this country can help us—Rey del Rey."

He whistled softer now, directing the horse to him. Nearer and nearer came the running hoofs. Then, presently, they could hear the brute snorting in the shadows.

"Come, *chamaquita*," he said, taking her hand. "We shall await our friend at the base of the cliff."

Quickly they went down into the valley. The hoof-beats had stopped. But at the Kid's whistle they were resumed. And then, out of the night loomed the palomino, head cocked to keep clear of the trailing reins, the silver of saddle rig and golden coat gleaming even in the darkness.

Straight to the Kid the brute came, its nose outstretched for a caress. It shied away from the girl. But the Kid quickly quieted its fears.

"*Caballo mio*," he crooned. "Always are you at hand. And now, *chamaquita*, do you mount the saddle." He helped the girl aboard the palomino who would have protested but for the Kid's steady hand on the rein. Then with a leap the Kid was up behind.

"Now for the Pillars of Hell, *chamaquita*, where we shall first find Toughy," he said. "And after that . . ." She gathered up the reins and the palomino sidled away into the gloom.

CHAPTER TWENTY-NINE

A S THEY rode through the night in silence the Kid kept his eyes and ears alert for sound or movement from the rancho. But apparently Rey del Rey's mad race in answer to his whistle had passed unheeded for the rancho was wrapped in the stillness of a tomb.

They were below the barns and headed down the trail up which he had so recently staggered, before he spoke.

"Lopez has not returned as yet, *chamaquita*," he observed.

"No." Again her voice was husky and musical, lacking the note of fear it had carried in the cave. "Had he come back he would have turned the rancho over looking for me. We cannot be too careful, Señor Kid. To fall into Lopez' hands now would be—"

"Have no further fear, *chamaquita*," he said, patting her. "We will only remain long enough to find Toughy, then shall I take you where you will be safe. My only hope now is that no harm has befallen the *chamaco*."

"That would be about—about the end of things

293

for me," the girl said. "For Toughy is all I have left now."

"All, yes?" There was question in the Kid's voice as well as his words.

"I didn't mean just that," she returned.

Again silence fell between them as the palomino picked its way carefully through the night. When they had ridden as far as he reasoned they should, the Kid pulled rein for her.

"We are nearing the Pillars now, *chamaquita*," he said. "It would be best, perhaps, if we stop here. The flames would only frighten the palomino. Already he grows nervous with the fumes of sulphur his quick nose catches."

By now Rey del Rey had fallen to curveting and mincing along the trail, almost stopping at times to throw up his head and send whistling snorts through his nose.

"He will remain here and wait our return?" she asked anxiously.

"Always will Rey del Rey wait," he assured her. "But this time you shall remain with him. No need will there be for you to enter that chamber of hell. Toughy would have made his way directly to the place where they left me. There he would have stayed close to search for me."

"You are not going to leave me here alone," she faltered, new terror in her voice. "Please, Señor Kid . . ."

"But the *chamaquita* has nothing now to fear,"

294

he told her. "You can rely on Rey del Rey. No *caballo* can out-race him. He dodges arroyo and barranca with the ease and sure-footedness of a deer. If you trust me, *chamaquita*, then also should you have trust in *caballo mio*."

"As you say," the girl replied with an attempt at bravery, but with a lack of assurance in her voice the Kid was quick to note. "I will place my trust in Rey del Rey. But only because of the trust you have in him."

"*Gracias*," the Kid said, slipping to the ground to stand looking up at her against the background of stars. "I will be away no longer than I can help. You are certain the *chamaco* will wait in there for me?"

"Positive," she replied. "He went for you. He will not return without you. But, Kid," she laid a hand on his arm, "—I am so afraid for him—and for you. Please hurry."

He gripped her fingers with a pressure that carried far more meaning than any word he could have spoken. Now that he had found her he was reluctant to leave her. He wanted to ride on and on into the night behind her in the saddle as did the Dons of old, riding with their brides toward the marriage altar. But there still was a duty to perform—the duty to the *chamaco*.

"I will return quickly," he said. "And when I am out from the flames with the *chamaco*, I shall whistle for Rey del Rey that we may be reunited quicker. Thus should you always be alert, *chamaquita*. For when Rey del Rey hears my whistle he is gone like the wind. Only death can stop him." With another quick grip of her fingers, he turned away. A loving caress on the nose of the impatient palomino and he was gone into the darkness.

Once as he moved along in his high-heeled boots toward the flaming Pillars of Hell, from which now arose a dull glow, he thought he heard a distant hoof-beat. He stopped to listen. But it was not repeated.

"You grow nervous as a woman, Kid," he chided himself. "Always now your ears hear hostile hoof-beats and your eyes see strange images of your fancy."

Thus he reassured himself as he tramped on. Had there been pursuit from Rancho Diablo it would have organized and sprung to the saddle before the outline of the rancho buildings had dropped away into the dark. In the three miles they had traveled the sound of galloping hoofs by now would be beating an alarm on the night air. But as he advanced toward the Pillars of Hell, he fought down a strange impulse to turn back— back to be close at hand should harm threaten the *chamaquita* whose very life now was in his keeping.

By the time he reached the outer fringe of smoke and flame, he had managed to get a grip on his nerves. Once he paused to look back. Nothing stirred in the blackness of the night. But now, he noticed with misgivings, the eastern sky was taking on a dull gray light, little lighter than the rest of the sky, but still enough to herald the approach of a new day. Realizing his need for haste, he plunged on into the Pillars of Hell.

Trusting only his sense of direction, he made his way through the flaming pillars toward where he believed had been the dugout. After what seemed an infinity of time in the stench and sickening heat, he succeeded in locating the place. The door to the dugout was still ajar as he had left it. But there was no sign of Toughy, no answer to his guarded call. Going inside, he groped around. But Toughy was not there.

Outside again his eyes attempted to pierce the eerie light. Nothing moved save the tongues of flame that licked into the sky, then died to a column of choking smoke. Uneasy now that something had befallen the boy, he made his way to where he was sprawled when Pearson fell under the bullet of Lopez. He bellied forward, to raise up, rub his eyes in amazement. Pearson's body, too, had vanished.

Satisfied now that someone had been in the Pillars of Hell since his own escape—it was foolish to believe that Toughy had come across the body of Pearson and had moved it—he took to calling loudly. His own voice beat back at him, but still no answering call from the boy. Thoroughly alarmed now, he moved through the pillars, calling his name. But his search of the smoke-choked inferno was of no avail. If Toughy had gained the Pillars he either had succumbed to the fumes and flames, or had been—

He jerked to a halt. Pearson's body had been removed. There was but one answer to that. Lopez! That probably accounted for the fellow's long absence from the rancho that had allowed him time to help the girl escape. Lopez had returned to the Pillars to drag the body of Pearson to some smoking fissure and dispose of it.

He strove to reconstruct the thing in his mind. Back in the Pillars, Toughy had seen Lopez at work disposing of Pearson's body, had learned of his own escape from the death Lopez was so positive had overtaken him. And again Toughy had fallen into the power of Lopez who now, with Pearson gone, would make short work of the boy who knew of his crimes.

But how long since the two had left the Pillars? The Kid had little doubt Lopez would take the boy back to the rancho, unless he had already done away with him in the inferno. But there was no way of knowing that. He had no idea of the time that had elapsed while he and the girl sat in the cave. Nor could the sky with only its spangle of stars help him. The lightening gray of the east warned him that dawn was approaching, that even before he could return to the girl it would be light enough to detect things on the desert.

For the first time fear for the safety of the girl assailed him. Before he was aware of it he was running and dodging through the smoke and flame toward the outer fringe from which he had entered. Breathlessly he ran out into the darkness. Once clear of the light of the hideous place he whistled sharply for Rey del Rey. Not waiting for an answer of hoof-beats, he started forward on a run.

Suppose by some trick of fate, Lopez had been leaving the Pillars as he had approached? The hoof-beat he had heard as he entered! Suppose that had been Lopez, who riding through the night, had observed him. Suppose Lopez had stumbled onto the girl? He had left her on the trail that ran to Rancho Diablo. Lopez would return to the rancho by that route.

He stopped again to whistle, wait with bated breath for the sound of Rey del Rey's hoof-beats. Still nothing but silence—silence that suddenly seemed ominous, sinister. Again he plunged on, halting only to whistle, then running along at the best speed he could in the high-heeled boots. By now he was certain—had somehow been fearfully certain from the first—that Rey del Rey would not answer that whistle. For while he dreaded to believe that the girl again had fallen into the hands of Lopez, from the outset some inner sense had warned him.

He pulled up short to whistle, again and again. But his efforts were wasted. The pound of the palomino streaking out of the night did not come. But, his quick ear detected a hoof-beat—a measured hoof-beat far up in the dark on the trail toward the rancho. Not of one horse but of two.

"*Sangre de Cristo*!" the Kid cursed, throwing himself on the ground. "Again you have proved how incapable you are of trust! You, the Mañana Kid, being thus outwitted by a . . . and Toughy gone, the *chamaco* who trusted you—the *chamaquita*!" He got to his feet, to stand staring at the now graying east. "The final showdown nears, Lopez," he said softly, but with the venom of a hissing snake in his tone. "If you have harmed the girl or the *chamaco* . . ." He whistled once again, knowing it was futile. Even Rey del Rey, the thing of greatest pride in all his life, was in possession of Lopez. For he doubted not now that he had reconstructed the thing correctly. Lopez again had played his hand and won.

But there would be a day of reckoning—the day that was swiftly approaching, the Kid thought as he set out again up the long trail that led toward Rancho Diablo.

CHAPTER THIRTY

D AWN had painted the east with fire yellow and the rising sun was shooting shafts of flame high into the coppery heavens when the buildings of Rancho Diablo took form to meet the bloodshot eyes of the Mañana Kid. Again he had stalked up the trail from the Pillars of Hell. But this time he had not stopped to rest on the way. Instead he had plodded through the darkness, death in his heart, besieged with fears that harm already had befallen the girl, or the *chamaco*, or Rey del Rey—for thought of the palomino in possession of Lopez maddened him beyond reason.

At the gate just below the barn he paused to sweep the yard with eyes that looked and saw red. But that yard was deserted save for one vaquero who was saddling a mount in the corral. And just outside was a gray animal rigged up and fighting a rope with which it was snubbed to a post. Another of the Rancho Diablo man-killers was the Kid's thought. For he never before had seen that gray. But by its actions it was plainly a brute which never yet had bowed to man.

Then of a sudden he caught sight of Rey del Rey. The golden rump of the horse was just topping an arroyo above the house. And the rider . . . for a moment the Mañana Kid lost his reason. His gun was in his hand. He was running toward the corral, shouting hoarsely. The rider of Rey del Rey was Lopez. Beside the palomino was another horse. And astride that brute . . . Lopez' companion was the girl he last had seen there in the darkened trail outside the Pillars of Hell!

The saddled gray was almost within reach. Just as the Kid gained its side, Toughy came out onto the porch of the rancho, heard his shouts, recognized him and came on a run.

Tearing a bridle from the corral fence, the Kid slammed the bit into the gray's mouth, jerked off the rope with which it was snubbed and vaulted into the saddle.

Toughy was crying something. But he did not hear. The boy was safe. But up there was Lopez and the girl. He would attend to Lopez.

Again Toughy yelled something. But again his words were lost to the Kid as the big gray threaded its nose between its fetlocks, let forth a raucous bellow, lunged into the air and shot away to land like a stone-crusher.

For the first time in his life the Mañana Kid set to work on a horse, his silver-mounted spurs tearing it from shoulder to rump, beating it across the ears to bring it quickly to its senses. But still the brute pitched—pitched, luckily, in the direction Lopez and the girl had taken.

And the Kid reckoned without the endurance of the brute. For a seemingly endless period of time it squealed and pitched. Then of a sudden it got the bit in its teeth and started to run. For all the Kid's sawing on its hammer-head the pace it set was terrific.

Presently ugly, weirdly shaped buttes rushed out of the heat-shafted air. The Kid's nerves tightened. The brute was running toward the badlands through which he had staggered the first day of his arrival at Rancho Diablo and somewhere ahead were Lopez and the girl—and Rey del Rey.

Once through bloodshot eyes he thought he caught sight of the gleaming coat of the palomino; but he could not be sure. The wind was whipping too furiously against his eyes to make sight certain.

Thoughts streaked through his mind like lightning—so many things had happened since his arrival at the rancho. But now he remembered that trip in—Rey del Rey wounded in the shoulder by the sweeping horns of the crazed bull. It had left only a slight scar, that wound. The Kid had determined some day to come back and square accounts with that savage animal, but thus far he had had no time. There had been so many other things.

As the hammer-head raced along the man tried to map a plan of action should he suddenly encounter Lopez and the girl. But he would need a lucky break, for he had no control over the outlaw. He could not use his gun aboard the running brute, which, lunging over arroyos with mighty leaps, would destroy his aim.

Ahead lay the great basin across which he had staggered. And again scattered herds of wild cattle, such as he had encountered that other time, left off their grazing to stare, then lumber after him. But the madly running horse quickly outdistanced them.

The gray's breath took to rasping croupily. Its lunges suddenly became uncertain. The Kid had time to look ahead for the moving dots on the dun earth that would be two horsemen, Lopez and the girl.

Then as he tried to locate them the gray went down, end-over-end. Came the sickening crunch of bone. The brute shuddered and stretched out, its head twisted beneath its neck. The Kid catapulted through the air to strike with a terrific impact.

How long he lay prone on the blistered earth the Mañana Kid never knew. He came to with a start, sat bolt upright, wiping dirt from his eyes and mouth. He expected to see Lopez bearing down on him. But neither Lopez nor the girl was in sight.

"*Pelado*," he spat, fingering his bruised head, which spun crazily. He got stiffly to his feet to survey the region. Bawling cattle were lumbering in from every direction. Toward the ranch he sighted one horse racing along madly, its golden coat gleaming in the sunlight. That would be Rey del Rey, with Lopez aboard, fleeing from the maddened cattle. But the girl. Slowly he turned in every direction. Then, presently, some distance above, his gaze fell on a human figure stretched on the ground, inert, motionless. Bawling cattle were running toward it from all sides. His gaze flew to his horse.

"*Sangre de Cristo*, Kid," he cursed. "The breaks ever seem against you. The caballo is dead."

Wasting no time, he lurched toward the prostrate figure. Even before he reached it he recognized it—the *chamaquita* he had left near the Pillars of Hell. Her pony stood off a short distance, grazing.

At that moment the bull which had wounded Rey del Rey so many weeks—years it seemed—before, attracted by the raucous bawling, rounded a nearby *penasco* to throw up its gigantic head, sniff the breeze and amble toward them.

Against the dictates of reason, the Kid whipped out his gun. But he held his fire; to kill the bull meant spilling blood. The scent of blood made tame animals dangerous and would drive the wild brutes about him frantic.

He staggered on to the girl, dropped down beside her, lifted her head. She was unconscious, but breathing. A deep bruise discolored her forehead.

The Kid mastered his dizziness. Again his lithe body moved with puma swiftness. He was on his feet, waving his arms and shouting at the bull, which had broken into an awkward run. Beside the dead horse the brute slid to a halt. For an instant it loomed a huge, stationary target. The Kid fired. The bull dropped in a kicking heap.

Bedlam broke loose. A whiff of the fresh blood set the cattle to running about, pawing dirt and bellowing. They crowded around the dying bull, horning it savagely.

Satisfied that the girl was safe for the moment, the Kid attempted to secure her pony. But the horse started to run, bridle reins trailing. The Kid quickly abandoned pursuit, went back to the girl.

"There is one chance—to make the *penasco*," he muttered. Lifting her limp form, he moved with what speed he could. A few paces and he stopped dead in his tracks. From behind the butte another and even larger bunch of cattle came running toward them, wild-eyed and snorting.

The Kid's brain shuttled; hundreds of schemes crowded through it. Out of the maze of thought flashed a maxim of the range: No matter how wild cattle are, they will not touch a dead man unless he has blood on him.

The Kid's one thought was of the unconscious girl. The idea of lying down in the trail was horrible to contemplate, thought of her risking her life was . . . yet there was no alternative. The moment demanded action. He laid her down, dropped down beside her on his back, arms folded across his chest, forty-five ready for instant use.

Weary of their bloody orgy, the first bunch of cattle suddenly quit the bull and came on a run to meet the newcomers. Almost over the motionless forms of the girl and the Kid the two bunches met. It took every ounce of the Kid's self-control to lie still, eyes tightly closed.

Now the cattle were sniffing at their forms, now bawling deafeningly, pawing dirt in their eyes and mouths. A brute licked him in the face. Its rough tongue all but brought the Kid to his feet.

Then the herds were circling them. He dared a glance through squinted eyes. Every critter within the range of his vision was branded. That brand was a Pitchfork!

The breeze shifted suddenly. The cattle caught the scent of blood. They broke in wild stampede toward the dead bull.

Once they were gone, the Kid sprang up, seized the girl, stumbled around the butte. He dug out a hand-hold in the corrugated 'dobe. With a strength born of desperation, he lifted her dead weight above him and climbed. Panting, sweating, choking with dirt that showered down upon him, he pulled up out of reach of the deadly horns and onto a narrow shelf.

Stretching the girl out, he slid back down and coaxingly approached her pony. When finally he succeeded in catching it, he led it around the butte and tied its head to its stirrup so it could only move in a circle. Then he crawled back up.

After a time the girl opened her eyes. They grew wide at sight of him.

"Kid," she whispered, "where—am—I?"

"Safe, *chamaquita mia*," he smiled at her. "You had a nasty fall."

"My horse bolted." She shuddered, sat up, holding her head.

"Please to exercise care, *chamaquita*," he warned, laying a hand on her arm to steady her. "You are seated on a ledge."

"I—do not understand. . . . How did I get up here?"

"The cattle—they became threatening. I brought you here."

"But where did you come from? I thought . . ." She was gazing at him as though still unable to believe that he sat there beside her.

"I came on a horse, *chamaquita*. And such a horse—a caballo possessed of all the devils that ever cursed Rancho Diablo."

"Where is he?"

"Gone to the abode of devils, *chamaquita*.

He broke his neck trying to follow you and—"

"Lopez." She covered her eyes with her hands. "He was forcing me to accompany him to Guadalupe."

"To be married," he supplied grimly. "I thought as much. He found you there near the Pillars of Hell where I had left you, yes?"

"Only a few minutes after you rode away," she said hoarsely. "I was waiting on Rey del Rey, when suddenly he came out of the dark. He seized Rey del Rey's bridle, pulled me from the palomino. I was so startled; before I could scream he placed a hand over my mouth. Toughy was with him—attempted to fight him. But Lopez struck Toughy and knocked him unconscious. He gave me my choice of going back to the rancho with him or seeing Toughy . . . Oh, Señor Kid, I can't stand more of this. . . ." She burst into tears—wild, uncontrollable tears that racked her body.

"Lopez threatened to kill Toughy if you did not accompany him quietly?" he asked so softly she scarcely heard him.

"Yes, and thinking Toughy was badly hurt, I went with him back to the rancho. He allowed me to care for Toughy, who was just stunned. And then this morning . . . he . . . he . . . Why must I always fear that man? Why do I never seem able to escape from this place?"

"You shall, *chamaquita mia*," he said. "Forever

the breaks cannot be against us. Now perhaps—yet still we face another problem. You must return to the rancho."

"If you are with me—but never alone, Señor Kid."

"Before we have ridden double on a caballo, *chamaquita*. Again we thus shall ride. But before we start, one more thing. Why did Lopez ride away on my palomino and leave you here to die?"

"As I said, he was taking me by this short cut, to Guadalupe."

"Then he did not bring the priest?"

"No."

"You know why, of course?"

"No."

"He did not go for a priest. He returned to the Pillars of Hell to dispose of the body of Ross Pearson."

"Oh!" A little scream escaped her.

"There he encountered Toughy, who was searching for me."

"And there he found me as he was leaving. He was furious. After he had choked me and struck Toughy he raved like one who was stark mad. He demanded to know how I had come by the palomino."

"Did he ask of me?" the Kid asked easily. "He usually inquires concerning my well-being."

"I—I—lied, Señor Kid," she returned. "I

told him I had stolen the palomino—that I had escaped from the room alone."

"And he believed it."

"Yes. For he told me you were dead—gloated over the fact that he had killed you. He even promised me the palomino if I would marry him without a scene."

"Then he has yet to settle with one whom he believes dead," the Kid said. "Which is well. For men fight not their best against ghosts who shoot straight."

Once she had rushed into the thing, the girl apparently was determined to tell him all.

"Then this morning he came to the room where Toughy and I had remained on watch all night. He forced me to mount the pony—he would not allow me to ride the palomino, knowing I could out-distance him. He made Toughy stay behind, and we set out. Then, out here in the desert . . . do you remember I told you that once Rancho Diablo had only great herds of cattle?"

"*Si, chamaquita,* I know what you would say. For I, too, noticed the brand on these animals."

"Rancho Diablo vaqueros have been forbidden to ride this way for years. Because of old Grizzly—"

"That is the bull which gored Rey del Rey the day I arrived at the rancho—the bull I shot and killed today."

"He is dead?" she breathed thankfully. "For he

311

has been the terror of the desert. The vaqueros were not allowed to come. . . ."

"The reason is obvious," he said scornfully. "Old Grizzly was a rustler."

She nodded. "I noticed it. I accused Lopez."

"Lopez knew old Grizzly had coaxed your cattle into the desert and herded them into his wild bunches. And Lopez was playing for these herds which some day will bring much *dinero*. It is so simple, *chamaquita*. For here are the Rancho Diablo cattle."

"My brother discovered it—he hinted to me . . ."

"But you? Why did Lopez desert you?"

"Lopez was deathly afraid of old Grizzly. After I had noticed the Pitchfork brand on some of these cattle, old Grizzly suddenly appeared. Rey del Rey—"

"The palomino remembers always—remembers the feel of that bull's horns. And he bolted."

"Straight back to the rancho. Lopez tried to turn him. But he was no match for Rey del Rey. The horse ran like one possessed."

"And your pony could not keep pace?"

"He fell far behind. And then, when I had all but out-distanced the brutes he stumbled. And— that is all I remember."

"That is enough for now, *chamaquita*. Now we must think of getting out of here." He stood up to look around the butte at the cattle, which in their eagerness to gore the fallen bull, had forgotten them altogether. "Come! The cattle are occupied; we shall go."

He helped her down and onto her pony. Then again he vaulted up behind. But this horse was not Rey del Rey. It made several strong lunges. He rode with his spurs hooked in the brute's flanks, while he clung to the girl. But she herself was a rider of ability. Tiring of its pitching shortly, the animal sidled along.

"Must we return to the rancho, Señor Kid?" she asked fearfully, as they dropped into an arroyo at his direction to circle the cattle, which with the breeze away from them, paid no heed.

"Of a certainty, *chamaquita*," he said decisively. "Never shall we leave without Toughy and Rey del Rey. There are many things there we need."

"I'm so afraid, Kid," she whispered. "Lopez will be there—or we shall meet him returning for me."

"It is the one wish I have at the moment, *chamaquita*," he told her quietly. "For I have much to say to Señor Lopez."

CHAPTER
THIRTY-ONE

THE TRIP the Mañana Kid and the girl made to Rancho Diablo that day was slow and silent—the girl silent because of fear, the Kid silent in his own thoughts. The sun had blazed a path through the metallic sky when finally the buildings of the rancho danced out of the shimmering heat, now to seem near, now seeming to recede as they approached.

Hoping to spare the girl in the showdown he now was determined to force, yet unable to hit upon a way, the Kid attempted to map a course of action as he rode. Then, presently:

"Just below the hacienda, I shall dismount in a barranca, *chamaquita*," he told her. "You shall ride around to the front alone. Then shall you go directly into the house, there to remain until I call for you."

"Kid . . ." Her lips were white on chattering teeth. "I—can't go back there. Lopez will kill me."

"No longer will Lopez kill anything with the gun of the Mañana Kid flaming," he assured her. "Every step you take shall you be protected. It is the only way, *chamaquita*. I only ask this for Toughy's sake."

"Then I'll go, Señor Kid," she said bravely. "For Toughy's sake, and for . . . because you ask it."

"*Gracias, chamaquita*," he said.

They rode on, circling the ranchhouse and coming in from the rear—as he had come that first day leading the wounded Rey del Rey. From the corrals arose the shouts of the vaqueros. But there was no sign of Lopez.

A few hundred feet from the house the Kid slid to the ground. He stood for a moment beside the girl, looking up into her eyes which met his bravely. She placed a shy hand on his shoulder. He covered it with his, gripped it strongly.

"*Adios, chamaquita*," he said softly. "For only a short time!"

"Be very careful, Señor Kid," was all she said as she returned the pressure of his fingers and rode straight for the ranchhouse.

When she had moved from sight around the corner, he went forward at a swift pace. Then again, as he had done the day of his first arrival, he flattened himself against the wall, went forward stealthily. Below now, at the corrals he could see the vaqueros. And Rey del Rey, with his own silver saddle rig gleaming, was grazing, bridle reins trailing. His heart leaped. At least the palomino was safe. He came near whistling for the animal, but checked himself.

Then he had rounded the corner only to stop short at the sound of angry voices. He checked a curse that sprang to his lips, dared a glance. The girl had ridden up to encounter Lopez, sprawled on the steps of the porch. Satisfied that she had not been harmed in this short time, the Kid waited. Their voices came to him plainly. Lopez was speaking.

"The señorita will do well to heed me," he was threatening. "Now that you claim to know so much of what has happened on the rancho, then shall you probably claim it for your own. But I happen to hold a mortgage on it."

Not until then did the Kid recall the money Lopez had seized from Toughy after the wager. He remembered now that he had determined to demand the Lopez mortgage in return for Lopez' own note. Now was his chance. He strained for Lopez' words.

"Should you lay claim to the rancho, then I shall only foreclose. However, should you use judgment, then the mortgage shall be destroyed and together we shall rule this great estate like king and queen."

The Kid caught sight of the girl's face. She was white. Fear flamed in her eyes. Even her voice trembled when she spoke. But her words were brave.

"I will kill myself before I will marry you, Juan Lopez."

Lopez sprang off the steps, to leap before her.

"You've played the hell-cat long enough," he lashed out. "I am the real owner of Rancho Diablo. You shall do as I say or . . ." He seized her roughly in his arms, spun her around, attempted to kiss her while she beat at him savagely with her fists.

The fear in the shrinking girl's eyes goaded the Kid to action. He bounded around the corner.

"The señor would do well to let the señorita alone," he said softly. "It is plain that the attentions are not welcome."

Lopez leaped onto the porch. Once it seemed he would go for his gun. Then a strange look crossed his face from which the color fled until it was yellow beneath the tan. A whistling sigh escaped his lips.

"Johnnie Bender's brat . . ." he got out through white lips.

"The one who is dead," the Kid shot back in a tone that purred. "The one you killed, Lopez. See, back from the grave I come to . . . and now to prevent trouble, Lopez, it is best that you throw down your gun, yes? And the *chamaquita*, please to go in the house. I have much to say to this—this—*pelado*."

Lopez recoiled, his face now ashen, his lips twitching. "You . . . I—thought—you—"

"The *pelado* thinks like he moves," the Kid said, "too slowly. Please to go, señorita."

With obvious reluctance, the girl did as she was bid. But the Kid noticed she was uncertain of her footing as she mounted the steps—noticed that she was swaying on her feet. She gained the house. The door shut behind her.

"And now, señor, who strikes in the dark," the Kid said. "We have much to settle. First shall you return the money of the wager you stole from the *chamaco*."

"I'll see you in hell first," Lopez exploded.

"Then there we shall meet, but still I shall collect the wager," the Kid said. "As I came up just now I heard you mention a mortgage on the Rancho Diablo. Please to turn over this mortgage too, señor."

Lopez' face was working nervously. Fear suddenly had flamed into his eyes. Sight of it brought a cold smile to the Kid's lips.

"I'll bargain with you," the vaquero said. "The mortgage for the note."

"Both I shall take, señor," the Kid shot back. "For then you shall have no further claim on Rancho Diablo—Blackie Ware. . . ."

Lopez started violently.

"You are—an—officer—of—the—law?"

"Little have I to do with the law. I only heard what you and Pearson spoke of there in the Pillars of Hell—the night you murdered Pearson. I only recall the reward notices I saw for Blackie Ware when first I came into this country accursed. I heard Pearson accuse you, Lopez."

"You'll be sorry for this, *pelado*—you can't get away with it. I own this rancho. I'll—"

"You will spout words only as a whale spouts water, señor. For I know all. Know of your theft of all the Rancho Diablo cattle, by use of the bull. . . . Know of your theft of the wager money. . . . Know of your murder of Ross Pearson and of Ortega Garcia. . . ." He wondered as he recalled the name. Yet a mystery was that name. Ortega Garcia? He had heard Lopez admit that murder there in the Pillars of Hell.

A scream came piercingly from the house. The girl sprang onto the porch.

"Ortega Garcia," she screamed. "Lopez killed Ortega?"

"By his own confession, *chamaquita*," the Kid said. "But please to be calm. It means so much, that name, yes?"

"Ortega Garcia was my brother," she cried.

"Then you are—"

"Maria Garcia. . . ."

"*Gracias*, *chamaquita*. Such a pretty name. But always to me will you remain *chamaquita mia*. But from Lopez' own lips I heard him confess the killing of your brother. Later I shall prove to you—for I have yet to see Lopez draw his gun. Always has a cloud of dust been between us.

But I saw the gun that killed your brother pulled back from the door at Cantina El Paseo. I tried to catch the killer. I will know him because . . ." He looked at her for a second, ". . . your brother was killed because he had stumbled onto the secret of the stolen cattle. And perhaps because he had uncovered a murder or two. But please to retire, *chamaquita*. For I have not yet finished with this one."

"Bravo, *compañero*," came a voice from the door. "Make him come to you now. He's abused everyone on this rancho until he's got us all scared to death. Now, *compañero*—"

"Brat!" Lopez hissed at Toughy, who stood framed in the open door.

"*Chamaco*," the Kid smiled. "I shall do as you say. For now the Señor Lopez no longer rides the trails rough-shod. His hand is called. Please to go, señorita."

The girl went back into the house. Out the corner of his eye the Kid saw the door close on herself and Toughy.

"And now, señor," the Kid said. "Time speeds. I grow impatient that you delay, for I have much to do. Such as turning you over to the sheriff and collecting two thousand dollars reward for you. And counting the thousands you stole in wager money."

"You don't dare turn me over to the sheriff," Lopez lashed out. "I have known you from the start, you damned fugitive. You killed Ortega Garcia."

"The señor but makes idle talk—talk to waste valuable time. Now I count—only to three, señor. Then down shall go your gun, or . . . One!"

Lopez took a backward step. The porch creaked ominously. His face was ghastly.

"Two!" The Kid stepped forward a pace.

"You can't shoot," came from Lopez' dry lips. "Your gun arm is stiff."

"That is for the señor to prove," the Kid said quietly. "For he has but one more count— one more chance to throw down his gun or . . . three!"

Two forty-fives barked. The smile on the Kid's face widened. At last he had found the gunman of Guadalupe. For Lopez had gone for his Colt with his left hand!

Lopez staggered, stepped back. His knees seemed to sag. The Kid shook his head, came on, his face set in cold, lifeless lines, his narrow eyes glowing red.

Again two shots. Lopez' knees buckled. His legs gave way. He went down on his side.

"Bravo, *compañero*," came Toughy's scream from the doorway. "He deserves it—the mur- derer."

The Kid came on, half crouched, his taut body bent like a catamount ready to spring. Lopez dropped his gun.

"You've got me," he snarled. "Now what are you going to do?"

"You are scarcely fit to live longer, señor," the Kid said, kicking the forty-five aside. "And too vicious to die. Therefore I shot low to wound you, not thinking to take your life. But first you shall return the money of the wager, together with the mortgage you claim to hold on Rancho Diablo."

"It's all in the saddlebags on that damned palomino," Lopez said.

"Then you figured to leave the country—and steal my golden *caballo*," the Kid accused. "For that alone I would have killed you." He whistled sharply. The palomino threw up his head and came thundering to the porch. And, the Kid was quick to note, his holstered gun slung at the horn.

"Please to feel in those saddlebags, *chamaco*," the Kid told Toughy who had come out on the porch. "And recover for yourself the money this *pelado* stole from you."

The boy bounded across the porch to Rey del Rey, who turned his head to watch quizzically. Quickly he found a bundle, ripped it open. As Lopez has said it contained the money, the note and the mortgage on Rancho Diablo.

"*Gracias, chamaco,*" the Kid said as Toughy rammed the packet back in the saddlebags. He half turned to the vaqueros who had slunk up, but who sensed the end of the battle for Lopez had made no hostile move. On every face now was something of sympathy for the Kid.

"Now please to see to the *pelado*'s wounds, vaqueros," the Kid ordered quietly. "He shall be treated well. But he shall be bound in the same bed upon which he bound the helpless *chamaquita*. Then shall you send for a doctor, for he is bleeding badly. But he will not die. I saw to that—me, the Mañana Kid, who cannot shoot because of a stiff arm, Lopez. Quickly, vaqueros!"

The men did as they were bid.

Then Toughy and the Kid stood alone. With fingers that did not so much as tremble, the Kid found his tobacco and papers, twisted a cigarette, lighted it, let the smoke drift through his nostrils.

"Now shall we have water to quench our thirst, *chamaco mio*, who now owns Rancho Diablo."

"Me? I own Rancho Diablo?" the boy's eyes grew wide in wonder. "Are you joking, *compañero*?"

The Kid squatted on his heels beside the boy, threw an arm about him. "Never does the Kid make fun with one he loves, *chamaco*," he said gently. "I have solved the riddle of this rancho accursed. You own it, *compañero*—you and the *chamaquita*, Maria Garcia. . . ." He rolled the name on his tongue gently. "You and the *chamaquita* here shall rule like king and queen."

324

The boy threw his arms around the Kid's neck, clung to him.

"But you. Kid. You will stay here with us?"

"I have done my work, *chamaco*. The cattle are ready to gather. From every part of the Cuyamas shall I send *Rancheros Visitadores* to help you with your rodeo, as once my father helped others. The men who made this rancho accursed are gone. I shall take Lopez to Guadalupe myself, that I may testify against him, and thus clear the record for the rancho, which now is shunned. First I shall drink, *chamaco*," he said, releasing himself from the boy's arms and rising to his feet. "Then shall we find food."

"But Kid!" Toughy was crying, tears trickling down across his cheeks. "You can't leave Maria and me—we love you, Kid. You're the only one who ever has been kind to us. We want you to stay. Please, Kid. You promised you and me could be partners."

For a moment the Kid stood looking out across the valley where the shadows of evening now were creeping. "It is probably best that I go, *chamaco*. Always I long for the open trails— the places where other men live not, where only Rey del Rey and myself can wander at will. And you don't need me now. But of that we shall speak—Mañana."

"We'll do nothing of the kind, Señor Mañana."

The Kid whirled. The *chamaquita* stood there

on the porch. And she, too, had been crying. Tears were glistening in her lustrous black eyes, had trickled down across her cheek. "You will remain on Rancho Diablo as the major-domo. For—"

"For . . . ?" There was a note of mockery in his tone.

"For—we need you." She came down off the steps, moved over beside him, stood looking up into his eyes. "Can't you see—anything—Kid?" she whispered.

"I see only an adorable *chamaquita* whose name for weeks I did not know—with pretty lips that should be kissed. Perhaps—Mañana . . ."

"Mañana nothing," scornfully. "If I saw any pretty lips that should be kissed, I'd kiss them. Oh, Kid, are you really going now?"

Then his arms were about her. She was clinging to him frantically. And Toughy, too, was hanging onto him.

"*Si, chamaquita y chamaco*, shall I be going." He lifted her head, looked into her tear-filled eyes. Then he bent his lips to meet hers, in their first kiss. Her eyes closed under the caress. Then presently he lifted his lips. Again their eyes met. "*Si chamaco y chamaquita*," he repeated softly, "shall I be going from Rancho Diablo. But—now—that leave-taking will be . . . Mañana."

| Books are produced in the United States using U.S.-based materials | Books are printed using a revolutionary new process called THINKtech™ that lowers energy usage by 70% and increases overall quality | Books are durable and flexible because of Smyth-sewing | Paper is sourced using environmentally responsible foresting methods and the paper is acid-free |

Center Point Large Print
600 Brooks Road / PO Box 1
Thorndike, ME 04986-0001 USA

(207) 568-3717

US & Canada:
1 800 929-9108
www.centerpointlargeprint.com